CRIMES OF THE BLOOD CULTS

AN OCCULT NOIR SHORT STORY COLLECTION

FREDRICK NILES

FEVER GARDEN PUBLISHING

Copyright © 2022 by Fredrick Niles

All rights reserved.

No part of this book may be reproduced in any form or by any electronic or mechanical means, including information storage and retrieval systems, without written permission from the author, except for the use of brief quotations in a book review.

CRIMES OF THE BLOOD CULTS: AN OCCULT NOIR SHORT STORY COLLECTION

First edition. June 1, 2022.

ISBN: 978-1-950021-13-0

Fever Garden Publishing

Cover design by

TheCoverCollection.com

❀ Created with Vellum

CONTENTS

SIGN OF THE GREY CLOAK

It began here, in the rain-sodden streets of Blackburg.

It began with bodies in the streets. Slash marks across the necks so deep you could drown in 'em. Friends, family, and neighbors were lying out like cold slabs of meat, reminding everyone of the stuff they're made of.

Flesh, blood, bone, cartilage, hair, and spit. When these things stop working, so do you. The soul and the stardust drain out and you slip into something else. What? I can't say. But it ain't here. It ain't now. Here you're just a tin can with its lid peeled back.

The girl was 16. Shit, maybe 14. Blonde hair like golden seaweed in the rainwater, blood already down the sewer and halfway out to sea. She was just old enough to hold her future in her hands, to know what she was losing as she lost it.

Her fear wasn't just animal fear—the kind you feel as a child without understanding it. No, her fear was a holy fear, existing in the tension between what is and what could be. Yes, holy fear. It makes me wonder if that's what they wanted.

Because the killings were random and seemingly without motive. The victims were mostly young, but not all. The oldest was 45. A man who played cello in the Blackburg Chamber Orchestra. His solitary life almost completely removed from this girl lying face-up in the street. Her neck gaping wider than her mouth.

The longer I looked, the stonier I felt. I knew the law, but people forget that there are two laws: the law of men and the law of nature. People forget that hundreds of years ago, nature meant something different than it means today. Back then, nature referred to something like reality. The way things were. The obvious right and wrong of the world.

That's the law I followed. The nature I lived by. And I swore to God above that I would be the arm of it. And I swore that when I found the ones who did this, they'd gape as she gaped.

THE RAIN MADE the crime scene miserable to process. I headed home around 1:15 am and was just coming out of the bathroom when the phone rang.

"Still up?" It was my new partner, Nora. From what I could tell, she never slept, which made for frequent middle-of-the-night calls like this one.

"About to go down. Why?"

"Did I wake the wife and kiddo?"

I leaned around the corner and peered into the bedroom where my wife, Samantha, was sleeping.

"Don't think so. What's up?"

"A uni scored a hit in the initial canvassing. Guy who owns the quick mart 'round the block said he saw our vic hanging with a couple kids that frequent his place. Doesn't know 'em by name but it might be easier to approach them out on the street than get their names and go through their parents."

"You sure? People are getting wary of strangers who

approach them on the streets. Especially if they're kids and the ones doing the approaching look like cops."

"I don't look like a cop."

"Yeah, you do," I said.

"What? Bullshit."

"It's in your step. The sense of authority you walk with."

"What, a girl can't walk around confidently without being a cop?"

"When do you want to meet tomorrow, Nora?"

"5:30. I'll pick you up."

"Christ, in the morning?"

I could practically see her rolling that toothpick around in her mouth like she always did. She was buzzing.

"You're lucky we're not going now," she said. "Figured I'd cut you a break."

"Barely." I rubbed the bridge of my nose. "You don't think kids are up that early do you?"

There was a beat of silence and I realized that she had probably shrugged. Nora wasn't always great at speaking with people like they were humans.

"6:00," I countered. "And you bring the coffee."

"Deal. And the coffee's already made."

I sighed. "Nora, don't you dare bring me precinct break room coffee."

Another beat of silence. She had probably smiled.

"See ya tomorrow," I said and hung up the phone.

ROUGHLY 4 HOURS LATER, I found myself sitting in the passenger seat of Nora's '97 Cadillac DeVille. The seats felt like they were made of the same material they used to make Halloween masks and the interior smelled like a pack of gum.

"Where'd you get this thing?" I asked. I was holding a paper cup of coffee in my hand but hadn't tried it yet. I wasn't sure how long this stakeout was going to be and I didn't want to find myself with a full bladder a quarter of the way in.

"Car store."

I turned and looked at her. She was wearing a pair of aviators and a black peacoat. Her dark shoulder-length hair was tied loosely behind her head. She wore no make-up or earrings, from what I could tell, and there was a firm set to her jaw. We hadn't been working together long, but everything combined gave me a strange impression of her.

She was serious but not inflexible. Stylish but not uncomfortable. I knew she carried a handbag in her car and a wallet on her person. Seldom wore heels. Cursed occasionally but always sounded like a high schooler trying it on for the first time.

"Car store?" I asked skeptically.

"Yeah, got it for about six."

"You paid six thousand for this thing?"

"Six hundred."

"Well," I said. "That worries me even more."

"Less gadgets," she replied. "I don't do gadgets."

"No exploding pens for you then?"

"Huh?"

"Nothing." I tapped the side of my coffee absentmindedly. "From a movie."

"I don't really do movies either."

A couple of kids walked into the store across the street. I squinted.

"That them?" I asked.

"Nope. Guy said there were usually three of them. One has a red backpack and another carries a skateboard but never rides it. They come in to buy soda every day before school."

"And they were seen with our victim last night?"

"Allegedly."

I looked at the clock on the dash. 7:14.

"Could have told me we were catching these kids before school. Probably wouldn't have given you as much guff last night."

Nora blew a small breath out her nose in the way of a laugh. "I do guff."

"Tell me," I said, leaning back. "What do you do and not do? Sounds like you have a solid list."

"Hmm." She pursed her lips, the sunglasses and peacoat making her look briefly like a caricature of a model. "I do cop stuff, tape-record soap operas, drink wine but not beer, whiskey but no other hard liquor. I shoot, mostly handguns and rifles. I swim. And uh... that's about it."

"And *guff*," I added.

"Right. And guff."

I nodded, then caved and took a sip of coffee. I was already exhausted and didn't see myself making it through the day without a steady stream of caffeine.

"That list brings up a lot of questions, I suppose. But what about your *don'ts*."

"That list is a little easier," she said. "No smoking. No gadgets. No pork. No movies. No books. No brawls. No dating. And go nowhere without a gun."

I laughed. "Okay. Let's start with the one that bothers me the most."

"And what's that?"

"No movies, but you tape soap operas."

"Movies take themselves too seriously. I want something I know is fake."

I shrugged, smiled, and shook my head.

"And books?" I asked.

"No books."

"Why's that?"

"Too long," she said. "Don't have the time."

"Because of the cop stuff."

She nodded. "Because of the cop stuff."

I thought about what I was going to say next and if I should. I hadn't known her very long and it seemed a bit early to be digging into her personal life, but Hell, we were going to be sitting in this car together for countless hours in the future. Might as well get everything out in the open.

"You know, I read your file when you were assigned to me." I turned and looked at her.

She was still, her expression unreadable.

"So?"

"So it sort of sheds some light on those lists of yours."

"How so?"

I took another sip of coffee, beginning to regret going down this path. I forged on anyway.

"Your aunt stole you from your parents when you were three. You lived somewhere off-grid with a cult for 15 years before they brought you back."

"They didn't bring me back," she corrected. "I left."

"So?"

It was her turn to look at me. Her face was serious at first, then it softened.

"So I'm not some cult follower if that's what you're wondering."

"I'm not. It's just-"

"Yeah?"

"Well, your list-"

"Yeah?" She cocked her head.

"No pork? No smoking? No dating? No movies? You shoot guns?"

She was shaking her head, so I relented.

"Well, it sort of makes you sound like a religious fundamentalist."

She raised her eyebrows, then started laughing. I started laughing too, though I wasn't quite sure why.

"Eh, I think you're more of a fundamentalist than I am, Richard."

It was almost jarring hearing her use my name. She rarely addressed me. She usually just walked up and started talking.

"How's that?" I asked, indignant.

But just then, she seemed to focus on something past my shoulder. Three kids were walking into the convenience store. One with a red backpack. Another with a skateboard.

WHEN THE KIDS WALKED OUT, we were there to meet them. There were two girls and a boy. The boy, a rough-looking kid of about fifteen with shoulder-length black hair, was the one carrying the red backpack. The girls were both dark-haired as well, and the one with the skateboard looked Nora over and leaned in to the other and whispered something. I just barely caught it.

Cops.

I tried not to smile.

"We weren't doing nothing," the non-skateboarder said, a note of indignation in her voice. "We were just off to *school.*" She twisted the last word as if we might be the school police.

"We're not looking to bust your chops," I said. "Just want to ask a few questions about the girl they found last night. That okay?"

At this, they all seemed to shrink back slightly, the boy visibly wincing. A beat of silence passed and someone shouldered past us into the convenience store.

Nora tilted her head sideways and we all moved out of the entryway.

"You saw her last night, right?"

"Was it Alena?" the boy asked. Skateboarder turned slightly in his direction as if to tell him to keep his yap shut.

"Alena Shepherd," I said. "Yeah. Her parents ID'd her early this morning."

The boy worked his mouth a bit like he was chewing on something.

"C'mon, Ricky," Skateboarder said. "We don't need this shit."

"You knew her?" Nora jumped in before they could walk away.

Ricky nodded. "She was—we were-"

"They were fucking," Non-skateboarder said. "Don't tell her daddy though or he'll come down out of that white castle of theirs and beat his ass."

"Mr. Shepherd do that sort of thing?" I asked.

"What, beat asses?"

"Or faces, or kidneys. Even drywall. He that sorta guy?"

I hadn't seen him the night before but it would definitely be something to keep in mind when we questioned him later today.

"He wasn't that bad," Ricky said. "He was just very... controlling, I guess."

"How so?"

"Curfews. No dating. No drinking. No smoking."

"What about movies or brawling?" I asked, and saw Nora turn slightly to look at me.

"What?" Ricky looked genuinely confused but I let the question hang there. I was genuinely curious after the discussion in the car.

"We could watch movies, but he didn't really like me hanging out there."

"Not a fan, eh?" Nora asked.

"Of me? No, not really."

"You could say that again," Skateboarder said, rolling her eyes. "He offered to pay him off."

"Pay him off?"

"Yeah," Ricky said. "He offered me two grand not to see his daughter anymore."

"Did you take it?" I asked, raising my eyebrows.

"No way, man," he was suddenly passionate. "What Alena and I have for each other is real."

I noted the use of the present tense, guessing that the Shepherd girl's death probably hadn't quite sunk in yet. That, or their relationship wasn't quite as "real" as he was making it out to be.

"Let's get outta here," Non-skateboarder said.

"Wait." Nora took off her glasses. "Ricky, what were you doing here last night?"

Ricky shrugged. "We were just gonna hang out and catch a flick, but she seemed to get skittish at the last moment. Kept looking around her like she was being followed."

"Did you ask her about it?"

Ricky blinked a few times, thinking to himself.

"She wouldn't say," he said.

"You say you were going to a movie together?" I asked.

"We were planning on it, yeah."

I waved my finger at the three of them. "All of you?"

This seemed to catch them off-guard. I leaned into the silence, Nora doing the same.

"We all hung out together," Skateboarder finally said. "So what?"

"Nothing," I said, shrugging my shoulders. "Just seems..."

"What?" Ricky said, his impatience growing. "Seems like what?"

I blew a breath out my nose. "Look, all I'm saying is that

there would be some tension between my wife and me if I hung out with a couple of other women all day long."

"What, like your partner?" Ricky said. "How does she feel about that?"

I shifted on my feet. "She's leaving me, actually."

I felt Nora tense beside me. The kids stared at me awkwardly.

After a few moments, I smiled. "Kidding," I said. "You guys are fine. We just gotta ask these sorta questions."

Everyone seemed to sigh a breath of relief, including Nora.

"Look," I said, squaring up. "Who do *you* think killed Alena?"

Ricky's face seemed to fall a bit.

"I don't know," he shook his head. "I honestly have no clue who would want to kill her. She was just—I don't know. It was like she was everybody's friend, you know?"

As he was talking, I caught Skateboarder nodding along.

After that, we nailed down a sequence of events. They were going to catch a 9:00 movie but Alena ducked out at the last moment. I asked if they still had the tickets and after a minute of searching, Ricky was able to dig his out of his wallet.

Alena's body was found around 9:45.

I gave each of them my card, telling them they could use me as an excuse for being late to school. Five minutes later, we were headed to the Shepherd house.

On the way there, Nora asked me what I thought of the kids.

"They seem a little hinky," I answered.

She nodded. "Why do you say that?"

"Ricky didn't seem as broken up as you might expect. He seemed shaken, but he'd be shaken if he killed her too."

"Yeah. The girls were a little strange as well. Like they didn't really like Alena at the beginning of the conversation, then by the end, they're agreeing that she was the kindest person around and everyone loved her."

"Mmmm." I looked out the window. Something about the kids' story wasn't adding up.

"Slick move with the wife-leaving-you bit. I even bought it for a second."

"The idea is to get them to tighten up and then instantly release the tension. Shakes something loose occasionally, for all the good it did this time."

Nora accelerated at a yellow light, not-quite-making it. I involuntarily gripped the armrest a little harder.

"I think we got enough," she said. "And without really spooking them. A more formal interrogation might be warranted in the future, but let's burn that bridge when we come to it." She took an on-ramp, the tires squealing briefly beneath us.

"You know we got to make it there to question the Shepherds, right?"

"We'll all make it to the afterlife someday," she said. "Can always question them there."

I grunted a laugh.

"What do we know about them?" I asked. "Shepherd seem like the heavenly sort?"

Nora tilted her head back and forth a bit.

"Hard to say. He's the CEO of Heffer Lumber. One of those 'family values are key' sort of guys who also has a few leaked *home videos* floating around the web, and the co-stars aren't his wife."

"Ah, he do the whole *'back in my day we were courteous to each other, ya fuckn' imbecile'* bit?"

"Pretty much."

"So lots of enemies then?"

Nora nodded. "Also, don't think I'm letting you get away with that dig about no dating and no movies back there."

"Just making sure y'all weren't in the same cult, is all."

The air in the car seemed to tighten and I instantly regretted the comment. I pushed on.

"What was that you were saying earlier about *me* being cultish?"

"I said you were a fundamentalist," she said, her voice neutral.

"How's that?" I tried to put a casual edge in my voice. Let her know we were just busting each other's chops.

"Oh, I know your sort," she said, a grin cracking the side of her face.

I turned slightly in my seat. "And what sort is that?"

"Country, God, and family," she said. "Roughly in that order. Those are your fundamentals."

"God comes before country, thank you very much."

"Does it?"

"What's that supposed to mean?"

Nora shrugged. "All I'm saying is I've met a lot of people who are Christian because they're conservative and not the other way around."

"Does it matter?"

"Most of the time, yeah. It does."

"Explain," I said, not unkindly.

"Look, all I'm saying is that it's pretty easy for someone to stand up there and say 'under God' then make themselves the sole arbiter of the truth. This basically makes *them* God, all the while claiming some sort of humility. Happens on both sides of the aisle, really. Oldest trick in the book. I should know."

"It's not like that," I said. "And don't think I didn't notice you putting country before family."

"You think differently?"

I chewed it over in my head for a bit, then said, "No."

Nora laughed. "Oh?"

"Sometimes country comes before family. Or the laws of it, at least."

"Really?" Now it was her turn to look at me. "You'd place the law over your own family?"

"I *do* place the law over my own family. It sucks sometimes, but I don't think I'd be able to have a family without law and order. My daughter's future is everything to me and I can't put that in jeopardy by letting the streets of our city drown in chaos. That's something we take for granted."

"What is? Law?"

"Stability. And stability comes from law. The whole reason we've been able to have such breakthroughs in medicine, philosophy, and what-have-you is because we don't have to worry about our next meal or if something is sneaking up on us to turn us into lunch."

"Hmm," she said. "You know, I once heard someone say that the reason we're more advanced than, say—dolphins or something else—is because we can manipulate our surroundings. In turn, the ability to manipulate our surroundings and provide security for each other and ourselves is what allows us to stack layers of knowledge."

"What about squid or other tentacled creatures? They're said to have brains that surpass ours, and they can also manipulate their surroundings."

"Who knows," she said, smiling. "Maybe they're manipulating our world more than we think."

WE GAVE each other shit for another minute or so. She continued to press me on the "law before family" thing while I grilled her on her *don't* list. Before I knew it, we were pulling up to the guard shack that sat at the entrance of Evergreen Place, the wealthy community where the Shepherds lived.

Nora showed them her identification and the gate arm went up.

I pointed at the small security camera wired to the corner of the shack's roof. "Remind me to check that camera's footage on the way out. I want to know where each member of the Shepherd family was last night."

"Good call," Nora said. "You really think we're looking at this guy? The father, I mean?"

"I don't know," I said. "But I want to keep my options open."

THE SHEPHERD'S house was large and ornate. I'd seen bigger on lakes and stuff a few towns away, but nothing like it inside the city limits. While something like this may have gone for 650 thousand somewhere else, it would be worth millions here. Possibly even tens of millions.

We parked and got out of the car, our doors *chunk*ing closed in quick succession, the sound reverberating through the warm afternoon air. As we walked up the drive and got closer to the house, Nora quickly reached over and tapped my shoulder.

I followed her gaze up to the front door, which was hanging slightly open.

"Shit," I said, reaching down to unsnap my holster.

"Lock's busted," Nora said as she pushed the door open, her other hand on her own sidearm.

I looked and saw she was right. Tiny splinters lay on the floor from where the locking mechanism had been busted inward. Whoever had done this must have hit the door with something hard. A battering ram, maybe.

Or it was just someone really big and strong.

A light was on in the entryway. The area was small but

seemed like it opened in a few different directions. I went right and Nora went left.

She was the one that found the body.

THE WOMAN HAD LITERALLY BEEN TORN APART and piled in a heap on the floor. It looked as if every joint had been snapped and severed. Her legs and feet lay at the bottom of the pile, then her arms and hands, then her torso, and finally her head. Her blank eyes stared upward, her cheeks slashed and jaw hanging open.

The pile was lying in the center of the living room and around it, a strange symbol was drawn in blood. Like an infinity symbol with extra accents. Or possibly an hourglass.

Nora stayed with the body and called for backup while I cleared the rest of the house. Nothing. Mr. Shepherd was gone.

"You think this is the wife?" I asked once I returned to the living room. The area smelled horrible. Not quite like rot or decay just yet but like raw meat, gut sack, and something else I couldn't quite put my finger on. What came to mind first though was seaweed.

"Pretty sure," Nora said. "I hung around a bit last night while she gave her statement. Husband gone?"

"Yup."

"We think it's him?"

"At this point, not really. I doubt he'd need to bash down his own door."

"Unless she locked him out," Nora countered.

"Maybe. Crime scene will be here soon. Hopefully they can give us something."

WE SPENT the rest of the day chasing down small and tedious leads. I helped canvass the neighborhood with the uniforms while Nora procured the security tape and started going through the footage.

It seemed like nobody saw anything. No strange cars entered the whole morning and the neighbors were either at work or weren't paying attention. There were the few odd sightings, of course, but most turned out to be gardeners or mail carriers who walked too slow down the sidewalk.

After ensuring that those leads were truly nothing, I caught a ride back home with the uniforms and rang Nora.

"Got anything?" I asked.

"No, just running plates through the database one-by-one, hoping to get lucky. Nothing stuck out immediately though."

"Hmm. Well, keep at it. Or don't. You slept yet?"

"What, you mean like, ever?"

I wanted to react but caught myself. I could practically hear her grinning over the phone.

"Look, don't stay there all night," I said. "Who knows, you might fall asleep and miss something important on the tapes."

"Good point," she said. "You got plans this evening?"

"Not much. Hannah's going to a friend's house, so I'm planning on a quiet night with Samantha."

"Friend's house, eh? How old is she?"

"16, like I need reminding."

"I'm sure she'll make good decisions," Nora said, which was about the worst thing she could say.

"I'll tell her you said that. She's just about to leave." I lowered the phone. "*Hey, Hannah sweetie?*"

"Yeah?" Hannah called. She stepped into the living room from the kitchen.

"Nora said she's sure you're going to make good decisions."

"Only always," she said, turning on her heel and walking back out.

"What'd she say?" Nora asked as I brought the phone back up. "Was she sarcastic?"

"I'm not sure...Hey, I'm gonna let you go. Get some sleep, yeah?"

"Sorry, going through a tunnel."

"In the station?"

"It's a proverbial tunnel," she said. "I'm entering a liminal space."

Then she hung up.

MY PHONE RANG JUST before midnight. I rolled over and picked it up, my mind already moving at a hundred miles per hour. Something was wrong, I just didn't know what yet.

"Yeah," I said into the phone, rubbing my eyes.

"I got a hit on one of the plates." It was Nora. I looked at the clock on my nightstand. 11:53 pm.

"Yeah?" I repeated, this time with a question mark.

Silence.

"What?" I asked. "Who is it?"

"Do you own a red 2014 Nissan Maxima?" Then she rattled off the plate number. My plate number. I felt the world tilt underneath me.

"Hold on," I said. "Are you saying someone stole my car and drove it to the Shepherds?"

The other end of the line was as quiet as the grave, and this time, I didn't think it was because of some gesture she was forgetting to verbalize.

"Richard, I'm looking at the photo from the security cam and..."

"And what?" I practically shouted. Then I quickly turned over to check on Samantha. She was gone.

"It looks like Hannah at the wheel. She must have talked her way in."

The blood turned to ice in my veins. "How could that be?" I asked.

"I don't know," Nora replied. "But it looks like someone is sitting in her backseat. Looks like a woman but I can't see her face."

"I'm going to get her," I said. "Right now. We'll sort this all out."

"Okay, text me the address and I'll meet you there."

We hung up and I threw some clothes on. I pulled my pistol from the drawer next to my nightstand and loaded it. It was a 9mm Beretta. I had used it twice in the line of duty, but only to provide cover fire on raids that had gone sideways. I'd never killed anyone. Hoped I never would.

My conversation with Nora earlier flashed through my mind. What mattered more: family or the law? Hopefully, it wouldn't come to that.

"*Sam*," I shouted. Shit, where was she? She needed to know what was going on. I rubbed my face for a second, then called out again. Still no answer.

"Goddamit," I said to myself as I punched her number into my cellphone. It started ringing as I stomped down the steps and that was when I realized I could hear her ringtone coming from the living room.

"Sam, I-" But stopped as I stepped into the room.

Candlelight suffused the dark area, the flickering flames deepening the shadows of the cloaked figures standing in a half-circle. In the middle of them stood a figure, its face completely hidden by its hood. The cloak it wore was grey, as opposed to the others which were black. Not an inch of skin was visible, as if the clothing were suspended upon a ghost.

And standing before it was Samantha. She was bound and

gagged in her nightwear, tears streaming down her face. I imagined her hearing a noise and coming down here to find this —whatever this was. Them binding her against her will. I drew my sidearm and aimed at the figure in the center of the room.

"Leave now and we won't have any trouble," I said. The words were hard because I didn't actually want them to leave. I wanted them to pay for what they were doing. For what they had likely done to Mrs. Shepherd and her daughter. I wanted them to die.

The sights of my Beretta lined up on the grey figure's head and I felt my finger begin to apply pressure to the trigger. It would be close with Samantha in front of him but there was just enough room. I could make the shot.

"It's okay, daddy." The voice was startling, not just because of how calm and serene it was but because it belonged to my daughter. One of the figures on the end drew back their hood.

My legs went limp.

"We will all be ascending," she said dreamily. "When the streets flood and the city sinks. When the pillars break and the saltwater washes clean. We will ascend to our chosen place and the pain of this life will be but mist banished by the sea breeze."

"What are you talking about?" I said, adjusting my grip on the pistol. I tried to make eye contact with her but her gaze was distant.

"All things pass," she continued. "The pillars of this age have corroded. The keepers of fleeting ideals have abdicated their work, giving way to selfish ambition and petty squabbling. It's nothing to be sad about. It's the way that civilizations age. And now comes the plunge back into the void from which we crawled so long ago. It's happening. It's been happening. And we are the doctors, here to bless the world with a merciful passing into its final slumber."

The words had the quality of a script being read by a first-time actor. They were over-annunciated. Overly sincere. I got the impression that Hannah was performing, but in what way? Was she trying to deceive them or convince them she was one of them? The part of me that loved her—that was her father—wanted to trust her. To believe she had some plan.

I looked at Samantha and she looked back at me, despair plain in her features. I tried to send a silent message to her, to communicate how sorry I was. That I loved her. That I loved our daughter.

"You will join us," Hannah said, looking at me. Then she turned toward her mother. "And she will light the way."

The grey robes of the figure behind her rippled and the room was suddenly permeated with the stench of brine and seaweed. Long, glistening tentacles emerged from the sleeves of the cloak, slowly wrapping around Samantha's arms and legs. When they first touched her skin, she recoiled and let out a long, muffled moan through the rag that had been shoved in her mouth.

"Why?" I yelled, suddenly frustrated. I tried to steady myself. The sights of the gun were now bouncing around in front of me as my hands trembled and sweat poured out of my body. I wanted to ask a million questions about the Shepherds and the kids and what was playing out right in front of me. But I couldn't form the words, the necessary thoughts. So I just repeated myself. "Why?"

"Because it's your time," said another voice, this one male. "The young who refuse to walk the path will perish. The old who refuse to lay it out will become beaten Earth. You are lucky your daughter has chosen as she has, for it is a blessing."

It took me a second to realize which of the other hooded figures had spoken, but when I did, I could picture the face beneath the robe. Ricky. And the two shorter figures to his right and left. The shapes and builds were right. The two girls.

Fuck, where was Nora? Then I remembered, I had sent her the address of the house Hannah had been supposedly staying at. Lord, what would she find when she got there?

"Mother," Hannah said. "Will you light the way?"

"No!" I pulled the trigger before I knew what was happening and the top of the grey figure's robe plucked as the bullet passed through it. I pulled again and again as I saw the tentacles tighten and begin to twist.

The gunshots drowned out the sound of breaking bones and ripping muscle as Samantha's body was twisted apart. But the scream sliced through everything. Through the gunfire, through my mind, and through my soul. It cleaved me apart as her limbs separated.

I'm not sure if it was a subconscious act of mercy or a fortunate mistake, but one of the rounds struck home just above her left eye, spraying the figure behind her in blood and bone. If nothing else, I could claim responsibility for her death. Strangely enough, this felt right. As if I had robbed them of something important.

The gun clicked dry. My body felt numb, like it was floating. Hannah smiled and the robed figures began walking slowly toward me. Their hooded forms blotted out the monster behind them as its grey cloak slid to the ground and it continued its monstrous work.

FEED 'EM TO THE STARS

The white rabbit showed up at my door wearing a pair of soiled marigold swimming trunks and smoking a cigarillo that smelled like grape.

"What the fuck are you doing here?" I hissed. "Do you know what'll happen if my roommate sees you?"

It was past midnight and the streets were empty. But if my neighbors saw some bedraggled creature slinking around, I'd be neck-deep in cops before I could blink.

"You gotta stop," it croaked, the cigarillo shaking in its little paws. "You gotta stop *now*."

I moved out onto the step, closing the door behind me. The night was warm but I could still feel a slight chill through my robe. I hurried the rabbit down the steps, across the yard, and through the doorway of the detached garage that sat adjacent to the house.

The sound of chattering buck teeth permeated the darkness as I fumbled for the light switch and I didn't think it was because of the cold. Something had him spooked—spooked enough to come knocking on my door right out in the open.

The switch clacked as I flipped it up and a single bulb in the center of the ceiling blazed to life, casting light on my 2002 Chrysler, stacks of boxes, a workbench, and a tight area where I worked a heavy bag every morning.

"Okay Rico, what the fuck do you want?" I asked.

"You gotta stop," he repeated, his huge eyes bulging out of his face. His little snout twitched and he reached down to pull up his ill-fitting swim trunks. He took another nervous drag on the cigarillo, then blew grape in my face.

"I can't," I said, waving the smoke away. "You know what'll happen if I do."

"And *you* know what'll happen if I get caught narcn'," Rico shot back. "That's how you know it's important."

"How about you *tell* me why it's important, or I'll bring you to the big guy himself."

He shrunk back and looked away.

"I can't," he finally said. "It's not that I don't want to. I literally can't. I don't know what's coming down the road but I think it's bad. What he's doing with the-" The word caught in his throat. "The *packages*. I don't think he's doing what he says he's doing. I think he's building something."

"And what does he say he's doing?"

"You didn't ask?" Rico looked incredulous.

"I didn't care. I *don't* care."

"The story he spun us is he's using the shipments as currency. Lots of people willing to pay high prices for some ivory. Lots of people doing lots of dark shit."

"But you don't think that's what he's doing with it..."

"No, see, one of these cult fellas come to me looking for some *product,* ya know? And I says I can hook him up. But when I go and tell the boss, *he* says we're all out."

"All out?" I asked. "I just delivered a shipment yesterday."

"Yeah, and that's not all. He's been talking big lately. *Fuck the pinkies* and all that."

Pinkies were what they called people.

"You know we ain't actually pink, right?" The slur had always grated on my nerves. "I seen tan and olive, but I ain't never seen pink."

"It's 'cause you all pink on the inside," Rico stammered. I noticed he had a hard time keeping the grin off his face.

"How about I see what you look like on the inside? I bet it looks pretty fuckn' close to pink." I straightened up. "Plus, I've heard you say worse about us. What's the big deal with the boss runnin' his mouth?"

"I was just blowing smoke," Rico said, then blew some actual smoke as if to drive his point home. "Truth is, I don't give a fuck. Pinkies got the three B's."

"Three B's?"

"Babes, booze, and blow."

I made a face, thinking about Rico using his wretched rabbit body to partake in *babes*.

"But you think he wants to get rid of us."

Rico nodded. "Yeah, he's been talking about feeding you to the stars."

"Feeding us to the stars? What does that mean?"

"Dunno. But there are worse things out there than me and the boss. Bigger things. Hungrier things."

I shuddered involuntarily, thinking about what sort of "worse things" he could be talking about. Rico was pretty bad, had done some wicked shit in his time. And his boss, Beaky, was on a different level.

"So you think I should stop." It wasn't a question.

"Gotta," the rabbit said. "If they're planning on doing something to y'all, then I'm next. There's no place for me in their world."

What I took that to mean was that there was no place for *debauchery* in their new world, but it might as well have meant the same thing. Take away the substance abuse and Rico was nothing but a husk. Without the *three B's*, he'd probably die.

"If I stop, they'll drop me in the fuckn' ocean with a cinderblock life-preserver," I said. "You know that."

"You can run. Canada, Mexico, or-"

"You ever know anyone to get out alive? The position I'm in? The things I'm doing?"

"Sure," Rico said, the word slipping out of his mouth as easy as the truth.

I shook my head. "If I run, I'm dead. And I don't see a point in saving a world I don't get to live in, do you?"

"Awfully selfish of you, Gary."

The use of my name unsettled me, bringing with it the feeling of being implicated. I smacked the rabbit across the mouth with the back of my hand, the cigarillo arcing across the garage. I had planned on stopping there but I didn't. The feeling was too satisfying.

As he regained his composure, looking somewhat shocked, I planted my knuckles in his left kidney and he doubled over. I worked him with my fists, then my knee, and finally my foot. Wearing nothing but slippers, I had to use my heel.

When I was done, he looked up at me pitifully with those big brown bunny eyes.

"Don't give me that look," I said. "I know what you've done to them girls. Some of 'em not even in high school yet. Maybe I'll tell their parents where the bodies are buried. Then if Beaky doesn't get you, the town will. It'll be a rabbit hunt like no one's ever seen. They'll skin you and hang your hide in a fuckin' museum. Charge ten bucks a pop to come see it."

"I was saving them kids," Rico pleaded, blood coming out from between those two big gravestone teeth.

"If that's how you save people," I said. "Then I sure as shit ain't helping you save the world."

. . .

I WENT out the next night, my knuckles still raw. This was when joggers were out, the ones who had worked late and didn't feel good until they got their run in. I walked with my hood up, hands in my pocket.

The park was massive, a maze of trails winding in and out of the trees. It had two parking lots, but on the south end there was a small rest stop across the highway that no one ever used. I parked my car there, just enough dirt on my license plate to obscure the numbers without drawing suspicion.

I was lingering in a patch of heavy woods when I heard the huffing of a jogger a few hundred feet off. The sun was down, the paths lit up with trail lights. Even so, there was still the occasional dark nook to hide in.

She came around the corner, swinging her elbows side-to-side in wretched form, expending more energy with her arms than with her legs. She was tired. Out of breath.

She was perfect.

I began to move in just as something on her person chimed. The noise threw me off and I hesitated. She half-turned toward me as she drew her cell phone from its carrier on her arm. I stepped slowly back into the brush, watching.

"Yeah?" She said, panting.

Someone said something on the other end and she looked around.

"I'm by the bridge. Yeah, the walk bridge." She stood on her tiptoes and looked down the trail. "Oh hey, I think I see you."

Another woman came trotting around the corner. This one moved more gracefully, less hunched. They chatted for a bit and then set off together. I cursed.

I went another hour without seeing anyone, then decided to call it quits. Every minute I spent skulking around here was a risk and I still had another night to procure the goods. I would be okay.

As I was about to cross the lonely highway back to my car though, I saw a camper pull into the slot next to me. I waited in the woods and watched. No cars coming. I could cross at any time.

The door to the camper opened with a light slap and an elderly woman tottered out, followed by a man of about the same age. They conferred for a second and then moved off toward a thick brick building that served as the restrooms.

Him or her? Him of her? It was a toss-up, really. I had brought them a woman last time. Maybe they'd appreciate a man now. I didn't know how the spells worked that the cult assholes used; maybe the sex mattered. Who knew?

I went with the man.

The door to the restroom creaked open and I was surprised to find him already washing his hands. *A fine prostate in you, sir.* I nodded and went to move past him toward the stalls. He was wary, I could tell, but his body relaxed a little bit once I had passed.

That's when I struck, the hunting knife sliding into his right kidney. I clamped my hand over his mouth, smothering the scream. The flush of a toilet sounded through the walls from the women's restroom. I had to move quickly.

The man was light, his blood soaking my shoulder as I hustled him out into my van. It was risky. The whole thing was. But I only had to do it three times, that's what the boss said. And this was my last. It was worth the risk.

Two weeks from now I'd be set up richer than I'd ever been. I'd still have a job with old Beaky—you never really got out and to be honest, I didn't want to. I just wanted something where the risk of getting caught and sentenced to lethal injection was a little less.

The old woman moved slowly, a good hand washer. And by the time she was stepping back out into the night air, I was already on the highway.

The back seat of my car was covered in plastic and I had just enough room in the cluttered garage to pull all the way in and get the door down. All I had to do now was roll the body up and carry him over ten feet of open ground before I could breathe a sigh of relief inside.

I unlocked the front door first, then went back to the car to retrieve the body. The night was dark, the neighborhood asleep. Still, I didn't love walking out into the open with a body slung over my shoulder, even if it just looked like a roll of plastic to whoever might be watching.

Last one, I told myself. *Last one and you're done.*

My roommate, Chris, was gone, working the night shift. This meant I had the entire house to myself, even though I really only needed the bathroom.

Once inside, I dumped the old man's corpse into the tub with a loud clunk. The body was already growing slightly cool. Best to do this now before *rigor mortis* set in.

Using the same hunting knife, I cut off all of the man's clothes and bundled it up with the plastic. Then I went into the bathroom closet where I kept the bleach and began unscrewing bottles.

Twenty one-gallon containers to do the job, and even with the windows open and the fan on I could feel the fumes burning the nose hairs out of my nostrils. I was wearing rubber safety goggles, which helped, but last time I swore I was going to get a full-sized face mask.

Just one of the many things I never got around to.

.   .   .

IT TOOK eight hours when all was said and done. Six hours to dissolve all of the soft tissue. About thirty minutes to wash all of the grimy, red soup down the drain, and then another hour and a half to bleach and clean the remaining bones.

Chris wasn't home yet but even if he rolled in a little early, I would still be okay. Despite the heavy fumes in the air, his living area was downstairs and he often used the basement door to come and go. He'd never know.

The urge to turn in and get some sleep was strong. I had been up all night and now that the sun was out, I felt weary. There was still work to be done though, so I bundled up the bones in a navy-blue duffle bag and stashed them in the back of the van where I had put the rolled-up plastic while I was waiting for the flesh to dissolve.

Beaky and Rico would take the whole lot, including the van, when I dropped it off tonight, giving me a loaner in its place. Shit, they'd probably have to torch the whole vehicle. The old man had bled *a lot* and the plastic didn't quite catch all of it. The vast majority of it had pumped out as I dragged him to the van at the rest stop, but the human body held a lot more blood than I had thought prior to taking this job and the old man was determined to get as much of it on me and my backseat as possible.

The thought reminded me to take off my clothes and throw them in there too. I had already taken off my shirt, which was soaked all the way through, but there were some definite stains on my pants and probably my socks and shoes. It would all have to go.

I had seen the cop shows, the ones where they crack a case by finding a single hair or drop of blood. If they ever searched my place, I'd be fucked. This was only my third kill, and while it hadn't been pretty, the first two had been even worse.

If the cops ever went over my place with a fine-tooth comb,

they'd find blood, hair, fibers—the whole shebang. I just had to hope they never did. I had been careful but not skillful. A number of things could have gone wrong but to the best of my knowledge, they hadn't.

No one rolled up on me while I was hauling a dead body somewhere. I had ditched the cell phones of the first two women as soon as they died so I hadn't carried a *tracking* beacon home. No flat tires or getting pulled over. It had all gone according to plan, more-or-less.

And now it was over, thank the stars.

For some reason, I had never had any qualms about killing people and when Beaky offered me the job and told me what I'd be making, I jumped at it. It was risky, sure, but not as risky as running dope for twenty years on the streets. Not as risky as boosting cars in middle-class neighborhoods or running guns or some shit.

No, this was tight. It was short, relatively easy, and Beaky did the worst part: he got rid of the bones.

After this next payment, maybe I'd get an old Mustang or something. Something with a lot of get-up-and-go. Or maybe I could get one of those cool guns the cops used. The big handguns that looked blocky and plastic and held a million bullets.

First thing I'd be doing though would be getting a new house. Maybe in Florida where the rest of the operation was. Beaky hadn't said so precisely but it sounded as if they had operations all over the country, maybe even the world.

Which made sense. Hell, I hadn't even known him and his kind existed until an old friend showed me in the basement of a strip club on the South Side. We were playing poker when Rico came through a door that I thought was a closet and I almost shit myself.

The closet wasn't actually a closet but a hole that apparently led down into the ground. I had only been there once to meet Beaky, but the place was wild. It was half-jungle, half-wooden city. I didn't get a good look at the place as I moved from one structure to the next, but I would have killed to see what lay beyond the city limits.

Maybe I'd see if I could move *there.*

I fell asleep on the couch thinking about living in a wooden city populated by giant animals that played poker and did blow. It wasn't a nightmare, really, but it was unsettling. The creatures kept looking at me with wild animal eyes. Some wanted to eat me while others just wanted to kill me and dump me by the side of the road.

There my body would lay, flies buzzing over my corpse as giant rodents scurried around me with bags of bones. Building something.

I AWOKE to a pounding on the door. I shot up and made my way across the living room to unlock it.

"What the f-" But the word died on my lips as I stared into my roommate's pale face.

"Dude, you gotta see this," he said.

A draft of wind blew through my legs and I realized I was standing there in my boxer shorts.

"Hold on," I said, ducking back inside to grab my robe and slippers. I tried to remain calm but my heart was hammering.

Did I miss something? Did he find the bones in the back of the van? The garage was mine, he was just renting the basement. We had agreed that that part of the property was off-limits, but what if he had gone in any way?

"Okay, what's up?" I asked, sounding calmer than I felt.

"You just gotta come see," he said, his head shaking from side to side.

I followed him out as he began to explain how he had stayed at his girlfriend's that morning after getting off of work. Apparently, they had slept together for about six hours before he got up and came back here to grab some stuff. That's when he found the body in the backyard.

He had then panicked and run to knock on my door. There was a basement door he could have used inside the house that connected the two floors, but the staircase was piled so high with shit he couldn't get through there if his life had depended on it. The situation made for a sort of fire hazard, but honestly it was a nice assurance that he'd never come stumbling upstairs some night.

"What do you think it is?" Chris asked, staring down at the dead thing.

And it was definitely dead. The creature's stomach had been punctured and gouged open, its head torn completely off. I swallowed.

"It looks like a deer or something, but some sick fuck put swim trunks on it."

"Not many deer got big thumpers like that," I said quietly.

"So what then?" Chris said. "A rabbit?"

A rabbit in dirty yellow swim trunks, I thought. *And I bet he smells like grape if ya lean down and sniff 'em.*

"Looks that way," I said, trying to react how one might expect a normal person to react. One who had never seen man-sized rabbits before. "Pretty big though."

"I mean, this is a hoax right? This has gotta be a hoax, like them pictures of Bigfoot?"

I didn't answer. Instead I continued to stare at the gaping wound where Rico's head should have been, the tough gristle sticking out into the grass.

What the fuck was this? I asked myself. *A message?*

It definitely felt like one. Did they know he came and talked to me yesterday? Were they reminding me who was in charge and not to get any wise ideas?

Must be. I reached up and ran a hand through my hair.

So what, I thought. *This doesn't change anything. I still got the package. This is still my last one.*

"So who do we like...call?"

The question caught me off guard. "What?"

"Like, the police? Animal control?"

But I was already shaking my head.

"I'll take care of it," I said.

Chris hesitated. "Well, how are you gonna-"

"I'll take care of it," I snapped. "It's my property, my responsibility."

This answer didn't seem to satisfy him, but I drilled the point home with the deadliest stare I could muster. He finally nodded and turned away. For a second it seemed like he was going to go inside, but then he turned back.

Neither of us said anything, we just looked at the giant white rabbit, its head nowhere to be seen.

"Hmm," Chris said after a minute.

"Yeah?"

"It's just..." He waved his hand.

"Just what?"

"It kinda smells like grape."

I took care of the body, or at least, that's what I told Chris. Truth was, I just dragged it to the back of the van and jammed it inside with all the rest. If I got pulled over and searched or something, I'm not sure if the extra corpse would help or hurt my case. Hell, maybe I could play it off as movie props or something.

It was evening now, the sun just beginning to dip below the horizon. I cruised slowly down the backroads of the city until I reached Kessler's Bar and Grill. The establishment was shoddy with bad siding and a bunch of burnt-out neon lights in the window. It did maybe...sixty grand in a year after taxes.

Good thing booze and burgers weren't the only sources of cash flow.

When I walked in, there was a girl on the tiny stage singing to an empty room. She wore cheap bedazzled sunglasses in the shape of stars and looked to be about nine months pregnant. I stopped and watched her for a second but her gaze never fell on me. Instead, she looked from empty seat to empty seat, making eye contact with no one at all.

The song was a classic that I couldn't quite remember the name of. She hit the notes just right and had great control over the microphone position. I watched her lumber around the stage for a few more seconds and then made my way back into the corner office.

"How'd it go?" asked Beaky. He was seated behind a desk in the backroom, his denim jacket pulled tightly over his feathered chest. The membranes that served as his eyelids flashed. He clacked his beak and tilted his head, assessing me.

"Good. No one saw anything." I learned a while ago that straightforward answers worked best.

Two giant taloned feet appeared up from behind the desk and deftly worked the cork out of a bottle of Jack and poured two glasses just a little higher than I was prepared for. The feet disappeared again and he used a wing to nudge a glass in my direction.

I picked it up and took a sip. The burn was welcome, nothing compared to the bleach fumes from earlier.

"The van?" He asked, piercing me with his raptor eyes.

"Around back, like you said." I waited a beat. "You'll find another body in there too."

The boss tilted his face toward his own glass of whiskey, his tongue flicking out a few times once he was close enough. He blinked and shook his feathers.

"I assume you're keeping the head for something?"

"Yes," he said. "Nutrients. If you really want it you can find it in the milky white splatter I leave on the hood of the Mayor's Jag tomorrow morning."

"He wanted me to stop."

"I know."

"Look in the trunk of the car and you'll see I didn't."

"I know that too," he said. "That's why your face isn't mixed in with his in my gizzard right now."

I nodded. "So this is it then. The job's done."

"This one is, at least," he said. "I'll have more stuff coming your way."

"Hopefully with a little less risk," I said. "I'll do whatever dirty stuff you want but the more I roll the dice the bigger chance of getting smoked. Maybe something a little less visible next time?"

"You're not the one who gives the assignments," he said, clacking his beak in irritation. "And I don't take orders from pinkies."

"I wasn't-"

"Shut the fuck up," he snapped. "You'll do what I say. You're a tool. If a tool gets broken on a job, it can be replaced. Maybe you need to be a little more *careful*."

I tried not to let him hear the grinding of my teeth.

"Come back here tomorrow and I'll have something for you. That is, of course, if you brought the goods tonight like you said."

"I did," I assured him.

"Good. This shipment is the last piece of the puzzle. I have someone that I answer to and if the package isn't in pristine shape then it won't be me you're answering to, it'll be him."

"They're exactly what you asked for," I said, putting on my kindest voice. I knocked back the rest of the drink and stood up. "Am I good to go?"

"For now."

"When do I get paid?"

"Once the package is delivered and okayed by the big guy. If all goes according to plan, we should have the money by tomorrow. Oh, and Gary?"

"Yeah?"

"Next time someone goes behind my back, you come and tell me before I have to get my beak dirty. You understand?"

"Loud and clear."

I left the bar with my fists clenched at my sides, the pregnant girl with the star sunglasses still belting away at an empty room.

THE CAR they loaned me was a piece of shit. The thing had been Frankensteined together out of a bunch of different vehicles and lurched down the road like a three-legged cow, sputtering black smoke and backfiring every 200 feet.

It pissed me off. The whole interaction pissed me off. I had done a good job for Beaky. A *damn* good job. And he treated me like some lowlife scum bag running crank. Better than Rico, though. Geez.

When I got home, Chris was still freaking out about the body.

"What'd you do with it?" he asked before I could make it to the door. He had been in the backyard with his girlfriend having a small campfire. Empties littered the ground and picnic table and I couldn't help but notice he had dragged the table about as far away from the place where the body had been found as possible.

"I got rid of it," I said. "Why?"

He threw a glance over his shoulder at his girlfriend who was reclining in a lawn chair with a beer in one hand and a cigarette dangling from her mouth.

"Carrie wanted to see it."

"Why?"

He shrugged. "I don't know. She was curious."

"Did you go and call all your friends and tell them we found a man-sized headless rabbit in our backyard?"

"Of course not," he said, his darting eyes betraying the lie.

I turned towards him to face him square.

"Chris?"

"Yeah."

"Keep your fucking mouth shut about this. I looked into it and it's not a person. You have nothing to worry about."

"Fucking obviously it's not a person," he rambled. "It had goddam rabbit legs."

"So we agree then."

"Agree on what?"

"That it wasn't a person. No one is in danger. And we're dropping the whole thing."

"What?" Confusion blazed on his face, enunciated by how drunk he was.

"That's what the DNR told me."

"DNR?"

"Yeah. Department of Natural Resources? I called them and they told me it was a deer with a genetic mutation that had escaped a facility a few miles away. It sucks but it happens."

"A genetic mutation?" He scrunched up his face. "Was it born without a *head*?"

"No, they said that was probably done by another deer." The lies were flowing freely now. "They do that, you know. They kill other deer with genetic defects."

"Is that true?"

"I don't know. That's just what they told me."

Chris looked dejected, like he wasn't quite ready to buy it.

"I can give you their phone number tomorrow if you'd like. They'll tell you all about it."

"Why not now?'

"Because you're drunk now. You going to work like that?"

"I'm not drunk," he slurred. "And I took the night off."

"Chris." I grabbed him gently by the shoulders. "Go sit back down with Carrie. We'll talk tomorrow."

I WASN'T QUITE sure what I'd do if he asked for the DNR's number tomorrow. Hopefully, he'd just forget. If he pushed it though, I could always give him the number to someone down at Kessler's and tell them to tell Chris what I had said. They could even answer like a DNR receptionist and everything.

Maybe. With Beaky acting the way he was, they might just as soon eat his head like they did Rico.

Like I gave a fuck. Chris was okay as far as roommates went but he was becoming more and more bothersome by the day. I just didn't want to have to clean up another body.

MY EYES SNAPPED open in the middle of the night and I sat up listening. Something was wrong. Something I couldn't quite put my finger on. It wasn't anything obvious, just a low tone that hadn't been there before when I had gone to bed.

It took a few minutes to place it, but when I did I threw off the covers, hopped into my robe and slippers, and padded out into the hallway.

I flipped the lights on as I made my way through the dark house, my suspicions slowly solidifying until they were confirmed in the kitchen. The noise was coming from the overhead fan on the stove, a low grating sound as the air was sucked up into the ventilation system. I moved hesitantly in and clicked the button off, the sound dying away.

Then there was a click from behind me. The sound was distinctive. Metal on metal. Someone had just pulled the hammer back on a gun.

I turned around slowly, my hands raised.

Sitting at the dining table was a massive figure, its silhouette framed by the yellow light from the window behind him filtering through the shades of the blinds. The orange glow of a cigarette lit up a furry face with black beady eyes and a whiskered snout beneath a tilted fedora. There was also the smell of something wet and musty in the room, like standing water from a previous night's rainstorm.

"I'm unarmed," I said weakly.

"I know." The voice was deep and husky.

"What do you want?"

"The package you delivered to Beaky's last night. It was defective."

Defective? What the fuck did that mean?

I tried to formulate the question but couldn't quite verbalize it. The creature saw me struggling and spoke to what I had been thinking.

"The bones were weak. Brittle. Cancerous."

"So?" I asked, just a sliver of incredulity sneaking into my voice. "Aren't they going to be ground up for spells or something anyway?"

"It's not that kind of spell," the creature grated. "I need new bones."

"What about the second body?" I tried. "The rabbit."

"Did I ask for rabbit bones, motherfucker?"

I pursed my lips and shook my head, my gaze falling down to the gun. It was big and heavy, the barrel a dull silver. The hole at the end seemed to stare out at me like a hungry eye.

"You know you're not the only one doing this," the thing said. "The others have finished gathering bones as well. And some of them *failed* as well."

Sweat soaked my back, clinging to my robe. I couldn't move very fast in these slippers if it came to it. I was a sitting a duck.

"They paid from their own pockets, ya get me?"

I nodded.

"You gonna pay from your own *pocket,* boy?"

"No, sir."

"I ain't a fuckin' *sir.* You pinkies are *sirs.* I'm a builder and I'm a killer. Got it?"

I dipped my chin in acknowledgement.

"You have until nine o'clock tomorrow night. That's about 18 hours from now. Bring the package to Kessler's or it'll be me coming to get ya. Now say it."

"Nine o'clock tomorrow night," I croaked.

"The whole thing."

"Nine o'clock tomorrow night at Kessler's or it'll be you coming to get me."

"Good." The chair he was sitting in creaked as he stood up, something heavy slapping to the ground behind him. "Now walk back to your room and close the door. Don't come out for five minutes or I'll shoot you in the tummy. After five, you can come out and I should be good and gone."

I did as he said, not sure if I could go back to sleep. My heart was hammering, my teeth chattering away. I had about 18 hours to procure another body. I had to get started now.

My thoughts were moving like glaciers but thirty minutes later, I had my plan. Taking another jogger close to dawn was risky. I could get caught and even if I got away, I wouldn't be able to haul a body with me. What I needed was a sure thing and enough time to process the body in the tub.

The answer was Chris. Being his roommate, suspicion would fall on me quickly. By the time someone noticed he was gone though, I would be too. Hopefully, down in Mexico or maybe the Philippines. Somewhere warm and far away from here. The only problem right now was his girlfriend, Carrie.

Chris had driven her over here and she was probably pretty drunk. Chances were good she'd be staying the night. If that was the case, I'd do them both. Hell, maybe even get paid double.

I moved quietly to the seldom-used basement door, turned the handle, and eased it open. The hinges didn't creek but even in the dark I could see that getting down the stairs would be a problem. Shit was piled everywhere. Boxes and bags and empty bottles. I'd have to move slowly and carefully.

After about four minutes of easing up and over the piles of trash, my slippers finally landed on the cold cement of the basement floor. There had been a few close calls. A bag that rustled as I knocked into it with my leg. A box that tipped, only for me to catch it in the last moment. But once I was down the steps I was home-free.

I gripped the hunting knife in my hand.

The door to the bathroom was half-ajar, the light turned out.

Good, I thought. *No one catching me from behind.*

Even so, I quickly glanced down the hall to see if any other lights were on that might indicate someone somewhere I didn't want them. All was dark and quiet.

Continuing to move carefully, I made my way to Chris's room. The basement was dark, only a little bit of streetlight coming in through the egress windows from outside. I knew the place well though and managed not to run into any walls. This was my house, after all.

Unlike the basement door, the hinges to Chris's room did creek as I pushed it open. I stopped, not moving. Nothing.

I would have to move fast. Flip the light on or no? If I flipped it on I could shock them and see what I was doing. If they were still half-awake though they'd be able to respond to an attack much better.

No. I knew where the bed was. I'd just stride over and sink the knife into whoever was sleeping there over and over again until they stopped kicking. I prepared to move.

A heavy body suddenly knocked into me from behind and we both grunted.

"Fuck," I heard a woman's voice say.

The feeling was mutual. She must have used the bathroom with the lights off, not wanting to disturb anyone. She had just padded in and done her business and padded back out. No lights, no flushing, no handwashing.

Without thinking, I rushed forward and thrust the knife into where I thought she would be. She whimpered as the blade stuck home and something hot and warm ran over my hand. Then she started thrashing.

"Jesus. What the fuck. Holy-" And on and on like that, shock and pain etched into her voice. As if she had just stubbed her toe.

I pulled the knife out and thrust again. Once again, I felt the knife go in and this time she screamed. I pushed forward, knocking her to the ground.

It was dark and she was flailing her arms and scratching at me as I jumped on top of her and straddled her like a mechanical bull. I turned the knife around and brought it down hard over and over again while she screamed, warm drops of blood spattering against my face.

Then the light flipped on behind me, ripping the world back into visibility.

Carrie looked bad. She was wearing an extra-large t-shirt with a beer logo on it, the fabric soaked with blood and puckered with holes. Her face was wild, like an animal. Her eyes bounced around the room until they landed on me. She brought her nails up to rake my face in a sudden fury at the same time I felt something crash into the back of my head.

Pain seared across my scalp as I tumbled off of the madwoman. I rolled and saw Chris standing there, still drunk but sober enough to realize what was going on. He was holding a shotgun across his chest, presumably having just used the stock to bludgeon my head.

"Gary, what the fuck?" He screamed. Then he aimed the gun at me.

I moved fast, hoping surprise was still on my side. Chris hesitated just enough, the gun going off as I pushed it up toward the ceiling. Plaster rained down on the three of us. I brought my knife up into Chris's gut once, twice, three times.

But Chris was a big dude and still a little drunk. He managed to push me off of him, then brought the gun to bear on me as I fell to the ground. I brought my hand up to shield my face, just barely managing to get out the first half of "*wait*" before he pulled the trigger.

There was a flash and I saw my right hand disappear as half of my field of vision went dark. It felt like bees were inside my face, buzzing and stinging. The pain was bad but more surprising than debilitating.

Later, I would think "birdshot." Chris had just blown off my hand and half of my face using birdshot. But right now I wasn't thinking, I was reacting.

Screaming wordlessly, I pushed myself up and charged out of the room, half tripping over Carrie as she rolled around. I heard the *chunk* of the shotgun as it pumped behind me. I tried to duck and doing so probably saved my life.

There was a giant boom as I felt the top of my scalp rip away. I continued on, turning at the basement door, fumbling for a second with the lock, and then charging out into the open street.

I looked around frantically, not knowing where I was gonna go. The cops weren't on their way yet but they would be, if not from Chris then from the neighbors hearing a shotgun being discharged in the middle of the night.

The streets were empty, so I took off down the road.

I DON'T KNOW how long I ran before I heard sirens, but as soon as I did, I ducked into a hedge on the side of the road. Blood streamed down into my one good eye and the pain in my face was growing steadily in intensity. I didn't want to reach up and touch it for fear of finding it worse than what it felt like, which was pretty bad.

A couple cruisers screamed on past with their lights on, followed a few seconds later by an ambulance. They'd be looking for me soon. I had to get the fuck out of here.

Maybe I could steal a car. Even as I had the thought though, I realized that my knife was gone. I must have dropped it at some point in the melee and I doubted I'd be charming any cars to the side of the road looking the way I did.

I crawled backward through the brush, the twigs and branches scratching the good side of my face. Once I was through to the other side, I stumbled to my feet, my head swimming.

Shit, how much blood had I lost?

I reached down and took off one of my slippers, which had miraculously stayed on, and pressed it to my face. The rough texture stung a bit but if it could slow the bleeding then it was worth it.

I looked around the yard I had crawled into. The house was a two-story with white siding. They had one of those little signs that indicated they had a security system set up for their property. Did those just work for the house or the yard as well? Either way, I had to get out of there. I had to get far away and get some help.

Maybe Beaky would help.

Fat chance, I thought. *He'd just as soon hand me over to the guy he answered to. That monstrosity that had been in my kitchen.*

No, for now I just had to run and hope I came across some opportunity. Maybe someone just getting into their car for an early start to the workday. If I could just get some wheels...

I walked past the house and through the backyard, jumped a low fence, and then walked through another person's yard before I was back out on the street. I was just about to cross when a car suddenly screeched around the corner, bathing me in headlights.

I froze like a deer, watching it approach. Then, just as I was turning to run, it pulled up alongside me and threw open the passenger door. The overhead light was out but I didn't need it to tell who was driving.

"Get in," croaked a voice. It was a voice I recognized. The one from the kitchen, I turned on my heel.

"Get the fuck in," it hollered. "I'm not going to hurt you."

Despair flooded through me. I had nowhere to go. My face hurt like Hell and the cops were on my ass. I got in the car.

.   .   .

ONCE I WAS BUCKLED into the passenger seat, the pain in my face truly hit me. Exhaustion washed over me and I closed my one good eye.

"You look like shit," said the thing beside me.

I barely managed a groan in response.

"I take it things didn't go as planned." There was a soft click as the creature lit a cigarette. "Name's Nathaniel, by the way."

"Nathaniel?"

"Does my name shock you more than my existence, Gary?"

"I think it's the combination of the two," I admitted, then groaned. Talking made my face hurt.

"It's not actually as bad as you think," Nathaniel said. He reached over and flipped down the visor mirror. "See for yourself."

I couldn't see much in the dark car, but as we passed a streetlight, my face came into view. It was simultaneously better and worse than I thought. Better because I thought the entire side of my face had been blown off. It was shredded, for sure, but it wasn't pure gristle. Not like my hand.

And worse because it was me. Seeing my own face like that was shocking beyond anything I could remember.

"It won't matter soon," Nathaniel said.

"Why's that?"

"Because of this."

There was a loud bang and I felt something ripple in my gut. I raised my hand and it came away sticky. I looked over at Nathaniel and saw the gun now, held tightly with his left hand between his big hairy belly and the steering wheel.

"Wh-Wh-"

"Why?" Nathaniel asked for me. "Because I'm sick of you pinkies, that's why. Sick of your soaps and detergents and all that shit. Sick of what you do to the water. Sick of you wearing us as coats."

A streetlight flashed by, illuminating the interior of the car for a second. That's when I finally realized what he was. Nathaniel was a beaver. A huge fedora-wearing, cigarette-smoking, beaver.

I groaned. My gut hurt worse than anything, even my pulverized hand.

"It'll be over soon," he said. "You can consider this a mercy, actually. Being spared from the stars."

Those were the last words I heard from him before I passed out.

I FADE in and out of consciousness now. I am being dragged across the ground. It's cool and wet and particularly rough. It smells like swamp here. My face is burning and my stomach has started to spasm. The pain is almost unbearable.

I WAKE up for what I believe is the last time. Nathanial is hunched over me, gnawing on something. I feel a pull and realize the thing he's gnawing on is me. There is a thick squelching sound and then I see my leg in his hand, chewed off at the knee. He turns it over and begins to remove the flesh with his paws.

Past him is a giant mount of bleached bones. Hundreds of bodies' worth. Maybe thousands. Beaky wasn't kidding when he said they had people working this thing everywhere. Even so, it's not until I see Nathaniel take the bone and place it among the heap that I finally realize what it is.

He's building a dam. Has *built* a dam, actually. I'm the last piece.

I turn and look behind me. The sun is just beginning to rise, revealing a large lake. On the other end is a fire burning out on a beach. A large black building stretches up behind it and if I'm not mistaken, I can hear the sound of a woman screaming.

The screams are certainly screams of pain but as I listen it becomes clear that she's not being murdered or tortured. No, the cadence of the screams is something I've heard before. There's a certain swelling and rhythm to them. They come in between the pushes.

Whoever it is, this stranger is giving birth. Down at the other end of the lake where a fire burns against the black hills of the coastal landscape, something is coming into this world. Something new. Something old. Something I had a hand in.

Nathaniel comes back and starts chewing on my other knee. The sound is so horrendous that darkness overtakes me. No stars for me. No revelation. Only the sick, wet gnawing of teeth on bone and cartilage.

I slip away.

BLUE CHAMELEON

THEY WAITED UNTIL THE SUN WAS DOWN AND THE STREETS WERE empty, then they came for me.

I knew they would. I had something of theirs. Something valuable. I didn't know what it was quite yet but I recognized the packaging. Small blue gel tabs with the image of a purple lizard on them. Couldn't be anything else but designer drugs.

I came upon them quite by chance. Stuck my nose where it didn't quite belong but hey, in this day and age you gotta be on the lookout for opportunities because they sure as shit ain't gonna advertise themselves.

Mine came in the form of a small tan briefcase left in the mens restroom of a subway station. I was the only one in there, so I decided to give it a peak. After quietly sitting down on the toilet and locking the stall door, I tried the small metal clasps. Locked, of course.

This wasn't anything beyond my capabilities, however. I had been on the streets for as long as I could remember and you don't do so without picking up a few valuable tidbits.

The combination dial read 6-7-0. Bizarrely enough, I had

come across very similar dials before on briefcases. Maybe 0-4-4 or 1-9-9.

What this usually meant was that they had just bought the case. Most modern briefcases came with the ability to set the combination and therefore defaulted to 0-0-0 with its factory settings. If people didn't plan on using the case for a while or simply didn't care to learn how it worked, they never bothered changing the combo, opting instead to leave it on 0-0-0 and give it a quick twist of the thumb before they set out. Their thumb pads were usually only good for two individual dials, hence the similar numerals right next to each other with the occasional third dial being moved either one or two notches.

6-7-0. I tested out the handle and positioned my thumb. Interesting. Chances were good that the person who had held this last was left-handed. Most dials had the last two digits changed rather than the first two.

Either that or I was full of shit and the pattern of two high numerals next to a single low numeral was just a coincidence. I didn't think so though, so I quickly thumbed the dials back until they read 0-0-0. I popped the clasps.

Voila.

However, the sense of triumph was displaced once I saw what was inside. Laid out in six neat rows were piles of grey tube socks. Socks. What a joke. I almost put the case back.

But then I stopped myself.

The idea of carrying around socks in a briefcase seemed ludicrous to me. So ludicrous that it gave me pause. Now, if I were trying to conceal something, what would I use to hide it. Something boring, right?

And what was more boring than socks? Hell, it was practically the go-to joke for boring kids' presents at Christmas time. Opening up a beautifully wrapped gift just to reveal a pair of socks was almost an insult. A slap in the face. The perfect anti-gift, because that money could have been used buying something cool like an air gun or video game.

This was all stuff I had picked up from listening to rich kids talk, of course. I didn't receive a birthday present myself until I was seven and that turned out to be a hand-knit sweater. Not quite socks, but clothes nonetheless.

The thing is, I loved it. Winters in Blackburg were notoriously rough on the streets so getting thick warm clothes was about the best thing I could have asked for. Though I'd have taken socks too if they'd been presented to me.

But to most people—people who carried briefcases on the subway—socks were boring. I hefted the case and shook it a little. Something rattled inside. Not as loud or heavy as coins but definitely not socks.

I opened the case back up, removed the socks, tapped out what ended up being a false bottom, and looked at my catch. The real catch. The thing the socks were meant to conceal.

There must have been a hundred of the tiny bags, each one with roughly ten of the blue tablets inside. The case had been left here on purpose, for a pickup probably. Any minute, someone would be walking through that door to find me with their drugs sitting in my lap.

I took one crucial moment to think about the situation. A small case with a combo that hadn't been changed. The most obviously boring thing to cover up the goods. A significant gap between the drop-off and pickup.

The people facilitating this little handoff were amateurs. If they had been pros, it would have been a more secure case and it would have never hit the ground. It would have transferred from one person to the next while something distracting happened elsewhere. Or the exchange would have taken place in a more secluded area.

No, these weren't pros. Far from it. The people they

answered to though, were probably a bit more serious. And if that was the case, then what I currently had in my possession was a boat-load of drugs that was about to hit the streets. Or maybe it already had.

A new drug. A powerful one, probably. That's how it always started. Flood the streets with the most potent version of the drug you can, get the people hooked, then remove it from circulation, driving everyone to a significantly less potent product that was far easier and cheaper to produce.

That meant that this case was worth more than its weight in gold and would likely be worth twice as much once it got pulled by whoever was producing it.

I didn't think twice. Like I said, street rats like me gotta keep their eyes out for opportunities and this was a big one.

Three minutes later and I was walking up and out of the subway station. The case swung casually at my side, my grey hoodie draped over it. Boring. Invisible. Like socks.

I smiled to myself, walking back to my apartment. An invisible target on my back.

I'M A NIGHT OWL, always have been. It's the only time I can think properly. When the sun is out and the streets are full and everyone is going on living their normal lives, I feel like the noise is too much for me to handle. Too much is happening and it makes me feel like I have to shrink down and hide in a corner until it's over.

I was awake when they came, the soft plodding of boots thumping through the floor as they approached my door. The rattle of gun straps. The hiss of breath through tight lips.

I didn't hear it as much as I felt it. I had been living in this building for close to twelve years now and it gave off certain rhythms. During the day, it sang with the activity of fifty families locked in everlasting turmoil. At night it creaked and thumped with the comings and goings of single men and women or folks working the night shift.

Now it was yelling. Practically screaming as the men approached. And by the time I heard the scrape of the automatic lock pick in the door, I had the case in my left hand and a small 9mm Firehawk in my right.

I didn't want to use the gun for a number of reasons, first and foremost being that I was extremely unlikely to survive a firefight with what sounded like a team of professional hitters. Then there was the fact that I had used the gun before. I had been in a tight spot much like this, and I was gone before I could tell if anyone had been killed.

If they had, however, and the police processed the crime scene, then there would probably be forensic evidence tying the gun to the crime. And if I used it near my apartment, they could match the ballistics to those other crime scenes and link the gun to the occupant of the room where all the shooting had taken place.

The little 9mm was what people on the street called "hot," but I hadn't gotten rid of it. Guns were expensive and I was perpetually three months behind on rent. And these days, nobody dared travel the streets at night unarmed.

So when they came in, I was already headed down the fire escape. I had left quickly, not bothering to shut the window. I should have, I know, but I heard the door opening as I climbed out and didn't want to make any noise pulling it down behind me. They'd know where I went but hopefully not until they cleared the apartment, which gave me a couple of seconds.

As I moved, I reconsidered my situation. The handoff earlier had indeed felt amateurish but this didn't. A whole squad of armed men? I hadn't seen them yet but I'd have bet both of my thumbs these were professionals.

So what did that mean exactly? If they used amateurs to hand off the product but were willing to send a whole squad of goons after me, that meant a new player was in town. Someone with considerable resources who was just beginning to implement them but hadn't quite developed a sophisticated network on the ground level yet.

Furthermore, an organization couldn't just pull a bunch of street thugs out of their ass. Street rats like me had *loyalties.* Well, okay, *obligations* maybe. But those obligations were pretty binding and there were tons of folks you didn't want to cross by bringing in a new product.

Considering that and the particularly sloppy work that had allowed me the opportunity to get my hands on this case, I was willing to bet the new "street thugs" were actually just kids. Green and impressionable, this wouldn't have been the first time a bunch of teenagers had been roped into something nefarious like this.

But if my hunch was correct and the runners on the streets *were* kids, then this could only end one way: badly.

This all flashed through my mind as I scurried down the metal steps. Once I had made it to the floor below mine, a voice drifted through the open window above.

"Fire escape."

The words were clipped and tense. Shit, I should have had more time. How had they cleared the apartment so fast?

They hadn't, I realized as I looked down at the street below. On the side of the road opposite the apartment building was a black van. Its windows were up and they were too far away to see through to the inside but the moment I saw it, I knew.

They had been watching my room. Had probably seen me hop out the window and immediately radioed the guys inside. Damn.

I couldn't climb very fast with the case in my hands and by

all rights, I should have just dumped it and bolted. Considering how fast they had found me, that could only mean one thing: there was some sort of tracking device inside the case.

Of course there was. The product was valuable. Extremely valuable. No chance they'd entrust that to a few runners without a backup in place.

I couldn't let it go though. This was my chance. The drugs inside had to be worth a fortune. If I let it go now, I'd be right back where I was, scratching through the alleyways for cigarettes, barely able to pay rent or buy food. No, this was my ticket out and they'd have to pry it from my bloody hands.

Unfortunately, that's what they seemed hellbent on doing. Something red flashed across the metal rungs beneath me as I hurried down the escape, and before I could think twice about it, I jumped and hurled myself through the nearest window just as the rapid pops of silenced submachine gun fire clattered above me, chewing up the platform I had just been standing on.

Up until this point, I had jumped through exactly two other glass windows in my life.

The first had been as a kid in an abandoned house on the Southside of town when one of my friends had dared me to do it. I had hesitated just a little too much as I leaped and paid the price as my foot caught on the ledge and got carved up by the remaining glass still sticking out of the frame.

The second time had been from the second-story window of an industrial warehouse when it got raided by the cops. That time I had shot through the glass like a canon, suffering only a few scrapes on my arms and forehead. I dislocated my shoulder as I landed on the back of an empty delivery truck that had been parked down below, but that was a whole different problem.

This time was the best of both worlds. I sailed quickly and cleanly through the cheap pane, getting nothing but a scratch on my forehead. Better than the times before. Better than if I had been turned into Swiss cheese. Better than dead.

I hit the ground with a loud thud and rolled headlong into something solid. It was dark, only a little light streaming in from outside. I sprang to my feet, trying to catch my balance and orient myself. I could hear the occupants of the apartment scrambling and grunting in the next room over and knew I had mere seconds before they were out here.

Thankfully, every apartment beneath me was set up like mine. Wasting no time, I bolted toward the door and twisted the lock, the gun slippery in my hand. The door came open but slammed to a halt after a few inches.

"*Fucking dammit,*" I grunted to myself as I hastily reached up and pulled the chain out.

Two seconds later and I was out in the hall, running. A door clanged open behind me and I heard the shouts of multiple men as I flew around the corner. They knew which floor I was on, which meant they could have me surrounded within seconds.

The apartment building was shaped like an L, with one entrance facing the road and another facing a small alleyway. If they were watching my room, then it was probably safe to say they had people posted at each entrance. That meant I had two ways out, up or down.

So I went up *then* down.

At the end of the hallway was another stairwell and I burst into it, fully expecting to be mowed down by a hail of bullets. Nothing though. The stairwell was empty.

I had gotten lucky. The guys chasing me were prepared enough to block the exits but not smart enough to improvise. If they had been smarter, they would have split into two directions and taken both stairwells. Instead, they had simply gone for the nearest one.

My feet pounded up the steps as I passed my floor and then exited out onto the one above it. Nobody in the halls. Good.

Moving a little lighter on my feet, I scurried around the corner and down the hall towards the opposite stairwell. This time, I opened the door quietly and peeked downward. No one, which meant they were on my tail, probably already on the opposite stairs.

My heart hammered in my chest as I hurried down, the briefcase swinging in my hand. I moved past my floor and then past the one below it. Four more flights and I thought I heard a door open above me, but by then, it was too late.

On the ground level now, I turned left, heading away from the entrance and into the building. Halfway down the hall was a maintenance room I had scoped out when I moved in. And at the back of the room was another door that led to a sub-level where they kept the boiler and a few storage rooms.

I tried the maintenance door. Unlocked.

I made my way across the room and tried the sub-level door. Also unlocked.

Glee surged through me as I opened it and skidded to a halt as a bald man in a black jacket with a blue bandana covering his face swung in surprise to meet me. He had been leaning against the wall, obviously certain I was not about to come through that door. He was wrong.

There was a deafening *bang* as I fired the gun from hip level and the guy jumped, a small hole appearing just above his left hip. He seemed startled by it. He looked down quickly and then back up at me, shock on his face. Then the submachine gun he was holding at his side began to rise.

I thrust my hand out and fired two more times. *Bang bang.* The second shot went wide but the first hit him square in the chest. This time there was no look of surprise.

His body went limp where he was standing and he crumpled to the ground.

Shit. A body. The cops would have my ass for sure.

Whatever. Better than dead.

I stepped over the dead man, the sound of the shots still ringing in my ears. My hands were shaking uncontrollably now and it was all I could do not to drop both the gun and the briefcase.

I managed to hold it together as I made my way down into the sub-level. From there, I skirted along the wall until I hit a small closet with a wooden door. Inside was a bare cement floor with a square metal door in the middle.

Without thinking, I tried to tuck the gun into the back of my pants, letting out an involuntary yelp as the hot metal touched my bare skin. I cursed, then awkwardly switched the gun into my left hand, which also held the briefcase.

The door was hard to lift with one hand but not impossible and after repositioning a few times, there was a loud screech of metal hinges followed by a clang as the door fell backward and hit the cement wall behind it.

Fetid air washed up out of the mouth of the sewer. There was a steep metal ladder leading down and after descending a few rungs, I reached up and pulled the door closed above me.

If I had had my wits about me, I would have simply set the gun and briefcase down on the ground, opened the door, picked them back up, then descended down into the sewers. At this point though, my wits were so far gone I'd have had to pay long-distance just to check in on 'em. Men with machine guns had broken down my door, shot at me, and chased me down the stairs.

And I had killed someone.

I was pretty sure the guy was dead. He sure dropped like he was dead. Like I said, I had fired my gun before in self-defense but I had never stuck around to see who lived and died. For all I knew, I had never hit *anyone*.

This time was different. I had pointed my gun right at a man's chest and pulled the trigger. I saw where the bullet hit. Saw his eyes as he realized he was dying. Then watched him crumple.

It was something I'd never forget. Something I still think about even now, here in the woods at the end of the world. I think about what it would be like to know you're going to die. What do you do at that point? Pray? Beg to some higher power? Quickly evaluate your life and see what it's worth?

My brain buzzed as I made my way through the dark underground passage. I made it probably twenty feet before I stopped and doubled back. Once I was standing beneath the metal door again, I popped the case open and started jamming fistfuls of the tiny plastic bags down into my pockets. It was a tight fit but my jeans were pretty worn and loose at this point, affording a lot more space than some of my other pairs.

Once my front and back pockets were full, there were still a few handfuls of the baggies left. I considered them for a moment, finally opting to tuck the bottom hems of my pants into my socks and shove the remaining bags down the legs.

It certainly wasn't comfortable that way, standing there with bulging pockets and ankles. And I knew it would be even worse walking. I could make it though. Would have to if I wanted to keep the drugs but ditch the case with the tracker in it.

I briefly considered sitting down and removing my socks and using them to carry the drugs. The thought of walking through the sewers with bare feet inside my ratty sneakers sounded pretty unpleasant though, so I ditched the idea immediately.

Before leaving, I glanced up at the door and considered it. There could be people coming through it at any second and I was just standing here like a knob waiting to get shot. Near the handle was an interlocking ring meant for a padlock but as far as I could see, there was no lock in sight.

I had seen rings like this before, placed on sewer entrances nearly a century ago by the City of Blackburg in a controversial and unprecedented move to halt the underground distribution of bootleg liquor. It had violated all sorts of city ordinances, of course, but when you're the one writing the laws and you've got the right people on your payroll, then you're only accountable to yourself.

A number of the rings had been removed since, mostly by knowledgable business owners. Apparently my landlords didn't belong to that group, and for once, I was thankful for their ignorance.

I could have used my belt to secure it but then my pants would be falling down even more than they were now, being dragged down by who knew how many pounds of designer drugs. Plus, I was pretty sure they would be able to wrench it apart after a few good pulls. No, I needed something a little more sturdy.

Taking just a few more precious moments, I reached down and began to disassemble the gun I was holding. The light was almost nonexistent, except for what was filtering down through the storm drains from the streetlights outside. Thankfully, I had taken the gun apart to clean it enough times to where I *mostly* knew what I was doing.

There was a tiny snap as I heard a spring let loose and then a small clang as a knob slipped through my fingers. Oh well, didn't really plan on using it again anyway.

After a few seconds, I managed to pull the slide mechanism off the frame to look at it. Then I tried forcing it into the metal ring and was relieved when it just barely fit. I pushed it in and gave it a few good thumps with the handle until I was sure that no one could open the door without breaking the metal slide first.

Finally, I hucked the bottom half of the handgun into the water. The police might find it but maybe not. Either way, I would not be returning here.

"You smell like shit," Mia said after opening the door. She was wearing black jeans and a low-cut v-neck, as if it wasn't 4:30 in the morning. Another night owl.

"That's a relief," I said. "I was afraid you'd tell me I *looked* like shit."

"You always look like shit, Aldo. I thought that was a given."

"Thanks. Yeah. Hey, could you let me in before I get shot in the back?" I turned and looked down the street for effect. Mia lived in a small single-story home with two other girls. From what I could tell, the neighborhood was asleep.

"Sounds like a good reason not to let you in." She leaned against the door frame as if we had all the time in the world. "What's in it for me?"

I reached into my pocket and pulled out one of the little baggies. I held it up in front of her face and watched her eyebrows rise.

"Shit, Aldo, do you know what this is?" Mia held one of the pills about an inch away from her face.

I was standing in the middle of the entryway, trying to kick my shoes off without touching them.

"I don't know. Drugs?" I stumbled as I managed to free my right foot. I finally gave up and reached down to pull the other one-off.

"Obviously. Hey, don't you step into my living room like that. Those clothes are going straight in the garbage can."

"But... I'm in them..."

"Doesn't matter," she snapped. "Strip. Nothing I haven't seen before."

I hesitated and she jerked her chin at me. I did what she said.

"So, what is it?" I asked as I pulled my shirt off over my head.

"It's called Blue Chameleon. I just heard about it like eight hours ago at The French Press." The French Press was the name of a local nightclub.

"But the Chameleon is purple," I pointed out. "The background is blue."

"Yeah, it's like those colored word tests, remember?"

"Can't say I do," I said truthfully.

"Like when you have to say the color of a word but the word itself is the name of a different color. For example, you read the word 'blue' on a page but the color of the text is red. When you're asked what the color of the text is, you want to say blue because that's what the text *says*, not what it is."

"You lost me."

"Something about incongruence in the brain. Or maybe the world. I can't remember. Apparently the drug makes you trip balls though."

"Gotta be more than that," I said as I dropped my boxers into the pile of dirty clothes on the ground. I reached down to cover myself. "People at clubs don't just wanna see a bunch of weird shit. They wanna *feel* it. It's gotta give them that warm fuzzy feeling they can't get anywhere else."

"That too," she added, thankfully not looking in my direction. "Supposed to feel like slipping back into your mother's womb."

"Isn't that what they say about all narcotics?"

"Yeah, but apparently this one is the shit. It's like stepping into a different *world*. Gabriel made it sound like he was experiencing infinity."

"Infinity? Sheesh, what's coming down like?"

"Hard to say. When I spoke with Gabriel he was still tripping. He was babbling about seeing old gods and I kind of got the sense he was looking right through me as he talked." She pointed a finger down the hall. "Shower. Go."

"You got it." I turned and took a few steps, then turned back. "Yeah, nice try. No way I'm leaving all this shit out here with you."

Now Mia did look at me. She crossed her arms. "You think I would steal from you?"

"It's not impossible," I said as reasonably as I could.

She shrugged. "Yeah, I guess I can give ya that." She turned and rummaged through the closet for a second and then came out with a cloth bag that may have been used for groceries at one point. "Here, use this if you're so worried. You can even take 'em into the bathroom with you."

I nodded and began to reach down for my pants.

"Whoa, whoa, whoa," she said, reaching down with me. "Please don't bend over. I don't need one of my roommates coming out and accidentally staring straight up into a man bent over by the coat closet."

Hot water streamed down my face and chest, melting away the tension of the last few hours. I spent a considerable amount of time scrubbing the sludge off of my legs and then carefully inspected some of my wounds.

I had a cut on my head from the glass, friction burns on my thighs and ankles from the little baggies, and a few cuts along my left side. The cuts were small but numerous. I wasn't sure if they were from the broken glass or if I had taken a few bullet fragments when the guys had opened fire on me.

Either way, it wasn't a big deal. Could have been worse. A lot worse.

The image of the dead man's eyes flashed through my mind. The look of shock and concern. Of fear. Fear of what was happening and what was to come.

It was strange to think that he might know something now that no one living did. If there was an afterlife, then he was probably there. He had passed through the veil. Been let in on the secret.

What was it Mia had said? *Experienced infinity.*

I tried to put it out of my mind. I listened to the squeal of the shower, the hot water thrumming against my body like a heavy rain. I wanted to be thankful for my good fortune tonight but wasn't quite sure who to be thankful to.

I didn't believe in God and as far as I saw it, thanking *the universe* was just a way of thanking God without acknowledging his existence. No, I was in control of my own fate. That was the only way it could be. On the streets, you took responsibility for yourself because there wasn't room for luck or mistakes.

AFTER GETTING out of the shower and drying off, I walked into the living room with a towel wrapped around my waist and the bag of drugs hanging from my shoulder.

"You plan on going back like that?" Mia said.

"I don't know which *back* you're talking about," I replied. "But if you mean my apartment, no. I don't plan on going back there *ever.*"

Over the next ten minutes, I explained how I had come across the drugs, been chased by gun-wielding goons, shot a man, and trudged through the dark sewers. Mia didn't seem phased by the part where I talked about gunning someone down but then again, if what she had told me about herself in the past was true then she was hardly an angel.

"So what are you gonna do?" she finally asked.

"Sell it," I said. "Preferably once it gets pulled from the streets and replaced with something less potent."

"You gonna cut me in?"

"No real way around it." I shrugged, tightening the towel a little tighter around my waist. I was sitting on the couch now and while the towel was long and did a considerable job covering up the bits, I preferred to stay covered. I still felt vulnerable.

"Ten percent," she said.

"Six," I replied without thinking.

"Hey, I'm not looking to squeeze ya. I realize you're in a tough spot right now and took all the risk upfront but you *know* I could ask for as much as fifty right now. You got nowhere to go and it wouldn't be hard to figure out who's looking for you. All I'd need to do was point a finger."

"You wouldn't do that," I said, feeling my face flush.

"No. And I'm not, which is why I'm only asking for ten. Plus, I can help you. I have connections."

I mulled it over for a second, slowly acknowledging that I didn't have a lot of leverage sitting there naked in her living room with literally nothing to my name now but the pills.

"Eight," I said.

"Fine, eight. But we're renegotiating if I begin to feel like I'm in danger. I'll gladly take eight but the moment I see someone with a gun then my price doubles. Then it keeps doubling for every gun I see after that, clear? Gives you some extra incentive not to take any unnecessary risks."

"As if I need an incentive for that."

"I know you, Aldo. You need it."

I didn't have a snappy comeback for that. Instead, I nodded. "No unnecessary risks."

GREY MORNING LIGHT was just beginning to seep through the blinds when my head hit the pillow in Mia's guest room. I was asleep before I could even get under the covers.

Dreams plagued me. I wasn't sure if it was the events of the night before or sleeping in a strange bed, but for the next ten hours I found myself walking through a litany of bizarre scenarios.

The first one had me running endlessly up and down stairs. Somehow I knew that some version of Hell was down below and Heaven was up above. As I ran, my pursuers hot on my trail, I wasn't sure where I wanted to go. Obviously, I didn't want to go to Hell but I wasn't sure I belonged in Heaven either. So instead, I just kept running.

Next, I was down in the sewer being followed by something in the water. I was moving slowly now, wading through the scum with my pockets full of drugs. And every couple moments I would hear a soft swirl as something slid through the water behind me.

I caught sight of it a few times. Inky black hair slithering across the surface like a black snake. But when the figure rose up and I caught sight of its face, I saw that it was a woman with telescoping eyes. They bugged out of her head and moved in multiple directions, not all dissimilar from the images of chameleons I had seen on nature channels. Except one of the woman's eyes was green, the other black.

Finally, I dreamt I was walking through some old forest at night. The sky was brilliantly clear, the stars shining above me so fiercely that I suddenly understood why ancient people might think they were their ancestors.

Now, as I strode quietly through the trees, I realized I was hunting something. The only problem was I didn't know what. There was a loud crack up ahead as a big shape moved through the underbrush. I stopped and waited, listening.

While I stood there, it occurred to me that I was dreaming. Reality began to come apart at the edges and suddenly the thing I was hunting was gone, as if any semblance of control was bound to cause it to spook and go bounding off into the darkness.

This was the last thing I remembered when I woke up and for some reason, it left a hollow pit in the center of my chest. I wanted to go back, to forget. I knew something had been lost but I didn't know what.

MIA and I went out that night just to observe people. If she had already heard about Blue Chameleon then it was on the streets. The only problem was that we knew literally nothing else about it. We didn't know what it did or why people might want it. It was a hallucinogen, of course, and Mia had said that it made you feel like you were 'returning to your mother's womb,' but it was hard to really understand what that meant without experiencing it.

The thought did cross my mind to just take one of the pills and see what happened but Mia talked me out of it. First off, if this was indeed the next big thing then we could probably score some in a club without digging into our own stash. Second, it might be helpful to watch someone jump off that proverbial bridge first and let them tell us how far the drop was.

That prospect didn't bother me as much though. After all: nothing ventured, nothing gained, right?

My only concern right now was being recognized. I didn't know who these guys were but if they were as connected and organized as I thought, then their lack of seasoned street people was probably pretty offset by a healthy network of legal and political connections. And with those, it wouldn't be too hard to trace my apartment address to a picture of me.

The only thing worse than the risk though was the thought of sitting alone at Mia's doing nothing. Maybe she was right. Maybe I did need some incentive to be more cautious.

The club we were going to was six blocks east and two blocks south of the house. There was the distinctive sound of heels on the sidewalk as her roommates, Ali and Sabrina, walked out ahead of us. I slowed down just a bit to put some more space between them and Mia and me.

"What's this place called?" I rolled my shoulders a bit. The night was warm and the shirt Mia had found for me was so soft and silky that I felt like I was wearing nothing at all. It would have been nice if I felt like partying but I didn't.

"We're hitting up McDowell's first," Mia said. "It's a bit of a dive but that's where the guys go. They'll do a bit of pre-gaming to work up the courage to ask us to a real club. Then when we walk into wherever we're actually going already on the shoulders of a couple dudes, the heavy-hitters in the club will try and leverage us onto *their* shoulders with booze and drugs."

"Heavy hitters?"

"Yeah, ya know, the guys who are there to *hunt*. They think they can buy us with a good time?"

"You're making it sound like they can."

Mia flashed a smile at me. "Depends on how good a time."

"Geez, I never knew it was so complicated."

"It's not, really. Think of it like a marketplace: everyone wants something; it's just a matter of figuring out what it takes to get it."

"Wow, look at you: Mia the capitalist."

"Mia the *realist*," she corrected me. "I feel like you should be able to appreciate that."

"So what is it you want?"

"What, tonight? I suppose I want to get a better grip on our product."

"No, I mean, what do you want, generally speaking? This obviously isn't your first time doing this."

"I don't know," she admitted. "Sometimes I want a guy to take me home but other times I just want to dance and get wasted. Half the time I don't even know what I want until I'm halfway to getting it. That's the beauty."

"Sounds like a headache."

"What about you?" she asked. "What do *you* want? *Generally* speaking, of course."

"On a night like this?" I leaned back and looked at the sky. The city lights obscured everything overhead, making the stars above feel like little else than theory. "I'd like a cheeseburger, a pack of cigarettes, and a good book."

"That's it?"

"That's it."

"Sounds, uh..."

"Simple?"

"Boring," she said, a slight frown on her face.

"Exactly."

"So why are you doing this?"

"Doing what?" I asked.

"Going through all this trouble," she said. "Just to make some money."

"We've created a world where you can't survive without money," I said. "Even if you find someplace out in the woods to build a cabin and live off the land, you still have to pay taxes. Which means it's literally *illegal* to live without money."

"Never thought of it that way," Mia admitted. "That's pretty depressing, actually."

"It is and it isn't. We live in a world with over seven billion people. Some of them will have power over you. In fact, with that many people living on one planet, there will always be somebody who can simply kill you just because you're inconvenient to them. And it's not just America. It's everywhere, all the time. Hundreds of years ago, kings and queens would regard common folk as nothing but tools to fuel the engines of their kingdoms. And before that, you could be killed simply by being an outsider to a tribe."

"So what then, you just live your life as a part of this machine?"

"Hey, you're the self-described realist," I said. "And this *machine* isn't man-made. It's simply the way things are. The only thing that truly exists is power and I'm just looking for enough of it to be ignored and left alone."

"Then what?"

"What do you mean, *then what*?"

"Well, what happens after that?"

"What do you think happens?" I replied. "Then you grow old and die."

Mia was quiet for a long moment, then finally said, "You're kind of a nihilist, aren't you?"

"I'm an atheist, not a nihilist."

"No, *I'm* an atheist," she shot back. "But just because I don't believe in God doesn't mean I don't believe in anything."

"I believe in something."

"What? What do you believe in?"

"I told you. Power."

"Nah, you gotta believe in more than that."

"Like what?"

"Like, I don't know, making the world a better place or something?"

"Is that what you're doing?" I asked. "Making the world a better place?"

"In my own way, yeah."

"And you want to move past religion, right? Because it's antiquated or something?"

"And dangerous and oppressive and controlling, yeah. What's your point?"

"Well, let me ask you this: what do you think of all these rumors of cults floating around?"

"I think it's awful, obviously. That's the whole *reason* I'm an atheist. I think cultists are dangerous, even if it just so happens to be the cult of Christianity or Islam or whatever."

"Here's where you and I differ," I said, slowing down a bit more. "I take control of my life. I take *responsibility* for my life. And the only way to do that is to get just enough power to where no one will fuck with you. *You*, on the other hand, in your trying to make the world a better place, have actually made it worse."

"What?" She said, visibly angry now. "How so?"

"Because you're trying to make this utopia where everyone's nice to each other. Where there's no religion. No hatred. No oppression. But in tearing down the old world, you've let a hundred other oppressive religions rise. Religion rises out of humanity all the time, whether we like it or not. Modern society has torn down all the major monotheistic religions but in doing so, we've created a power vacuum. And now things are beginning to rise and take their place."

"What, you mean like murder cults?" Mia laughed.

"*Everyone* is in a murder cult," I said coldly. "If you think that violence is justified for *any* reason *ever*, then you will use it to preserve your sacred values. And what is that other than a murder cult? Sure, the sacred values are *different* for lots of people, but if they require the spilling of blood to preserve them, then how are they different from these cultists bleeding folks dry in back alleys in the middle of the night?"

"They're different because they're *wrong*," Mia said.

"Yup. And that's exactly what they think about us."

"Except they *are*," Mia said. "We're not in the middle ages anymore. There are things we know without a doubt."

"Like what?"

She threw up her arms. "I don't know. We know the Earth revolves around the sun and not the other way around."

"Does it?"

"Yes. Obviously, yes."

"Have you seen the edges of space?"

"What?"

"The edges of space, have you seen them?"

"No. Why?"

"Because a center is only a center in so far as it relates to the edges of a specified area. The sun is the center of our solar system, yes, but it's technically possible that the Earth is directly in the center of the universe. It could be sitting absolutely still while all the other solar systems and galaxies rotate around it."

"That's not how gravity works."

"Gravity is only measured in relation to other objects. Once again, we don't know what else is out there and how many degrees our system is removed from the edge of existence."

"Ugghhhhh," she moaned. "You're making my head hurt. So, what's your point?"

"My point is it's extremely unlikely that Earth is at the center of the universe."

Mia exhaled. "It sounded like you just agreed with me."

"Almost. I said 'unlikely' but not certain."

"Shit, Aldo. Certain enough."

"Right. We are certain enough. But it's still a matter of faith.

And a person's faith is defined by their personal experience, not facts alone. Some people believe in a talking snake and giants and a devil and a God that sends you to Hell just for saying a bad word. They believe it because all those beliefs are like planets in a galaxy, rotating around a central point. And people have different central points. They are almost *literally* living in different worlds than we are. Everything is related to everything else differently than it is to us. And that's just the way it is."

"And your point is?"

"My point is, my gravitational axis is power. Everything else exists in relation to it. Yours is happiness and the vision of some better world that will never exist."

"You know you're a real buzzkill, right?"

"I've been told that, yeah."

"Do you know what you need tonight?" Mia said, the tension suddenly melting off her shoulders.

"What do I need?"

"You need a spiritual fucking *experience*."

IF A SPIRITUAL EXPERIENCE is what we were looking for, I couldn't think of a worse place to have one than McDowell's Pub. The place smelled like sour booze and sweat and half the people there were over the age of forty and looked like they wanted to hurt me.

Mia was my guide now, so I followed her lead. We sat at a high top in the middle with Ali and Sabrina and ordered drinks. Then, sure enough, it wasn't long before a few awkward guys came striding over.

A few of them eyed me suspiciously, trying to decide if I was competition. I stayed mostly silent while they exercised their attempts at conversation, the sound of ice clinking in my glass as I drank my way through the painful stretches of dead air.

Twenty uncomfortable minutes later and we were headed off with the chumps to bigger and better locales. At least, that's what I thought before we arrived. The French Press was loud and packed and everywhere I looked there were dudes prowling the crowd for women. Some wore easy-fitting clothes with just a hint of drip while others wore tight shirts to show off cosmetically toned muscles.

I'm a small guy but I was pretty sure I could take most of these swaggering bros in a fight. An incredibly *guy* thing to think, I know, but so many of them seemed very concerned with advertising how strong they looked. I guess toned abs might be some sort of measurement of strength in whatever world these men inhabited, but in mine I had won fights by being the first guy to try and bite the other guy's eyeball.

And there's no ten-thousand-dollar gym machine to prepare a pampered boy from the suburbs for that.

To be fair, I did see a few guys walking around with a sort of understated strength. They moved gracefully through the crowd, not quite looking cut but definitely sturdy. It was the kind of strength one either got from moving a lot of free weights or working ten-hour shifts down at the docks.

These men were definitely stronger than me. It was possible that I'd be able to take them through sheer intensity but they'd just as likely wrap their arms around me and squeeze until I passed out. A number of them had bent noses and tiny scars around their eyebrows. Blue-collar guys then. Workers who got in the occasional fight and took some hits.

What I didn't see yet were guns. It was pretty easy to tell if someone was packing. They always moved with a certain *hop* in their step. They gave people space and their hands were always close to their sides.

None of that here, however. Lots of chatter and posturing and semi-aggressive body language between dudes but so far I hadn't seen anyone who looked as if they might have belonged to whatever organization was distributing the Blue Chameleon.

"I'm *going to step into the girls room for a second, cool?*" Mia tilted her head towards a hallway that branched off just to the left of the bar.

I gave her a thumbs-up, watching Ali and Sabrina trail after her. The guys, whose names I couldn't have produced with a gun to my head, stood awkwardly next to me for a few moments before hustling up to the bar.

That was the last I'd be seeing of them, I figured. They'd either get distracted by some other girls, spooked off by some other guys, or simply lose patience and return to the comfort of the dive we had come from.

And to be honest, I half-wanted to follow them back there. As much as I liked Mia, this wasn't my scene. Too loud. Too showy. Too...*competitive*. Thinking about it more, nothing made me feel more like I was watching some Nat Geo special than seeing a few stumpy rich boys quietly square off with each other while their girlfriends huddled off to the side with drinks in their hands, enjoying the show.

"What a bunch of animals." The voice was soft and velvety, and when I turned to see who had spoken I found a woman standing just inches away from me. I took a step back.

She was just a few inches taller than me, probably a bit under six feet. She had shoulder-length hair as black as crude oil and wore a slim red dress that hugged her hips and fell just below her knees.

The most striking feature of hers, however, was her eyes. The right one was as black as her hair and the left one was emerald green.

"Mind if I cut in?" Her voice was quiet but once again managed to cut through the noise of the club like a knife, as if half of its volume was coming from inside my head.

"Isn't that what people say while they're dancing?"

She shrugged and I found myself drawn to her thin shoulders. She saw me looking and tilted her head.

"I don't know," she said. "I think it's applicable in all horrible situations, not just dancing."

"Do you have something against dancing?" I asked.

"Only the kind of dancing that happens here."

"I see. So what horrible situation are you rescuing me from then?"

She smiled but it didn't quite reach her eyes. "The situation where you don't go home with me."

I laughed. "I've heard a lot of bad pickup lines tonight but that one might be the worst."

The smile slid off her face and she turned away. My heart fluttered in a sudden panic and my first impulse was to apologize. I managed to stifle it, not just for the sake of my pride but because there was something about this woman that gave me an odd feeling. And not necessarily a good one.

She swiveled her head from side to side a few times, as if considering what to do next. Then she slipped away through the crowd.

Once again, I felt a strong wave of panic wash over me and I had to remind myself that I was here for a specific reason. But a few seconds later, she looked over her shoulder and smiled at me. Then she lifted a tiny bag and winked.

At this point, I'd have recognized the bag anywhere. Two tiny blue tablets flashed against the skin of her palm and without a second thought, I pushed my way after her.

The crowd thinned somewhat as we approached the hallway that advertised the restrooms and as I rounded the corner, I passed Mia. I jerked my chin at the woman in red. Mia stopped and turned back toward her, seeing the woman push through the men's room doorway.

"What are you doing?" Mia asked.

"I think I'm about to find out what Blue Chameleon is like."

THE BATHROOM WAS LARGER than I expected, with a long mirror against the back wall and an accommodating number of urinals and stalls. The room certainly wasn't empty—a few guys hurriedly finished up at the sink while some others turned around at the urinals to look over their shoulder at the woman who had just walked past them to make her way down to the final stall.

Before entering, she cast a look back at me and even from here I could see the shine of her green eye flaring in the fluorescent lights. I followed tentatively, my palms sweaty and heart racing. The whole thing had the air of some sexual encounter, and I was convinced that's what the others in the bathroom thought was about to happen.

It also occurred to me that she could be the bait for some trap set by whoever had hit my apartment. For all I knew, there could be a man waiting in there with her to jam a knife into my neck. Hell, she could be the one with the knife.

I didn't think so. Surely it would have been easier to seduce me over the course of the night, get me drunk, and lure me back to an apartment or some dark alley to knock me off. Even failing to do that, they could just follow me back to wherever I was heading afterward and send a crew after me as they had before.

Escaping the first time had been pretty lucky and I didn't think I'd be able to pull the same moves twice.

Upon entering the stall at the end, the woman reached up and grabbed my shoulder. I involuntarily flinched away and she smiled.

"Jumpy, are we?"

"Sorry." I cleared my throat. "I'm usually alone in these things."

"You're *funny*," she said, crinkling her nose. She raised her hand and showed off the tiny baggy. There were two pills inside, each with the tell-tale chameleon printed on it.

"Where'd you get these?" I asked.

"A friend."

"Your friend didn't want to party?"

"Oh, we partied," she said. "But she let me take a few for the road."

"Something tells me you can't drive on these," I replied.

"I wouldn't, no. So what do ya say? You wanna meet God?"

The phrase pulled me up short. "If I didn't know better, I'd say that sounded like a threat."

"Oh no, babe." She opened the baggie and jostled the tabs out into her palm. "This god is like nothing you've ever seen before. This shit'll make you feel like you're laying in bed on a warm Saturday morning. It'll make time stop."

"That doesn't sound like a good thing."

"You're kind of starting to sound like a buzzkill." The woman's eyebrows furled. "You a cop?"

"Do I look like a cop?"

She studied me for a moment. "No, I guess not. So we gonna do this or what?"

"Sorry. I'm just a little afraid I'm going to have a bad reaction. Why don't you do it first?"

"Sure thing, babe." She tilted her head and popped an eyebrow. "But you gotta promise to take care of me."

And before I could object, she placed the pill on the flat of her tongue and curled it up into her mouth. She smiled, her throat working as she gulped it down.

"Now c'mon. You can't leave me hanging."

I hesitated, then I reached out and took the tablet.

. . .

AT FIRST, I didn't feel anything. We left the bathroom and the woman dragged me out to the dance floor. As she pulled me by the hand, I shouted, "What's your name?" But she just looked back at me with that single green eye.

The bodies pulsed around me as the music swelled and I wasn't sure if it was the drug or not but I began to feel warm. Not uncomfortably warm but definitely warmer than I had been. I threw my head back and felt the muscles loosen in my neck. The lights swirled overhead and I felt as if they were the pin-prick pupils of silent stars looking down at me. Watching me. Waiting for something to happen.

At one point, I saw Mia. She was dancing with two guys and I could have sworn I saw one of them palm her something. We caught each other's gazes a few minutes later and I saw my own smile reflected on her face.

All of a sudden, I had the immense urge to walk over to her and kiss her. We had never known each other like that but now it seemed like nothing else was possible. Like we were destined to be together forever. The pull was strong. Magnetic, even. I began to walk.

Before I got to her, there was a loud bang and everyone ducked to the ground. A few people screamed and the music played just a hair too long before it was finally shut off. Baffled, I turned and saw a group of men cutting through the crowd, directly toward me.

No, not men. They had the shape of men but they were anything but. All of them wore blue bandanas and carried submachine guns, but the parts of their faces that were showing were scaled and had elongated eyes like chameleons.

I blinked, trying to snap myself out of it. Warmth still radiated through me and I couldn't tell if what I was seeing was real or just a part of my imagination. As they got closer, it began to feel real. In fact, it felt more real than real. Like experiencing something in a dream that—were you to try and replicate the same scenario in real life—wouldn't even come close to making you feel as intensely as it had while you were asleep.

Emotions tore through me. Sadness, despair, submission, and ultimately acceptance. I felt as if I was in a myth. A lesson for readers in some faraway place. But for the life of me, I couldn't discern what the lesson was.

Tears flowed from my eyes. I looked across the sea of scared and frightened people as they crouched down on the floor, flinching away from the armed lizard people as they made their way through.

And the last thing I saw that night was the butt of a gun as it smashed into my face.

I woke up on a train. It jostled a bit and I felt my body bounce in the seat. Rivers of pain snaked out from my nose, merging with a sea of dull ache that occupied the rest of my head. I winced and pressed my eyes shut.

No, not a train. Too quiet for that.

I opened my eyes and looked out the window. Clouds as thick and vast as a rolling desert stretched out around us. They were so white and solid that I felt as if I could walk on them if the plane were to stop in this exact place and let me out.

I turned and looked at the seats around me. They were all empty but the one immediately to my left.

The woman was so close I could smell her. She smelled of moss or maybe seaweed. It wasn't bad but it was slightly unsettling, as if she had just crawled up out of the ground or up from the bottom of a river bed.

"Am I dreaming?" It was the only thing I could think to ask.

"Do you feel like you're dreaming?" She turned and looked at me. I was expecting to see the two eyes I had seen before, the green one and the black one. But now I saw that her left eye was covered by a patch.

"I do," I answered truthfully.

"And if you feel that way for the rest of your life?"

I swallowed. "Do you *expect* me to feel this way for the rest of my life?"

"I don't expect anything," she said. I noticed she wasn't smiling. "Blue Chameleon will do strange things to you. It will challenge your perception of time, which as far as you're concerned, is to challenge time itself."

"Excuse me?"

"Everything you know about time is what you've experienced. My guess is that you haven't experienced anything novel with regards to time for a while now. But you're about to."

"I still don't understand."

"You will," she said.

A loud beeping sounded overhead as the plane suddenly pitched forward. The air pressure began to squeeze me and I felt something just inside of my ears fold like a bad knee. I looked down to see my knuckles straining white as they clenched the armrests.

"What the fuck is happening?" I asked desperately.

"We're about to crash," said the woman.

"What? Can't you do something?"

"Tell me, are you in control of your own life?"

"What the Hell kind of question is that?" I swung to face her but she was gone. In fact, I suddenly got the feeling that she had never been there at all. That the pilots hadn't been there either. I felt as if, through some elaborate accident, I had ended up thousands of feet above the ground and reality had finally caught up to the situation.

We were going down. We would hit the ground at several hundred miles per hour and in an instant, the materials that comprised the plane would flatten around me and crush me like an insect. And it was that thought that really drove the situation home.

I leaped up from my seat and hobbled to the door leading to the cockpit. I tried prying it open but it wouldn't budge. I wrenched on it a few times, then began pounding.

It was no use. I was about to die.

Die. *Me.* I was about to get crushed into a gory smudge. My heart would stop pumping and that elusive electricity would flee from my brain. What would happen then?

Would I end up in the afterlife? Heaven? Hell? Purgatory? Would I simply cease to exist? Here one moment and gone the next? I tried to pray but I couldn't. It suddenly seemed as if I didn't know how. As if I had *never* known how.

Is this what ran through the man's mind in the basement of the apartment building when I shot him? Or did he simply go "Oh shit," and then blink out of existence?

Any second and it would all be over. I've heard it said that there are no atheists in fox holes, but I sure didn't feel religious. No, I tried forcing a prayer to my lips. A final plea for salvation. But the only thing that came to my mind was a phrase. Neither religious nor non-religious.

I couldn't tell if I was saying it out loud or if it was just something stuck on repeat as I hurdled toward the ground. I could be dead in the very next moment but all I managed were two simple words.

What next? What next? What next?

Then, impossibly fast, the plane itself closed around me.

· · ·

I WAS STANDING in the woods. No words. No clothes. No sense of self. No past or future. Nothing but the current moment. Somewhere deep in the back of my mind I felt as if something tedious was going on in some imaginary life leagues and centuries and lightyears away from here. A life that was practically nothing. As quick and inconsequential as the twitch of an insect's leg before it gets sucked down into the gullet of a frog. Seen by no one and acknowledged by nothing.

I couldn't step back into that life any easier than a tree could step into a fallen leaf. All I could do now was watch the scene playing out endlessly before me.

It was midday, the sun high in the sky. A gust of cool wind blew across the meadow, bending short blades of grass. In the center of the clearing was a mighty stag, struggling in a tarpit. It kept snorting and trying to pull itself out but it neither managed to get free nor sink deeper. It simply struggled for what felt like eternity.

No. Correction: it struggles.

I keep standing and watching as its black eyes roll, its massive rack of antlers rearing up and falling back down. It stamps its hooves in the viscous substance, never giving up.

I keep waiting for it to end and reveal itself as a dream. I keep staring and doing nothing as the scene plays out before me.

And I keep not waking up.

THE BLOOD CURE

I'VE WORKED A LOT OF CASES IN MY YEARS AS A PRIVATE investigator but if you had told me the one that would change my life forever would come in the form of a half-in-the-bag college kid knocking on my door at 1:46 in the morning, I'd have said you were off your rocker. I stared at the figure through the glass of my office/apartment door, wondering if he was blurry because of the frosted glass or because of the incalculable amount of whiskey I had used to put myself to sleep not two hours ago.

I opened the door.

"Are you Detective Jack Lawson?" The kid said, he was wearing baggy grey sweatpants and an old Knicks tee with the sleeves cut off, giving me a generous view of his fleshy underarms.

I must not have been fully out or I'd have never heard the knocking. Instead, I was hovering in that purgatorial state where you can think clearly enough but the room you're in acquires the motion of a cabin aboard a ship during a particularly raucous storm.

I prepared myself to speak but thought better of it at the last second, unsure if I'd produce a sentence or a wave of vomit. I turned and looked at the letters on the frosted glass.

The kid took this as affirmation and tilted his head forward, asking to come in.

"Don't touch anything," I mumbled, walking back to plop down on the couch I had been sleeping on until recent discourteous events.

He looked around for a place to sit and I gestured at the wooden chair that sat on the other side of my desk.

"Except that," I said. "You can touch that."

He sat down.

"Do you live here?" he asked, his face crinkling slightly around the edges.

"Is that how you want to start this conversation?"

The kid nodded in way of apologizing. "Jeremy. I mean, I'm Jeremy, that is."

"Thought so. Seein' as I'm not." I slouched down into the couch, my blankets bunched beneath me. I closed my eyes for a second, resting them. "What is it you want, Jeremy?"

I couldn't see him through my closed eyelids but I could practically feel him twisting in that chair. The idea flitted through my mind that I was dreaming, having a nightmare about what the next day might bring. Clients who have problems but won't fucking tell you what they are.

Whatever, I'd let the silence do the questioning from here on out.

"I have a—girl."

"Good for you. Make sure to treat 'er right, kid."

"No, it's not just—well, she's missing."

"Why do you say that?"

"Say what? That she's missing?"

The silence put his feet to the coals for a few more seconds and then he continued to spill.

"She's supposed to be at my place, but I haven't seen her. Not for three days."

"Cops?"

"They'll ask if I tried her place, back in her hometown."

"And."

"Well, that's the thing. I think she's in trouble there. With her parents, I mean. Like, *bad* trouble. And I don't know who to go to about it. I'm trying to do things-" there was a squeaking noise as he shifted in his seat. "-differently."

I opened my eyes. "Okay, let's rewind a bit here because that's quite a bit to chew on. Where was the last place anyone saw her?"

"My place."

"When?"

"Three days ago."

"She leave a note?"

There was a crinkling of paper as he reached into his pocket and pulled out a sheet of paper that looked like it had come from a notepad. He leaned over to hand it to me but there was a solid two feet of space still separating us. He waited for a moment and finally stood up, walked over, and dropped it into my hand.

I looked at it, turned it sideways.

In messy handwritten cursive, it said, *"Gone to Ate - RONNIE"*

"Ronnie your gal's name?"

"Yeah."

"Tell me, Jeremy: does Ronnie typically go out to *ate*? Possibly with her mommy and daddy and a stuffed bear named Giggles?"

He reached over and snatched the paper from me, a bit of frustration finally beginning to show through.

"It's not what you think," he said. "She's a sophomore at the

U. Going for a degree in botany with a minor in applied mathematics. She's way smarter than me."

I righted myself on the couch, shifting my ball of blankets to the side. I leaned forward, rubbing my eyes.

"So you tell me then: what do you make of that?"

Jeremy shrugged. "Dunno. I looked up 'Ate' online and aside from the obvious, I got a few companies specializing in things like software development or logistics. All out of state. Nothing that would interest her."

"Where she from?" I asked. "Originally."

"Georgia. None of the companies have operations there either."

"Now," I sucked in a bit of air through my teeth. "You said you were trying to do things differently. What's that mean?"

I saw him clench his jaw, his brow furrowing.

"Reason I ask is because I'm king of trying to *do things differently*. Your cheeks are a little flushed right now. Could be nerves but I don't think so. I think you're here riding a wave of liquid courage, or you finally had enough of doing shit *to* yourself that you thought it about time you started doing shit *for* yourself. But you wanna do it right. Or at least, 'differently,' like you say. So you come here looking to speak to a professional, because last time you tried to help in your blunt but well-meaning way, people got hurt. By you. When you lost control and hurt them. This ringing any bells up there?"

I could see in his face that every word had been spot on, more or less. I leaned back.

"I've been known-" He looked down and clenched and unclenched his fist. "-to hit people. It's been an issue between Ronnie and me. Not that I've hit her," he rushed to say. "She just doesn't like to see me fight. And I figured if I drove down to her place and found something I didn't like. With her family, I mean.

Say they were treating her bad or something. Well, if I lost it with them then it would be over with us. Hundred percent."

I nodded. "So you tracked me down. A professional. At nearly two in the morning."

He nodded back, like I had just said the most obvious thing to him.

"How many other guys' doors you knock on tonight, Jeremy?"

"Three guys and a woman. Except I didn't knock, I just left notes on their doors telling them to call me. I had to do something, even if it was just that."

"But you knocked on my door."

He shrugged. "Your light was on. I figured *what the Hell?*"

I reached up and rubbed the bridge of my nose, still unable to let go of the suspicion that I was actually dreaming.

"So what are you gonna do when they call tomorrow?"

"I'll tell 'em to fuck off."

"You don't have to go *that* far."

"Right. No, yeah, I'll tell 'em I already found someone."

I gave him a thumbs up then asked, "So you want me to do what I do then?"

Jeremy opened his mouth to speak but I cut him off.

"And you know what it is I *do,* right? I find people. I'll roll into her hometown, take a picture of her getting the mail or drinking a beer on the porch or something and that'll be it. Found her."

"I don't just want you to find her," he said, then stopped.

"What? You want me to investigate her? I gotta say, it wouldn't be the first time I've done that for a client, investigate their significant other, but it would be a first if that ended well."

"No, there's something going on with her. She's been spending a lot of time with this professor."

Ah, I thought to myself. *There it is.*

"You want me to investigate the professor," I said. It wasn't a question.

"Not *just* the professor," he replied. "I want you to find out where she's gone. *Really*, gone. Hell, maybe she is at home, I don't know. But the note's weird, right?"

"Yeah," I admitted. "It's weird."

"So let's put it this way," Jeremy squared his shoulders. "Find out where she went. Start with the professor. She probably went home to her place in Georgia but maybe not. Wherever she went, figure out why. And look into her parents a bit too. There's something hinky there."

"Hinky how?"

"I don't know, she just..." He pursed his lips. "I haven't met them. Not yet. But she used to get along with them really well. But lately they've been arguing about something. She won't tell me what, but they actually called *me* a couple weeks ago looking for her. Said she wasn't answering her cell. They sounded mad but didn't elaborate."

"You ask 'em to?"

"Not really," he said sheepishly.

"Okay, so let me repeat this back to you." I clapped my hands together. I had meant to snap Jeremy to attention but only succeeded in startling myself. "Investigate Ronnie. See where she's gone. See what her professor has to say. What's his name?"

"Leo."

"Leo..." I twirled a finger in the air.

"Dr. Leo Stonehouse. In the Cultural Anthropology department."

"Anthropology." I raised my eyebrows. "You study a lot of anthropology to become a botanist?"

"No, and that's another weird thing." His voice ratcheted up about six notches. "What's she care about anthropology? She never talks about it, only that she sees him after class in his office a lot."

"Mmmm."

"Yeah, *mmmmm*." He blinked and shook his head.

"I'm not sure we're sharing the same *mmmm* right now."

"What do you mean?" Then I saw it click in his eyes. "Nah, I don't think so. Not her."

"Wouldn't be the first time a student was seduced by a college professor. Believe you me, I've got the photographic evidence."

But Jeremy was already shaking his head and I felt for the guy. "Nope. She wouldn't do that. Not Ronnie."

"Look, all I'm saying is: be prepared for anything."

WE WORKED over a few of the finer details. Timing, billing, that sorta thing. Jeremy rolled out around 3:40 when I called him a cab. He said he'd pay but I shoved a couple twenties into the driver's face before he pulled out. My charitable giving for the month.

Once I was back in my apartment, I replayed the conversation in my mind. It was solid. Weird, but solid. Guy with anger issues wants to go kick down some doors looking for his girl but knows that won't impress her. He's trying to change. Trying to be better.

I walked over to the sink, ran the tap, and filled a glass with water. I took a sip, swishing the liquid around the inside of my mouth for a few seconds before spitting it back into the sink. I then reached over and poured a couple fingers of bourbon into the same glass. I knocked it back and returned to my place on the couch.

The gal was probably cheating on him with the professor. She probably found out she was pregnant. Her family wants her to keep it and she doesn't. She doesn't know who the father is so she takes a few days to get her head straight. Just takes off for a bit.

I'd seen it a hundred times. Would have put money on it.

Good thing I didn't.

I HIT up the professor the next day around four. He was in his office, and a student was just leaving as I arrived. The student was young, blonde, and looked a little happier than I would have if I had just left a college professor's office. We made eye contact as we passed and she blushed, finding the tops of her shoes very interesting all of a sudden.

"Professor Leo?" I tapped lightly on the inside of the open door with the backs of my knuckles. The man looked up from his desk.

He was attractive. Younger than I expected, with blonde shoulder-length hair framing a soft face with intelligent green eyes. He tilted his head, no trace of the usual frown I'm greeted with upon introduction.

"My name is Jack Lawson, I'm a private investigator. You got a minute?"

"I've got an evening class at seven but should be good until then. What can I help you with?"

He radiated optimism, the kind I immediately distrust. It was hard to say if the defect there was his or mine.

"I'm looking for Veronica Dobbs. Friends know her as 'Ronnie.' You know her?"

"Ronnie! Yes." A look of concern passed over his face. "Why, has something happened?"

"Unclear," I said as I sat down in the chair across from him. The seat was still warm, presumably from Miss Rosy-cheeks. "I've been hired to find her. Seems she's gone missing."

"Missing?" He leaned back, ever so slightly. "I got an email from her a few days ago saying she'd be out for a week. Asked me to forward her homework."

"How many is a few?"

He looked up toward the ceiling, his lips moving silently as he ticked off the days.

"Four," he finally said. "I saw the email Thursday evening and sent her this week's assignments. Normally it'd be a bit more of a conversation but she's a great student."

"Huh. So you haven't seen any slipping grades or anything? No last-minute visits to your office begging for an extension?"

"Nothing like that, no," he said. "I mean, she's been to my office plenty but that's because I was trying to get her to switch majors. She's still in her sophomore year; it wouldn't be too difficult for her."

"Interesting," I said. "To uh, psychology, is that right?"

"Anthropology, actually. It's a fascinating field and she'd be great in it. She truly has a researcher's mind. Great with people. And she has *vision*. She wasn't made to be stuck in some greenhouse all day."

"Is a 200-level anthropology class normal for a botany major?"

"It's not uncommon, but I recruited her. A colleague of mine mentioned that she lived in Borhead, Georgia which is home to the fabled Lavernasynthe."

"Landera..." I gave up trying to pronounce the word almost instantaneously.

"Lavernasynthe," he repeated. "Only grows at the southern base of the Blue Ridge Mountains. Greek travelers brought it to Ireland hundreds of years ago and Irish immigrants brought it over here. They use it for blood cleansing rituals and mix it into a wide range of herbal remedies. Super fascinating stuff."

"I bet." I quickly rewound my brain, trying to see if there was some fascinating tidbit he had mentioned that I had somehow missed. "So what did you two talk about then? Couldn't have just argued about her major the whole time."

He laughed. "We never *argued* really, but she got heated sometimes. She could be like that. But who could blame her? It was her future, after all."

He kept talking but my attention had shifted to the back corner of the room where I had noticed something that was becoming increasingly difficult to ignore. I felt my pulse slightly quicken. The muscles in my throat and sinuses contracted and then relaxed. It was too much. I finally raised a finger and asked.

"They allow you to have liquor cabinets on school grounds?"

Dr. Leo Stonehouse twisted around to see where I was pointing, as if he didn't know what I was talking about.

"Oh yes, well, they allow me to. Or at least, they haven't come down on me yet. I figure it's better to ask for forgiveness than for permission." He swiveled slightly in his seat. "Would you like something?"

Two answers immediately dropped into my mind, one in the form of an angel and another in the form of a devil. I chose the guy with the fork and tail.

Professor Leo picked out a square bottle and retrieved a few tumblers from the inside of the cabinet. He apologized for the lack of ice in the room, poured two fingers in each glass, and then threw a dash of water in each from a water bottle he had sitting on his desk.

"You need a little bit of water in this to truly appreciate the taste," he explained. "Most of the good whiskeys are between 85 and 100 proof but anything over 80 can be physically unpleasant. Some good ice from a filtrated water system would be best but a spritz of spring water does just fine."

He handed me one of the crystal tumblers and I swirled the

liquid a bit. I reached over and picked up the water bottle. "You really think this is fed from a spring?"

"Don't you?" He brought the glass to his lips and took a sip.

"I think they could just as easily have gotten this from a tap in a subway station and you'd never know."

"Maybe I prefer to believe." He smiled and raised his glass.

I did the same. The liquor was good. Smoother than I expected, the flavor blossoming and solidifying into a robust smokiness, as if I was drinking the distilled essence of some yet-undiscovered woodland. I leaned back in my seat.

The room came to me then. My body relaxed as the images flooded in. Sticky notes on the walls with indecipherable messages. Diplomas. Pictures of Professor Stonehouse from different stages in his life. Shaking hands with people. Family. Friends. There were also newspaper clippings of his accomplishments.

Most of the images meant nothing to me. Then my eye settled on something peculiar. I jerked my chin at it.

"That bottle says it's from Georgia," I said. The auburn label proudly proclaimed that it was a Georgian bourbon. It even said the name of the city it was distilled in but I couldn't quite make it out. "Anywhere near the town Ronnie is from?"

Leo turned and looked at it, once again giving the impression that he didn't know what was in his own office.

"Yes, actually," he said. "She brought me that very bottle when she came back last. Have barely had a chance to dig into it yet."

A long stretch of silence passed, the alcohol easing the tension between us.

"If I was a professor with my own liquor cabinet," I said. "I think it'd be awfully hard not to offer a pretty young girl a drink now and then."

The professor blinked, a small smile tightening both sides of his face.

"How thick are these walls?" I probed.

"Not thick enough to stop rumors," he said gently, still smiling. "Not thick enough to stop a pregnancy. Not thick enough to stop an entire student body who's already suspicious of young, handsome professors."

"Sorry, you know I gotta ask though."

"I do," he said, then released a quiet sigh through his nostrils. "I'll say it directly then: I have let a few students drink in this office, though never more than what you got there."

I took another sip. "If I was younger and less acquainted with such *elixirs*, one drink of this stuff might be enough to send me stumbling."

"Maybe," he said. "Most of the students I'm chummy with are well-acquainted themselves though. Maybe even more-so than you."

I snorted.

"What you have to understand though, Mr. Lawson, is that I have never and would never take advantage of a student." He looked me dead in the eye. "I can't. All ethical matters aside, my career couldn't sustain something like that. Best case scenario: it's still a distraction. Worst case?"

"Death."

He seemed to be stopped by that, then he began to nod slowly. "Yes, actually. Death. That's a good way to put it. Even if I didn't take a short walk off a high bridge, it would still be the death of who I *am*. What I was made for."

"And what's that?"

"I'm here to learn," he said. "Just like all of my students. I'm here to probe the inner-most depths of what it means to be human. Across all boundaries of space and time and culture and biology, I'm here to find the center. The axis of all mankind."

"The axis," I said, tasting the words.

"Yes, the thing that unites us all. My work here allows me the flexibility to do my research and the means by which I can sort through my ideas and begin to articulate them."

"Teaching, you mean."

"Yes," he said. "I've found that teaching is actually an integral part. I can bounce ideas off my students. They're smarter than they act, you know. Lots of them are even smarter than me in certain ways. They're good sounding boards, once they have a firm grip on the basics at least."

"Mmmm." I drained the last bit of my glass. "So what do you think happened to Ronnie?"

Leo rolled his tongue around his mouth, thinking.

"I'm going to tell you something," he said, "But you didn't hear it from me."

I gave the smallest of nods.

"She admitted to me that they—some members of her family—hurt her."

"Hurt her," I repeated. "Hurt her how?"

Leo spread his hands and leaned back. "It's difficult to say, which is why I've been so hesitant to bring it up. It didn't seem physical though. I've seen people suffering from physical abuse and they act differently. This seemed more psychological. The kind of damage that she was just beginning to understand."

"How did this come up?" I asked.

"We were talking about family cohesion, how it differs in America from other places."

"How's that?"

"They're smaller," Leo said simply. "Or at least, they are in terms of household. Most places all throughout human history saw multigenerational households. Tons of people all sleeping in the same room. Watching each other live and die right there in the flesh. It's different and the effects of the differences aren't fully quantifiable yet. The two kids, two parents, and two pets thing works but just barely. There's some deficit there, something that evolution has bred into us that we just suddenly yanked out."

"And this provoked something in Veronica?" I asked, trying to get us back on track.

"Sort of," he said hesitantly. "She wasn't very forthcoming. She just explained that her family had been bad to her. Made her do things she wasn't comfortable with. And not just her immediate family but her extended family. Aunts, uncles, and grandparents; it sounded like. Or at least, that's the feeling I got."

I probed the professor for another twenty minutes or so, trying to pry a few more details loose but I didn't get much. He admitted that my visit had made him significantly more worried than he had been and when he asked what I was going to do, I told him.

"You think that's wise?" he said. "Just going and confronting them like that?"

"I'm not exactly going to be confronting them," I explained. "I'll just head down there, watch for a bit, and see what I can see. If everything looks normal, then I'll simply go and knock on the door and introduce myself. If Ronnie's there, then I'll try and convince her to come back."

"And what about the abuse?" he asked.

"That'll have to be something she sorts out on her own," I said, getting to my feet. "She's an adult. She has a stable boyfriend and decent access to mental health professionals here in the city. It'll be tough, but there's not much I can do for her. And even if I could, I doubt kicking her parents' teeth in would help ease her problems."

· · ·

AFTER TAKING a quick detour across campus to make sure that Ronnie wasn't actually just in her dorm, I got back in my car and pulled out my cell phone. I pulled up Jeremy's number to deliver an update. At the last minute though, I found myself staring at the numbers on the screen, my finger hovering over the call button.

I hit the home button instead, locked the phone, and then jammed it down into my pocket. I still didn't have as good of a grasp on the situation as I'd have liked and maybe Jeremy could shed some light on the matter, whether he did it intentionally or not.

There's a lot you can tell by watching how people act, especially inside of their own homes. Every home is like a map to a person's personality. I've found that messy people are often messy. Overly clean people can be neurotic. And everyone in-between simply lays out their house in terms of what they want and don't want the outside world to see.

JEREMY'S HOUSE was just off-campus and looked as if it had been a very nice building about thirty-five years ago. Since then, it had been slowly ravaged into a paint-peeled haunted house with a sagging roof, rotting siding, and lawn whose 10-inch-long grass was covered by a heavy matte of dead leaves that had fallen over a month ago.

"You uh—live here?" I asked, trying to refrain from judging too harshly.

"With a few other guys, yeah. We rent it from the Bonsons."

Now things were beginning to make sense. The Bonsons were something akin to this zip code's slum lords, preying on college kids who didn't know the first thing about what a maintained property should look like.

"We alone?" I asked, stepping inside. The entryway was

surprisingly clean, though the living room beyond seemed to have the normal stacks of empty beer cans one might expect in a college household.

"Yeah, everyone else has classes. C'mon."

I walked with Jeremy into the living room, then said, "Before we sit down, does Ronnie have anything in your room?"

"Yeah, why?"

"I want to take a look at it. Get a feel for what she may have left behind."

"Sure, but wouldn't her dorm be better for that?"

"Tried it. She's gone and I think her roommate is too. Plus, whatever she left behind here may be more helpful."

"Why's that?"

"Because if this somehow involves your relationship, then she probably would have grabbed whatever valuables she had here before taking off."

The thought of that seemed to quiet Jeremy for a moment, then he brightened up. "Well, actually, she didn't really take anything that I know of. So that's good, right?"

"Maybe."

"Maybe?"

"Could mean whatever is going on with her is bigger than your relationship."

No college kid in love wants to be told that there's something bigger than their relationship, and Jeremy *was* in love, no doubt about it. He gave a curt jerk of the head and led me down the hall, into his room.

The room was slightly damp with an underlying scent of sweat. The bed was rumpled. There was a pile of clothes sitting on the floor next to an empty clothes basket. Receipts and beer cans cluttered a small end table with a few books and notebooks on it.

He went immediately to the closet and started flipping through the clothes.

"Everything in the closet is hers," he said.

I moved quietly over to a dresser that was standing up against the wall. I checked to make sure his back was turned and slowly pulled the top drawer open a few inches. Socks.

"She has a few favorite dresses though and I don't think she'd want to leave 'em here. I'm not seeing them though..." He drew the last words out slowly as he continued to look.

I gently shouldered the top drawer closed and peeked into the second. The breath caught in my throat.

Nestled amongst a few t-shirts was the dull shine of a gun barrel, and next to that was the top of a box of .38 shells. I nudged it closed just as he turned around.

"Found 'em," he declared triumphantly. He pulled a few dresses off their hangers and showed them to me. One was a white sundress with large yellow flower patterns on it and the other was a slimmer black and maroon number.

"Hmm," I stepped closer to look at them, as if they might suddenly explain the whole situation. They didn't.

"What's that?" I asked, pointing at a bag in the corner. It was half open with a white blouse sticking out the top.

"Oh yeah, this is her main travel bag. She brought it with her when she came back from break. Apparently wasn't that important if she didn't take it with her."

I clicked my tongue against my teeth. How are you supposed to tell a hopeful boyfriend that that wasn't a good sign, that most people didn't just leave a bunch of their stuff before they disappeared unless they were planning to cut all their ties?

I probably could have figured out a gentle way to put it but I didn't. After all, I didn't know anything yet. So I switched tacks.

"How was she the couple days she was back?" I asked.

"Frazzled. Unable to sit still."

"If I'm being honest, I usually feel that way after getting together with my extended family too."

He laughed, some of the tension sliding off. "Well, she could be like that. A little high-strung. She wanted the world to be a very specific way."

"And what way was that?"

"I don't know." He shook his head. "Different. Less terrible, I guess."

A laugh lurched out of me before I could snag it back.

"Where do we go next?" he asked.

"We don't go anywhere," I said. "I'm going to take a quick swing down to Borhead and see what I can see."

THE ROAD STRETCHED out before me as I made my way south. A winter chill had set into the city streets but as traffic thinned and the sun set, I took comfort in the fact that every rest stop I pulled into would be a little warmer than the last.

It was a long haul, close to thirteen hours with stops for food and gas, but the silence was a welcome companion as I chewed the case over.

Ronnie goes home on Thanksgiving break. Comes back for a few days all in a tizzy. Takes off. The holidays could suck, sure, but what exactly was doing the sucking? Or who?

I thought about Leo. He seemed on the level to me, at least as on the level as a college professor could be, and by that I mean I didn't think he killed her. It was a hard thing to consider but it was necessary.

A professor knocks up an impressionable student, his career begins to pull away before his eyes, he acts out of desperation. Wouldn't be the first time. Plus, keeping liquor in his office right out in the open was asking for trouble. He must have either had some pretty big balls or some fine-ass professorial chops to be able to get away with that. I made a note to do a little more digging into his background.

I flipped the radio on, the oldies station was still in range but I started flipping through the stations. I was going on a road trip. I needed road trip music. The swell of a steel guitar caught my attention and I let my hand drop away from the FM dial.

I had done a brief search on the professor, pulling up all the important stuff. No rap-sheet. No controversies. He seemed clean as a whistle and blew just as much hot air. Seriously, guy could have talked for hours, days maybe, without me saying a word. He wasn't the kind of guy you had a conversation with, he was the kind of guy who had a conversation with *you*. And maybe, just maybe, you'd be able to participate yourself.

The speedometer crept passed 80, outlaw country bumping along. Again, it wasn't my normal kind of music but if I was going to be somewhere rural then I needed to soak it in. Feel the dirt. The twang.

The bite.

MIDNIGHT ROLLED by and I took a quick power nap in the parking lot of a rest stop. One hour later and I was back out on the road, pushing it.

The sun was just beginning to rise as I pulled into Borhead. I had just spent the last 45 minutes on an endless network of two-lane highways, taking a right every ten miles or so. The town was small. Blink and you miss it along with the two towns after. Three bars. A church. A fast-food restaurant and a motel that looked like a very fine place to catch Hepatitis B.

As I pulled into the nearly empty parking lot, a sheriff's deputy pulled in behind me. I sighed and depressed the down button for the driver-side window.

His cruiser was nosed halfway into the spot on my right, as if he might need to quickly hop back in and ram me. I cupped my hands and checked my breath out of habit, instantly realizing that I hadn't had a drink since my afternoon chat with the professor.

The door to the deputy's vehicle thunked closed as he walked around to my side.

"Mornin," he said, his tone neutral. He was thin, a pair of aviators covering half his face. Lank hair hung down past his ears in wispy strands and I'd have bet good money he was bald as a river stone beneath that hat.

"Morning," I replied. "What can I do you for?"

"Just rolling through?"

"Pardon?" I cursed myself for instantly picking up his southern drawl.

"You stayin' or goin'," he asked, making it sound like a statement.

"Stayin' *here*," I replied. In other circumstances, I might have given the local authorities a heads up, maybe even tried to pick their brain a bit. But I didn't like this guy following me in here. It felt off. My guard was up, the exhaustion of the night's drive instantly pushed away.

"Better place down in Tyson. Got a swimming pool and everything."

"Terrified of water, unfortunately," I replied. "Almost died in a wave pool when I was a kid."

The deputy leaned in closer, placing his arms on the inside of the windowsill.

"You being a smart ass?" The words came out of his mouth like coarse gravel.

"I'm just tired is all." I reached up and rubbed my forehead. "Was I violating some traffic law or can I go check-in and get some sleep?"

My own reflection stared back at me for a few long moments as the guy considered me. Finally, he stood up.

"When you heading there?" he asked.

"Now," I answered. I tossed a thumb at the motel behind me. "I'm tired *now.*"

He shook his head slowly. "You can't get in. Roads blocked."

Now it was my turn to stare blankly at him. He didn't take the bait.

"Where?" I relented. "Where can't I go?"

Some small muscle in his cheek twitched as he continued to look at me. He tilted his head sideways and then back.

"You're not feeding me a line, are you." Another question that came out like a sentence.

"I'm really not," I answered, letting the weariness bleed into my voice a bit. "I just want to catch some Zs."

"Sorry for grilling ya," he said. "We get lots of people coming down here to make questionable decisions after the mine closed down."

"The mine?"

"Yeah, old coal mine collapsed a few years ago. Ever since then, all sorts of people been rolling through here, poking their nose where it don't belong."

"Ah, you got kids coming in and getting lost in some old mines?" Things began clicking together.

"Some. Adults too. All manner come out, looking to see if the stories are true."

I waited two full seconds before taking the bait.

"Stories?" I tried to make it sound innocent but it ended up sounding like what it was: Eager.

The deputy's face hardened slightly and I looked at the small nameplate pinned to his uniform. Schneider.

"Ghost stories. Bigfoot. Aliens. All the usual bullshit. Someone started some rumor about seeing weird stuff and just like that, you got every nut-job forum on the internet buzzing with creepypastas and directions to the site."

"Creepypastas?" I knew what creepypastas were but I was pretty excited to hear this man's description of them.

"You know," he said. "Like, made up stories. Campfire stories, I guess."

"Except it's pasta." I gave him my best innocent face.

"Look, I don't know why they're called that. All I know is that's why we get all sorts of people coming down here and getting into trouble. Dangerous trouble."

"You had any deaths?" I asked.

Deputy Schneider hesitated. "A few."

"And I look like one these *sorts* of people?"

"Borhead ain't on the way to nothing and this here ride-" he gave a light kick to my front tire, "-probably gets great gas milage, but it ain't going up no mountain trails anytime soon. So you're not camping."

"Hmm. Guess you're right."

"So why are you here? If you don't mind me asking."

"Checking out some property for a friend," I said. "Wants me to cosign but I said I wanted to take a look for myself first. Purely investment."

"In Borhead?" Schneider raised his eyebrows.

"Up the river a ways." I silently crossed my fingers, searching his face for a reaction. There had to be something around here that fit the description. Georgia was lousy with rivers.

"Ah, by the old Reynolds place?"

"Maybe. He said there were a few houses nearby."

"Well, be careful. Lots of yahoos on the road these days."

WITH THE DEPUTY out of my hair, I crashed down onto a queen-sized bed that smelled like the interior of my dead grandmother's purse and was immediately asleep. I didn't dream. Just blissful nothingness that seemed to wash over me in waves.

I awoke around two, head hammering. Coffee sounded good right about now but I doubted the room I had rented came with continental breakfast, especially past noon. Imagine my surprise then when I found a small 4-cup coffee pot on the table next to the television.

Moving up in the world, Borhead.

After the machine had finished doing its thing and I poured myself a cup, I pulled out my laptop to do some research on the mine collapse. There were some local news articles and even a few national ones. Not much for details beyond the fact that the mine caved in, killing a few workers.

As I continued my search however, I began to dig into the more sensational sites. Deputy Schneider hadn't been kidding about all the creepypastas. The threads were full of them, even featuring links to a few audio renditions overlaid with creepy music.

There was everything from hairy ape-men to tales about giant frogs that had begun to inhabit the surrounding swamps. Ghost stories. Alien stories. You name it. The idea of something being unearthed from underground had certainly captured the horror-community's attention.

What was it about this though? Mines collapsed all the time, didn't they? Why was there so much lore focused around this one?

About an hour-and-a-half into my search I stumbled across an old story that bore the distinct markings of truth on it. The details about the timing of the collapse and the people who had died were dead-on accurate, and judging by how long ago it had been posted compared to the other stories, it could very well have been the first.

It was a single post that had been shared a number of times. Aside from the known details, it was surprisingly light on the imaginative work that was characteristic of these sorts of things. The only significant new bit that worked its way into the narrative was the photos and their explanation.

I leaned in and enlarged the pictures.

The first one was a wide shot of what seemed to be some sort of flat, sandy beach with the Blue Ridge Mountains rising in the background. Apparently this was way up the river, beyond any sort of civilization, which made it difficult to explain the tracks.

There were hundreds of them, all overlapping. The area was supposedly south of the mine and the sheer number of tracks in that specific area was unfathomable in a town that size unless the whole of Borhead had been there. That's assuming, of course, that the photo hadn't been manufactured in any way.

As far as hoaxes went, it wouldn't be hard to pull off. Get a bunch of friends to take off their shoes and walk over the same patch of ground over and over again. Kind of a weird one as far as staged photos went but I had seen weirder.

The next photo was similar. This one was across a muddy area after it had rained, apparently further north. More tracks. The photo was of a slightly different quality, suggesting a different person had taken it. Still nothing too outrageous.

Then there was the third one, which was slightly more suggestive. In the foreground was the same pattern of turned-up earth suggesting a whole bunch of people had been through, and in the background was what looked to be a pile of rubble.

Further pictures focused in on the rubble, the photographer moving closer and getting it from different angles. There had definitely been some sort of cave-in and the second to last photo showed a gap in the rocks just barely small enough for a big child or small adult to fit through.

For the final one, the photographer had turned the flash on and stuck their arm into the hole for a better look.

I stared at it for a long time. The shapes were hard to make out but they seemed distinctly human. It was like looking at some abstract painting. I was unable to tell carved wood from stone. If it hadn't been for the lead up I don't think I would have been able to tell a thing about it.

The aesthetics of it began to turn my stomach. There was something about it. A sensual curvature combined with something else. What was it? Energy? Confusion? There was something uneasy about it. Something restless.

I scrolled back up to the top and tried to find the original poster. Doing something like that on forums where everyone is anonymous can be a bit of a crapshoot but this wasn't my first time taking aim.

Another hour later and I had come up with a face. She was pretty, with soft features and auburn hair. The picture looked to be of decent quality, suggesting it might be a senior photo. From there I searched photographers in town and found only one. I clicked on a button in the middle of the header entitled "portfolio" and went a few years back.

It took a little bit of scrolling but I eventually found a match for the photo, taken two years ago, around the time of the cave-in.

Mary Ketz. I searched the name and didn't like what I found.

Aside from a few successful state volleyball tournaments and some social accounts, the results were dominated by news articles about her. She was missing. Had been for about a year.

I drummed my fingers on the desk, thinking.

THAT EVENING I rolled through a fast-food drive-through and pushed down a greasy burger and some fries. From there, I hit the liquor store and grabbed a bottle of something cheap that came in a plastic jug the size of my right thigh. I thought about chatting up the guy behind the counter about Mary but decided against it at the last moment. In my experience, town locals don't take too kindly to strangers who go on talking about missing girls.

From there, I made my way to Ronnie's place, watching my rearview for headlights the whole time. Didn't want to get tailed there. At one point it seemed that someone was in fact following me, but they eventually pulled off before I got to the road the Dobbs property was on.

I turned my lights off after making the turn and crept up on the house. Windows down, gravel crunching softly beneath the tires. I didn't think they'd see me—my car was dark and too dirty at this point to reflect any sort of glare—but I thought of a cover story just in case.

I was a private investigator. No need to deviate too far from the truth. Only difference was that I was investigating the Ketz girl for an anonymous client. Someone had mentioned she had been close to Ronnie's age but when I tracked down Ronnie's number at college, her roommate wasn't sure where she was, so I thought I'd come and see what I could see.

I'd let the subtext hang there. If they were guilty of anything, they'd spit out all sorts of information. They'd be helpful, forthcoming. In my experience, it was the innocent people that got angry at this sort of personal intrusion, not the guilty ones.

I sank down into my seat, pulling my camera from my center console. I thought about the gun I had in the car: a cased Remington 870 12-gauge pump loaded with 3" buckshot shells. It was in the trunk, not a lot of good from where I was sitting but then again, I didn't plan on shooting my way out of anything.

A fellow PI had once told me that he always carried a loaded Smith & Wesson Shield in his center console, which seemed crazy to me. Not once had I ever needed to shoot someone on the job. Maybe scare a few people, sure. I had once used the shotgun to diffuse a situation where an angry ex-husband had shown up with a metal baseball bat, but that was about it.

A week later, I'd definitely be rethinking my stance on the matter.

A FEW HOURS crept by with little-to-no movement. Observing from the edge of a copse of trees, I saw that the property had a spacious lawn, lit up by the house's floodlights. The driveway was big and split between the garage and a large barn off to the side. Blocking my view of the porch was an older model pickup truck and a white sedan parked next to it.

Jeremy had said that Ronnie owned a white sedan, so this must have been hers. She was home. Or at least her car was. Still no movement.

Geez, didn't these guys have a dog or something? Didn't someone need to go out and feed the horses or whatever animals they kept in that barn? Everything was shut up. All doors, barn or otherwise, were closed. Curtains were pulled with virtually no light shining out from inside.

I made it 'til about ten o'clock before I packed it in. Then back at the hotel, I drank until I was standing right on the edge of being tipsy, and then drank a little bit more and went to bed.

THE NEXT MORNING, the Dobbs place looked almost exactly the same as it had the night before. The vehicles hadn't moved. No one out in the yard. The door to the house stayed closed and the curtains remained pulled. I tapped a light rhythm out on the dash with my fingers, working something up inside me. I got out of the car.

As I walked up the driveway, I noticed that while the Dobbs house was quiet the surrounding woodlands sure weren't. The morning songbirds were singing loudly, screaming almost.

Halfway to the door and the smell hit me. Hell, it almost staggered me. Sweet, sick...something. I wasn't sure if it smelled like death or what, but it was definitely unpleasant. I forced myself to keep walking.

Three steps up and I was crossing the porch. I raised my hand to press the doorbell, then hesitated. There was something else. Some sound in the background that I couldn't place. I pressed the button, sending a deep chime reverberating through the house.

I stepped to the side, just in case they decided to send a few 30-30 slugs into my gut before asking any questions. A full minute passed. Determined to do my due diligence, I reached up to press the button one more time when the door opened.

I blinked.

"Hello? Can I help you?"

"Yes, ma'am." I cleared my throat. "Are you Mrs. Dobbs?"

"Depends on who's asking, I guess." She smiled, sending shivers down my spine.

The woman bore some familial resemblance to the photos I had seen of Ronnie. But there was something off about her. Something I couldn't quite define. A sort of sinking of the skin beneath the eyes. A looseness around the gums.

"I'm a private detective," the words came out as a croak. I fumbled my identification out of my back pocket and showed her. She looked at it like a dog seeing something on television for the first time. "I'm investigating the disappearance of Mary Ketz. You have a daughter that went to school with her, is that correct?"

The woman craned her neck toward me, giving the

impression of some long-lost prehistoric bird hunting in a field of tall grass.

"Yes indeed, that'd be my girl Veronica," she said. "Why don't you come inside and talk to her? She's just watching soap reruns in the living room."

My brain screamed at me not to enter the house. I glanced at the pulled curtains, saw the corner of one jerk as it fell back into place. The woman smiled at me again and I tried to take a step through the doorway but I couldn't. Something deep down inside of me was howling now. Begging to get out and take control. To turn around and run back to the car as fast as I could.

"Sure thing," I said, conjuring the best most-damned-winningest smile I possibly could. "To be honest, I wasn't really expecting anyone to be here. Mind if I grab my laptop from my car?"

A shadow passed over the woman's face, but then it was gone.

"Of course," she said. "I'll go put the tea on. Just make sure to take your shoes off when you come in."

I nodded and smiled, then stopped smiling for fear it looked too fake.

My skin prickled as I made my way back to my car, feeling eyes on me the whole time. Suddenly, in the middle of the driveway, I stopped. I thought about the sound I had been hearing, the one that was too low and amorphous to place. My hand flew to my face and I slapped a bug off.

The heavy thing fell and bounced off the tip of my shoe. A blowfly. That was it. I looked towards the barn, the sound sharpening. Flies. Hundreds of them all buzzing at once. Maybe thousands.

I began walking again, picking up my pace until I was practically running back to my car. Somewhere behind me was the loud sound of a door slamming and feet pounding across the porch. I fumbled my car keys out, dropped them in the dirt, picked them up again, and dashed around to the trunk.

The tip of the key shook in my hands as I jammed it into the lock and twisted. I raised the trunk just in time to see three figures step into view. A man, a woman, and a teenage boy.

I bent over, reached into the trunk, and yanked the gun case out. I heard footsteps on gravel as I pulled the zipper down, getting it caught on the fabric twice. Then a thick, bearded man stepped around the side of the car and I was pulling the shotgun out and jacking a shell into the chamber.

"Get the fuck back," I barked. I felt the tension harden inside me as I gave the command. Somewhere in the back of my mind I was praying I had read the situation right, that I wasn't holding a family at gunpoint over nothing.

"Whoa there, son," said the man. "Why don't we put that thing down so no one gets hurt?"

I took a few quick steps back, just in time to see the woman trying to come at me from the woods to my right. After seeing me disappear behind the car, she must have gone left to try and blindside me. She stopped dead as I swiveled the shotgun and leveled it at her gut.

"Don't take another step," I ordered. I continued to walk backwards, turning slightly until I was in the middle of the road. Mrs. Dobbs was standing near the back of the car, the kid near the front. Mr. Dobbs was between them and he took a tentative step toward me, his hand outstretched.

"Think about what you're doing here, son." A muscle twitched at the corner of his lip.

"Where's Ronnie?" I asked.

"I told you," Mrs. Dobbs said. "She's inside watching the *soaps.*"

"The barn," I said, jerking the gun sideways at it. "Open it up."

The trio of them hesitated, then Mr. Dobbs smiled.

"Why do you wanna go in there?" he asked, his voice like some sort of artificial molasses.

"Just do it."

"You're not gonna like it in there," the boy tittered, speaking for the first time.

Mr. Dobbs gave a light chuckle, followed immediately by Mrs. Dobbs.

I thought about the gun in my hands. I made a habit of driving with the chamber empty and four shells in the magazine tube.

What the Hell was I doing? The thought shook me. I was holding a gun on a family. If anyone were to drive by right now, they'd doubtlessly side with the family. So what was it? Why was I so sure the people in front of me were not my friends?

Call it an animal instinct. Nothing I could explain, just a feeling and my feelings had gotten me pretty far in life. No way they'd hold up in any sort of court though. No way. Especially not with the kid here.

I raised the shotgun to my shoulder, placing the bead on Mrs. Dobbs' face.

"Go. Now."

We moved toward the barn. The kid walked out front, occasionally throwing sly looks back at me over his shoulder. Mr. and Mrs. Dobbs, however, walked half-backwards, half sideways. At least one of them had their eyes on me the whole time.

When we reached the door, the boy lifted his hand to the latch and jostled it.

"Oh, *dang.*" He chimed. "It's *locked.*"

A chorus of titters rippled through them like waves, as if I was a teacher who was trying to get a few troublemakers to stay quiet during class.

"Unlock it," I yelled. "*Now.*"

Something dark crept into Mr. Dobbs' face. He tilted his head sideways and then back again, and as he did so his whole face shifted slightly, like the warping of a mirror. I swallowed, feeling my slick hands on the grip of the shotgun.

The man slunk past his wife towards the door, pulling a key from his pocket. He reached up and unlocked the padlock, took it off the latch, and then swung the barn door wide.

The stench hit me like a truck, literally staggering me. The sound of buzzing flies was incessant. God, there must have been thousands of them. The interior of the barn itself was dark, only a few small rays of light drifting in from above. What I could make out though was some sort of mound in the center of the wide-open space.

I moved in, slowly. The Dobbs family drifted off to the right, a smile on each and every one of their faces. They were watching, absorbing my reactions. As my eyes adjusted to the dark, I was able to make out the shape in the middle a little more clearly.

The mound was made of bodies. It was difficult to tell where the animal parts ended and the human parts began, but there were definitely both. Near the top was the distinctly narrow shape of a horse's jawbone and near the middle a piece jutted out that unmistakably belonged to a human's leg.

What I knew for sure was that there was more than one person in there. Everything, man and animal alike, had been skinned, making it look like one amorphous pile of gore. But the mass was too big. Too many pieces for just one human body. I wondered if one of them was Ronnie. And what about Mary Ketz? Was she in there?

Probably not. She had disappeared nearly a year ago and this looked...fresh. Who was it then? Anyone who had the misfortune of knocking on the door? The mailman maybe or a lost traveler?

A disturbing thought suddenly entered my brain. I turned and looked at the Dobbs family who had moved in slightly and were skulking in the shadows of the barn, teeth glistening as they smiled.

But they weren't the Dobbs family, were they? Because the Dobbs family was right here next to me, dead and heaped in a pile with all of their animals. They were all dead. They'd been dead for days.

I looked at the thing wearing Mr. Dobbs' skin. He tilted his head again, and as he did, the edge of his eyelid slipped down, revealing something dark and glistening beneath. He smiled.

I didn't acknowledge the blinding flash of the shotgun or hear the deafening roar. I just pulled the trigger and saw the thing's smile explode as his head was blown apart. Black slime sprayed the barn walls, coating the other two monsters as the cap of the thing's skull twisted and snapped in the air, still attached to the neck by a long piece of flesh.

The body stood there limply for a second, then collapsed to the ground. A beat of silence passed, making me wonder if I had imagined the whole thing. Was I really the sane one here? Did I just kill a man in his own barn while his wife and son watched?

I looked at the pile of bodies behind me and thought *yes. Yes, I am.* And in that small movement of my head, they were on me.

THE THINGS RUSHED FORWARD, eyes blazing as I swung the shotgun and fired. They were close, very close. The tight pattern of buckshot punched a ragged hole through the kid's gut and he went down thrashing.

I pivoted to put down the last one, but as I did, something crashed into me from behind. Bright yellow and purple stars flared in my vision as I reeled. The shotgun thunked into the dirt floor and I sank down to one knee, disoriented and nauseous. I raised my head to see my new attacker and then a bright light was shining into the barn, illuminating everything. The bodies. The blood-spattered walls.

And at the top of the mound was something I hadn't noticed before. It appeared to be some sort of lance with carved images on the end. I couldn't make out the details, but they bore the same aesthetic as the shapes in the cave. Down there in that collapsed mine where some brave soul had jammed a camera and fired off a picture or two. Without a doubt, something had come out of there. Many things, if the photos were to be believed. And now one of them was standing over me.

I looked at my attacker. She was holding some large farming instrument. It had a long wooden handle with a curved metal end, and judging by the pain in the back of my head, she had hit me with the blunt end of it.

It was Ronnie Dobbs. I squinted, trying to look closer. I tried to see past the skin to the thing underneath.

But there was nothing underneath. Just Ronnie. She stood there looking wild, some unknowable fire blazing in her eyes. In that moment, I knew that she wanted me dead. Not just to cover up whatever had happened here, but because she needed it. She craved it.

She had done this. Killed her whole family and all of their animals. Probably right at the Thanksgiving table. Then she had nonchalantly driven back to her boyfriend's place nearly 13 hours away. But she couldn't take her mind off of it—couldn't compartmentalize it. This was a part of her now. She had done this for a reason and whatever that reason was, she was now closer to it than she was to her old life. She had crossed a line, one that she couldn't step back over.

"Drop it." Said a voice.

I turned and looked into a pair of headlights, the ones that had lit up the barn just as Ronnie was raising her weapon. The headlights belonged to a sheriff deputy's cruiser. Schneider stood there with his revolver drawn, aimed at Ronnie.

"I said, drop it," he repeated, and then she did. He looked at me. "Knew this was trouble, you coming in here like this."

"You followed me?" I asked. Thoughts were cotton inside of my head. I tried to get up but a wave of dizziness overwhelmed me and I sank back down.

He gave the slightest of nods. The car I thought had been following me last night, it must have been him. The deputy had followed me up here and then watched me like I had watched the house.

Schneider walked carefully over to me and kicked the shotgun my way.

"Cover me while I cuff her?" he asked, not taking his eyes off of Ronnie. She had lowered the tool but hadn't dropped it yet. The thing that looked like Mrs. Dobbs was a few feet away, and occasionally the deputy's gun would swing in a slow arc between the two of them.

"Sure, but I don't think I can-"

A shadow lurched behind the deputy and before he could turn, something sank into the side of his neck with a sickening squelch. His eyes bulged and then the tool was yanked out, sending a river of blood down his neck.

"Noooo," I yelled, going for the gun.

The last thing I saw before the stars flared in the back of my head and pulled me down into unconsciousness was Schneider's body sinking to the ground, revealing something wearing Mr. Dobbs' skin, the shredded face hanging down past his elbow like a braid of hair. The flap of gore twisted slowly as it dangled there, and as it did a single eye came into view.

It blinked, gaze fixed solely on me.

. . .

WHEN I CAME TO, the boy thing was holding me down. His limbs were strong, especially considering the loose bits of intestine that were hanging out of him.

He stared down at me with hungry inhuman eyes. His eyelids slipped downward, just like they had on the other monster. With the headlights still shining in, I could see more clearly the thing beneath the skin.

The flesh was dark and mottled green, like some sort of extremely old piece of beef jerky. I'm not sure what it was that had crawled out of that cave but it was old. Shriveled. Still alive.

A garbled cry came from somewhere off to my right and I saw the body of Deputy Schneider thrashing feebly on the ground. He was still alive, so not much time had passed. The wound in his neck was bad. He didn't have long.

"He will be clean," Ronnie said in an almost sing-song voice. As she did, the rest of the creatures who were currently wearing the Dobbs family like hand-me-down clothes began to chant softly underneath their breath. They closed their eyes and their bodies began to sway slowly back and forth.

"His schemes are through," Ronnie continued, as she pulled something from her pocket. It was a glass vial with some sort of brownish powder inside. "The curse of your line will end in ashes. Not a sacrifice. Not a disciple. But a beginning. A drop of rain in the storm to come."

With the last bit of strength he had left, Schneider flailed in the dust and dirt of the barn as Ronnie forced a small bit of the powder into his mouth.

Nothing happened at first. His body slackened as he finally slipped into unconsciousness.

Still, Ronnie watched over him expectantly, the things behind her continuing to sway and chant. Then a small trickle of white smoke began to rise from the deputy's ears and nostrils. Then his eyes. In no time at all, his whole body was smoking and charring as his insides boiled and burned within him.

When it was finally over, Ronnie frowned.

"Unfortunate," she said. "It seems my father was rash in his action. The deputy was too far gone to be cleansed."

She looked at me. I wanted to yell at her. Or maybe to plead with her. Something. But the intensity of the act I had just witnessed was too much. Too much to be reasoned with. Too much for me to begin to understand.

"The Lavernasynthe cleanses," she said casually.

"I got that."

"I don't think you did." She tilted her head. "It cleanses us of the one thing we cannot cleanse ourselves. The future."

"I'd say it worked pretty well on him," I said, wincing. "I'd say his future is pretty much gone."

"Yes, but he did not experience the blissful feeling of *soon* turning into *now*. No plans. No ambition. None of those gross human things that destroy our world. Just-" she spread her arms, "-this."

I remained silent, instead searching for a way out of this. The deputy's car was still running. If I could just make it to the driver's side...

"The cleansing ritual originally made its way into Irish remedies when Greek travelers brought it all the way from their homeland. The plant acts as a drug. A psychedelic that removes your entire past and thoughts of the future. It turns you into something purely sensory. Raw emotion and reaction. The animals we were always meant to be."

"Before your insides burn away, you mean."

"It's the blood that burns," she said. "That river of life flowing through you is transformed into mist and smoke. Static hanging in the hair."

"Who told you all this?" I asked.

"I have found it for myself," she replied, prickling at the question. "It is self-evident."

I frowned and shook my head. An argument sprung to my mind but I stopped. She wouldn't listen. She had already invested too much into this newfound belief of hers. Explaining that something had ahold of her, some force buried but still alive, wouldn't take. And even if it would, I was too tired to try.

"What did they do?" I asked. "Your parents. Your brother."

"What didn't they do?" She laughed. "They drug me to church every Sunday, where I listened to the preacher chant about Hellfire. About the cleansing of the world and God's wrath. Then when we'd go home they used it the same way they used timeouts." She pitched her voice up and did an impression of her mother. "Pick up your toys. The Devil loves dragging disobedient girls down to Hell. Make sure to say your prayers before bedtime or you'll be easy prey for the Gates of Hell. Everything I did seemed to be within the context of escaping Hell. Do you know what that does to a child?"

"Sorry to hear that but I think it happens to a lot of children. Children who still don't murder their parents."

"I didn't murder them," she said with absolute certainty in her eyes. "Murder is something you do out of hate. What I've done is an act of love."

"Love for what?"

But she just smiled. "If I have to explain it then you're already lost."

I didn't know what to say to that. And as I searched for a response, I saw something change in her demeanor. She seemed to lose interest in the conversation, which wasn't good for me.

"Do you accept the gift?" she asked.

It was hard to keep my eyebrows from shooting up off of my forehead. Was she asking if I wanted to die? For my blood to literally burn away inside of me? But the look on her face was so sincere, as if she had just asked if I wanted to drink from the cup of eternal life.

I thought about it.

"Sure."

She smiled and I grimaced. I imagined what it would feel like. Would the drug go down like a glass of scotch, burning me away into blissful oblivion? If it came to that then I hoped so.

I had a final play though. I ran through it in my head, hoping that the drug worked the way I thought it would. I opened my mouth and she placed a dab of the powdered herb in the center of my tongue.

A few crucial seconds passed as I gathered it up in my saliva. Then I turned and spat a wad of the stuff onto the pile of butchered bodies. It felt like spitting acid.

When the drug had been forced into the dying deputy's mouth, it had taken a moment to take effect. I assumed that was because it had to be absorbed through the cell walls in the mouth or possibly through the stomach lining if he had swallowed it. That took time.

This didn't.

The pile of bodies went up as if it had been soaked in gasoline. Ronnie and the others turned away and I dove for the shotgun on the ground. The thing wearing Mr. Dobbs' skin was the first to shake off the shock of what had happened and began turning toward me as I scrambled in the dirt. Wasting no time, I lifted the shotgun a few inches and fired, his right knee exploding out from under him in a spray of blood, bone, and cartilage.

I pumped the action.

With one shell left, I made it count. Ronnie fixed her gaze on me, her lip just beginning to rise into a snarl when I pulled the trigger for the last time. I hit her full in the chest. She didn't fly backward like I assumed she would, but rather, flinched as if I had slapped her. Then she crumpled down into the dirt.

I let the empty shotgun fall from my hands.

In the brief moments I had just used to eliminate two of my attackers, the flames had risen up and engulfed the roof of the barn. The two other monsters were howling now, clawing at the smoke.

Still on the ground, I hurriedly crawled my way through the dust, beginning to cough now. Even in the haze of the fire, the sound must have been enough to give me away. The other two were on me in seconds.

Thankfully, I had just made it to the open car door. I threw myself into the driver's seat of the cruiser just as I felt hands close around my right leg. I pulled it back and kicked, then kicked again, this time feeling the crunch of bone as my heel connected with the thing's head. One more boot to the face and I was inside the door, slamming it behind me.

I gasped as the final creature threw itself against the driver's side window. Black blood smeared across the glass as the thing beat against it with Mrs. Dobbs' stolen face. I reached frantically for a weapon but came up empty. Instead, I threw the car into reverse, floored it backward until both of the figures were in front of me. Then I whipped it back into drive and slammed my foot down on the gas.

The cruiser had a lot more get-up-and-go than any car I had ever driven and it hit Mrs. Dobbs like a steel fist. Her body smashed into the windshield and then tumbled up and over the roof of the car at the same time I felt the sudden bump of the boy beneath my left wheel.

After coming to a stop, I thought for a single moment and then flew into action.

I threw the door open and jumped out. Both bodies were lying motionless in the dirt and it took me no longer than ten seconds to drag the boy to the edge of the burning barn and roll him inside.

The structure wasn't fully engulfed yet but the flames were intense. I barely made it close enough to the building to accomplish what I needed to.

Mrs. Dobbs' body was somewhat more difficult. She remained limp until the last few feet and then began thrashing in my arms. There came an awful grinding noise from inside of her as she moved, as if multiple broken bones were grating against each other. I had her slung over my shoulder and managed to hurl her forward into the flames.

Her body caught almost instantly, the stolen flesh peeling away from her as she danced awkwardly inside the inferno. Within seconds, nothing was left but the shriveled figure of some long-forgotten corpse. Mummified and buried, but still alive. Doomed to face a future of solitude and inactivity.

It was then that I noticed a sound in my ears I had been hearing for a few seconds now. The sound of sirens.

I WALKED out of the station the next morning with bags under my eyes so large you could pack a week's worth of groceries in them. The questioning had been sporadic and intense, leaving huge gaps of time in between for me to doze off in the bright fluorescent light of the interrogation room. We went over the same questions again and again. Why were you there? How did the barn catch on fire? Were you sure that the Dobbs family had all been inside when the structure had burned down?

I told them the truth, mostly. I was there investigating Veronica Dobbs after being hired by her boyfriend. I knocked on her front door after staking out the house and they invited me in. Something felt wrong so I decided to leave. They attacked me.

I conveniently left out the part involving the unregistered shotgun I had in the trunk of my car. They'd find it, of course, and put two-and-two together when they did the autopsies. I'd probably have to show up in court for the whole thing eventually, or at least have to give another statement, but there was nothing connecting the weapon to me.

The only part that was difficult to explain was the fire. I told them that I wasn't quite sure how the barn had caught but that it may have been a stray oil lamp that had broken open. They were hesitant, but said they had forensics that could verify my story.

I knew they probably wouldn't find a lamp, but what would they find? The point of origin was certainly the center of the barn but there was no sign of accelerant or anything to indicate arson. As far as they'd be able to tell, it was just a fire.

Or at least, I hoped that's the conclusion they'd come to.

To be honest, I didn't really care at this point. After the whole ordeal, followed by hours and hours of sitting in that interrogation room, I could see how someone might be ready to sign anything just to get the Hell out of there.

They finally released me a few hours after the sun had risen the next morning. I promised not to leave town and promptly did just that. My phone was dead by this point and my car was still locked down at the crime scene so I walked to the nearest gas station, where they told me about a small car rental place a few blocks away.

Small was generous.

The place had about five cars jammed into their tiny parking lot, one of which I assumed was the owner's. It was still part of one of the big rental places in America though, with drop-off points in most cities. I signed a contract and rolled out onto the highway just before noon.

. . .

On my way back, I called Jeremy and gave him a summary of what had happened. He said that he had already been called by the Sheriff's department to corroborate my part of the story and that he had more questions than anything at this point. I told him I was gonna go home and get a few hours of sleep and then clean up a bit. I'd drop by his place tomorrow morning.

The drive back was brutal. My body was completely exhausted and I probably shouldn't have been on the road at all. There was something keeping me going though, some underlying tension that permeated the previous night's events and kept me on edge. I worked through it all in my mind but couldn't resolve the whole thing.

I got back to my place, grabbed a quick bite, and stood in the shower for twenty minutes. I shut off the water and padded naked into the kitchen where I poured myself a much-needed drink.

The whiskey burned my mouth and throat and something swam up near the surface of my consciousness. I grasped for it but it darted back down into the murky depths before I could get ahold of it.

I collapsed on the couch, immediately plagued by dreams of mummified corpses coming to life and skinning people. I saw Ronnie and the zealous look in her eyes. I felt the burn of whiskey as it was forced into my mouth, and when I spat it out, I breathed fire.

When I awoke to my alarm the next morning, I knew what had happened and what had to happen next.

Jeremy couldn't sit down. He paced back and forth in his bedroom as I awkwardly sat on his bed like a teenager, telling my story.

A conversation like this might have been better suited to

somewhere like a living room, but his roommates were all crowded in there watching some trashy daytime television. I could have asked Jeremy to make them leave—could have insisted on the gravity of this conversation—but the privacy of the bedroom suited my purposes better for the moment.

I wasn't sure how much he believed about my own explanation of events. I told him everything that had happened, sparing nothing. I figured I owed it to him to tell the truth. It's what he was paying for, after all. What he did with it was up to him.

The hardest part of the whole thing was having to explain my own hand in Ronnie's death.

I saw the emotions play out silently in his face. He was furious at me, which was predictable. But then that blazing fire quickly smoked out as all the other pieces of the story came crowding in to smother it.

Ronnie had murdered her entire family. Had stood here in *this house,* talking with him while they were lying dead a couple hundred miles away.

Soon the magnitude of what she had done dwarfed what I had done in response to it. Like a rabid dog being put down after mauling a child.

And I think that a part of him had expected this. Deep down past the suspicion that she was seeing someone else or in some sort of trouble, Jeremy had known. He hadn't known what exactly, but he had seen the change take place in her. Had known how it would end.

But the doomed outcome and the grief that came with it wasn't wholly devoid of anger. As he continued to speak, I saw those coals begin to flare up in him again as he searched for a reason why. How could this have happened? And who was responsible for it?

And as his anger slowly rekindled, seeking an outlet, I felt my protective side growing with it. Maybe I saw myself inside of him, the drunken brawler. The man who had finally taken his first few steps on the path toward betterment, only to have it snatched away.

"It's that fucking professor," he said, his hands clenched into fists. I saw his eyes dart toward the dresser where I knew the gun was and then back down at the floor. "He tainted her somehow. Warped her. He made her do all that shit."

"I don't think Stonehouse is involved." I said gently. "He's too...*academic*. I know guys like him. They talk a big game about the world and what they think needs to happen to it, but when push comes to shove they're just a bunch of pearl-clutchers. They flirt with ideas. They don't embody them, not like what I saw at Ronnie's house."

He seemed stuck though. He was frustrated, so much so that I don't think he had fully considered the implications of what I had told him—that there were monsters in the world. Killers that defied death and everything we knew.

These ideas were too big for him at the moment. They weren't something he could yell at—something he could hit. So, maybe against my better judgement, I gave him that.

"I don't know if you believe me or not about what happened," I admitted. "But something happened down in Borhead. At the dig site. What happened at Ronnie's house—I don't think that's the end of it. There were hundreds of tracks in those photos."

Jeremy stood there silently, continuing to clench his fists and stare at the ground. Even so, I knew I had caught his attention. In the years to come, I'd question if I did the right thing, setting him on that path like I did. But ultimately, it was his decision and there was certainly more good that could come from this than going and beating the shit out of some college professor. Or worse.

"I'll send you the link to the blog I found," I continued. "It's possible that forensics is going to match one of the bodies they find in the barn to Mary Ketz, but I'm not certain. Her family could use some closure and the people down there probably don't have a clue about the kind of danger they're in."

I handed him my card. "Keep this with you. If you ever need me for anything, feel free to call, email, anything. I'm pretty busy most of the time but I'll help you if I can. If not, I could always use an assistant. Show you the ropes of what I do. Won't pay very well but it could be useful, if this thing down in Borhead is something you decide to pursue."

He took the card and put it in his pocket. His face seemed uncertain, but I could see him working over the new options. Come and work for me or investigate Borhead on his own. I knew what he would choose.

"I think I'll take a swing by Ronnie's house if I can. See what I can find."

I nodded.

"Can I make a suggestion?"

"Shoot."

"Bring a friend. Doesn't have to be me but...well, I wouldn't go down there alone."

He nodded.

"Now," I slapped my legs. "Time for the hard part."

"What's that?"

I smiled. "Paying me for all this."

For the first time today, Jeremy laughed.

"Hey, tell ya what," I said. "I'll knock a hundred bucks off if you go grab me a drink."

A minute later, Jeremy stepped back into the room carrying a few glasses of whiskey. We spent the next hour drinking and talking.

I asked him about Ronnie, about who she had been before

all this. Over the course of the conversation, he swung back and forth between sadness and anger. When he was sad, I would listen. Then when he got mad, I told him about Borhead. Gave him something solid to focus on. Somewhere to direct his anger, rather than himself and those around him.

I'm still not sure if that was the right approach. In doing so, did I aim a cannon at the community of Borhead and light the fuse? Maybe. But I knew he would want to do something about it regardless. I knew because that's what I would have done.

He offered me a second glass and I declined, explaining that more wouldn't help my mind at the moment. I hoped he got the hint.

Jeremy paid me, we said our goodbyes, and I headed back to the apartment. I thought things over for a few more hours as I lay on the couch and stared at the ceiling. Finally, I grabbed a set of lock-picking tools from my drawer and headed out. There was still one more thing I had to do.

Leo Stonehouse lived in a quiet neighborhood on the west side of town. It was just past ten o'clock and most of the houses were already dark. I parked a block away and walked with my collar up. I saw no one and heard nothing.

"Jack?" Leo asked after opening the door. He looked instantly uncomfortable then quickly adopted a stance somewhere between generosity and curiosity. "What can I help you with? Is everything okay?"

"Ronnie's dead," I said flatly, watching him absorb the words. To his credit, he looked genuinely upset by the news. "Can I come in? I'll tell you about it."

· · ·

LEO'S LIVING room looked exactly like his office: comfortable but a little cluttered. He had a few awards in frames in the living room next to a giant flat screen and seemed to have a number of assignments spread out over a coffee table.

"Grading assignments?" I asked.

He blinked, then looked down at the table. "Yeah, sorry. I can move it." He began tidying up and while his back was turned, I saw what I needed to see and did what I needed to do.

"No problem," I said. "I literally live in my office so I understand the struggle."

Once he had everything packed up, he gestured at a leather recliner. "Take a seat. Would you like anything? Beer? Bourbon?"

"I'm okay but you might need a drink."

Leo hesitated, then grabbed a tumbler off the corner of an end table he had obviously been drinking from before I had arrived and rushed into the kitchen. I heard the rattling of ice cubes from the freezer and then the squeak of a cork. A few moments later and he was back in the room.

He took a sip of bourbon and then blinked a few times.

"Sit down," I said. "I have to go soon so I'll be quick."

Leo sat down and took another sip. I gave him a hard stare for a moment and then reached over to drop a handful of .38 cartridges on his coffee table. They clattered on the hard surface, some rolling around before coming to a stop at the edge.

"I don't understand," Leo said after a moment.

"These are for you," I elaborated. "Or at least, they were."

The man's eyes narrowed. "Are you threatening me?"

"You will hear no threats from me tonight. Only an explanation."

"An explanation? An explanation of what?"

"Of why these aren't all lodged in your chest and face right now."

Leo swallowed, then turned to cough into his shoulder.

"Ronnie's boyfriend would have killed you if he knew what you did to Ronnie. How you infected her mind and bent her into a weapon."

He got to his feet. "What are you-"

"Shut the fuck up," I said calmly but quickly. "Like I said, I have to leave soon."

Leo seemed to freeze where he was standing so I continued.

"You said Ronnie brought you the bourbon from back home the last time she was there but that was a lie. She left her travel bag at her boyfriend's house. I doubt she would have swung by your office with all that was on her mind to give you some booze."

"Of course she could have," Leo snapped. "She-"

"What was on her mind, you ask? I'll tell you what: she had just killed her entire family. Sacrificed them to an ancient Greek goddess. The goddess of mischief and delusion. The goddess Até."

"I don't know who you-"

"She left a note for her boyfriend," I interrupted again. "So she was still conflicted. Still uncertain about what she had done. She wanted to explain herself but couldn't figure out how so she ended up leaving a pretty lackluster message: 'Gone to Até.'"

"Well, I-"

"But she didn't come see you." I stood up out of the chair and checked my watch, then reached down and scooped the shells off the table and stuffed them back in my pocket. "The bag was what tipped me off, but the real break was doing a deep dive into your research. You rushed to fabricate a lie when we spoke a few days ago and said Ronnie brought you the booze but she didn't. You were just covering your ass so you made that up on the spot. You bought the booze yourself while researching the ruins of a lost civilization a year back. The ruins that had been uncovered by a mine collapse. In fact, you're working on publishing that paper now, aren't you?"

Leo's face had turned a bright red. Sweat was pouring down his cheeks and neck. He snarled, slammed the whiskey, and then suddenly rushed at me with the glass raised high.

I moved quickly aside and tripped him. The man went sprawling. I walked over and knelt down next to him.

"I found a draft of the paper on your computer when I broke into your office tonight. Do you know what else I found there?"

Leo coughed, grimaced, then coughed again.

I held up the clear glass vial with the Lavernasynthe in it.

"Hurts, doesn't it?" I sighed. "I put it at the bottom of your glass when you were cleaning up the coffee table. I knew you'd refill with the same tumbler and do so in a hurry, not noticing the brown smudge at the bottom. I knew because that's what I do. One tumbler for the day. Cuts down on dishes."

An awful stench of burning suddenly wafted up toward me. I saw thin streams of smoke beginning to come out of Leo's eyes and nose.

"I know you, Leo, because I know myself. We got the blood curse. The kind that makes you want to knock a few back and fight the whole world. You cover it up with your academic mask but you're the same. You're bitter. Angry. Vengeful. You hate this world you were born into and worship some golden age that either faded away long ago or never existed in the first place. I get it. I feel the same."

I looked up at the ceiling where some smoke was beginning to accumulate. Soon it'd trip the smoke alarm. But not yet.

"But Jeremy," I continued. "Jeremy's like us too. He'd have come over here and blown you away if I hadn't turned him toward something else. He'd have put six bullets through your head, reloaded, and then kept on firing. And he'd have done so without a single thought of what came next. So you see, this is what I can do for him. You and me—we're damned, Leo. But the kid doesn't have to be like us. Sure, he'll still bust some skulls but he won't be seeing life in prison. Not for you."

And with those final words, Leo burst into flames. White smoke turned black as the heaping amount of Lavernasynthe finally took hold and took over. The smoke alarm went off along with an automatic notification to the fire department.

And by the time anyone looked out their window to see what all the fuss was about, I was already gone.

PREY

The prey turned down the alley.

There was no sound as the men walked. None of the dark chuckling and elbowing that usually serves to work men up before they commit a heinous act. No cat calls or winks. No air of putrid excitement. These men weren't rapists. They weren't muggers. They weren't even murderers, in the biblical sense. But they were killers, nonetheless.

Felicity pushed her collar up higher, hoping to protect herself with what little she had. But there was nothing she could do to cover the fact that she was a woman. That she was slight beneath her coat. And that she was alone.

The men didn't wear the dark robes of the Cult of the Black Tide and they weren't as manic as the Children of the After Wood. But Felicity could sense their strangeness. Their unnatural stillness, even as they walked. They moved like shadows.

The city seemed to be absolutely brimming with wackos. Every other day she heard of some new fanatical group of people with obviously sinister intentions. And they weren't just naive teenagers on the streets or secret cabals of rich men that met in quiet rooms at midnight. They were taxi drivers, teachers, journalists, janitors, and CEOs. They were everywhere. Everyone.

And she could see why. Dark things were beginning to rise. She wasn't sure what or where or how, but they were. She could feel it. In a world that had supposedly cast off the shackles of religion, modern man had opened itself up to an unspeakable litany of horrors. New kings and queens taking stock of their kingdom, wondering why there were walls, and tearing them all down. Then the monsters come pouring in.

In this new enlightened age, people were as dangerous as they had ever been. Maybe even more so. Felicity knew that personally. Had seen it. Had experienced it.

She tried to hunch in on herself as the men approached.

The alley was dark but a fence soon materialized out of the mist around her and she realized she had hit a dead end. She was stuck. She turned around.

Despite what she had seen in movies, she knew that there was little a woman of 120 pounds could do against a man with an extra 80 on him. Sure, she could score points sparring in the Tae Kwon Do class she attended three times a week, but when it came to grappling on the ground there was no competition. No way she could win.

Not fighting fair, at least.

That's why when the closest figure reached behind him to pull out a long curved blade, he looked up to find Felicity had produced her own weapon, a modified Glock with an extended clip. He froze, the four other men freezing as well, their eyes fixed firmly on the pistol.

They didn't look like cultists. Most of them landed somewhere on the spectrum between truck driver and salesman. Average Joes with an average pension for murder and bloodlust.

And to be honest, she didn't find anything particularly weird about it.

People had been killing each other for hundreds of thousands of years. In every age and continent, people crossed each other off in droves without remorse or pity. It was their nature. Slap a suit and tie on an alligator and it'll still drag you underwater. That's what it was built for.

So no, Felicity didn't find it odd that these supposedly mild-mannered businessmen would suddenly start abducting people on the street and sacrificing them to some nameless god in their basement. Given the whole course of history, it would be strange if they didn't.

If the Glock had been semi-automatic, she still could have killed them all within seconds. But it wasn't. Instead, a wiry little man working out of his garage had filed a piece here and replaced a piece there until the "semi" part of semi-automatic had fallen off, leaving just the "automatic."

The gun was hard to control when fired and a full 40-round magazine could be emptied in under 2 seconds. Felicity held the trigger down for one.

The air seemed to rip apart as she swung the pistol, spraying the alley with bullets. It was a dangerous way to do things and she was reminded of this as she heard the tell-tale *zang* of a ricochet as it careened off a brick wall. Orange spots danced in her vision, blotting out the bodies as they twisted and rolled around on the ground.

The first man hadn't had a chance. He'd probably taken five 9mm rounds to the chest and was dead before he hit the pavement. The rest seemed to all be in some state of dead or dying. All but one.

A heavy man in a navy-blue suit screamed and rolled around on the ground, his arm pulverized from the elbow down. Felicity walked over and looked down at him. She had maybe a minute before the cops would arrive. Three years ago, it would have already been too late. But things were different now. Half of the police on the force had quit and the other half were either too strung out or crooked to care.

They'd still come. She had made too much noise to be ignored. But they'd take their time. Check in with a few important people first to make sure there wasn't anything going on in this part of town that might require one to turn the other way.

Felicity thought about questioning the man. He probably knew something valuable that she could use to climb the ladder and track down some more important people in whatever group he had gotten tied up with. But she was tired and he was hysterical. The screaming grated on her and when he finally looked up and saw her standing over him, a curse formed on his lips before she shot him in the mouth.

She wondered if anyone was left living in this neighborhood. Most of the storefronts had been abandoned and all the apartment buildings were beginning to empty. Soon, there would be no one left to hear a man screaming in the night, just to have it cut-off by the quick bark of a pistol.

With five bodies on the ground, Felicity set to her next task with great efficiency and speed. In the age of the internet, no one needed to be interrogated anymore. All you needed was their cell phones.

Felicity holstered her pistol behind her and pulled back her coat to reveal a large meat cleaver in a leather sheath. In less than a minute, she had found six phones and ended the suffering of three wounded men.

The marks left by the cleaver were large and gaping. Obvious to anyone who knew what they were looking at.

They were good enough. She was done here. The sound of

her heels clicking on the pavement echoed like an empty gun continuing to fire.

DETECTIVE BROSS LOOKED DOWN at the bodies. Five men, all dead from either a gunshot wound or a blow from some heavy-bladed weapon. Analysis at the other scenes deduced the weapon to be a ten-inch stainless steel meat cleaver.

"It's her," said Hawkins through a cloud of cigarette smoke.

Bross turned and nodded at his partner. Two weeks ago, the canvassing of a crime scene had produced a grainy ATM video of a woman in a trench coat hacking two men to death in front of a sandwich shop on 3rd Avenue. They had to use tweezers to pick pieces of brain off of the "Permanently Closed" sign taped to the front door.

The media had taken to calling her the "Blackburg Butcher." Despite the fact that they had a pretty solid leash on the news networks, journalists couldn't resist a vigilante on a killing spree. Dog's gotta eat, after all.

With that reality in play, the most they could do was spin it. Make her seem more like a serial killer than someone out for justice. It wasn't a stretch, considering the crime scenes, and people would buy the idea of a serial killer in their midst pretty easily these days.

"This guy's missing a finger," Hawkins said.

"What?" Bross walked over to the body. The man was indeed missing a finger.

"A trophy maybe?"

But Bross was already shaking his head. "I don't think so. She took the phones, just like last time."

"You think she wants it to access a phone?"

"Best I can come up with."

"Why not take everyone's fingers then? Why just take this asshole's?"

"Dunno. But like I said: it's the best I got."

Hawkins huffed noncommittally. He took out his phone, scrolled to a name in his contacts, and dialed it. There was silence for a moment, interrupted occasionally by the sound of snapping cameras and muttered remarks as the crime scene crew went about their work.

"Yeah," Hawkins said into his cell. "It's her."

He listened to someone speaking and as he did, Bross wondered if she had finally pushed them too far. Five dead men, their bodies on display for all to see. This couldn't go on.

"Okay. Understood." Hawkins rang off.

"What'd he say?" Bross asked.

"You ain't gonna like it."

"I don't like most things these days. Spit it out."

"We're gonna give her what she wants."

Bross chewed on that for a second, then said, "You're right. I don't like it."

FELICITY DUMPED the six cell phones out of her coat pockets onto the table. Roscoe, the man who helped her live her double life, looked up at her. He was scrawny with long frizzy hair and slightly cross-eyed, the glasses that rested on his nose making his eyes seem about twice as big as they were.

They had met in a chat room on the dark web less than a week after it had happened. Felicity had been drowning in grief and desperate for answers. Roscoe had provided them. Now they hung out together in his garage/workshop drinking beer and trying to figure out how they were going to bring down one of the largest criminal organizations that had ever existed in the city.

"Please tell me you turned all of these off," he said as he poked at one. "I don't need the fuzz triangulating our position and sending a hit squad to knock my door down."

"What, don't you have a plan for that?"

"I do," he replied hesitantly. "But it was very time-consuming to set up. Plus, I'd have to leave this place and I've grown to like it quite a bit."

"You like Blackburg?" Felicity raised her eyebrows.

"Fuck no," Roscoe said. "I like my *house*. It just sucks that it's *in* Blackburg."

"Could always move."

"Yeah, well, so could you and I don't see you packing any bags."

"That's because there's work to be done."

"Exactly." Roscoe picked up one of the phones and inspected it. "So, what would you like me to do with these?"

"Pull all of the contacts and cross-reference them with each other. See if you can find the names of the since-deceased owners and remove them from the list. Chances are good that whoever works above them is in more than a couple of these phones. I want their name."

"Easy-peasy. Anything else?"

"Yeah." Felicity reached over and picked up a black flip phone. "I want everything you can possibly get off of this. I pulled this off the body of the guy I shot first along with a smartphone. I think he was probably leading this crew and used this to get ahold of someone the others probably didn't have access to. I want as many names as you can track down and I want their addresses."

"Might be a bit harder, but not impossible." Roscoe started scooping up the phones and shuttling them over to a set of monitors in the corner. "How'd the gun work out?"

"Worked okay," Felicity said. "I can still hear a faint ringing in my ears."

"That's because you listened to about a billion 9mm rounds going off. It's loud."

"It also fired a little too wild. Bullets were bouncing up and down the whole street. Last thing I need is for a stray to go through a window and hit some kid in their bed."

"Press would eat you alive even more than they are right now if that happened."

Felicity exhaled. "Yeah, I don't give a shit about that. I just want to find these guys and put 'em in the ground."

Roscoe walked over to the mini-fridge and pulled a couple of beers out. He twisted the top off one and handed it to Felicity then they both sat down at the picnic table he had pulled inside.

"So why are you doing this?" she asked.

"What, helping you?"

"Yeah. What's in it for you?"

Roscoe shrugged. "I feel like it was something I was uniquely made for. I spent my whole life researching cults and conspiracy theories. Now that there actually is one, no way I'm turning tail. Even if it is in fucking Blackburg."

"Hey, this city ain't all bad."

"Name one good thing about it."

"They make good pizza."

"Wouldn't know." Roscoe sniffed. "Lactose intolerant."

"Bullshit. I saw you eat a cheeseburger *yesterday*."

"Sometimes I'm willing to take the hit."

"So cheeseburgers are worth it but pizza isn't?"

"Yup."

Felicity shook her head and tilted the beer back. She took a long drink, swallowed, and blew out a breath. They sat there quietly for a minute, each thinking to themselves.

"You still think you're gonna find her?"

Felicity thought about that. Her impulse was to say, "yes." To be optimistic and say that of course they'd find her three-year-old niece, Presley, that had been taken from her home more than a year ago now.

But she had been there. She had been the one to walk in and find her brother and his wife flayed and nailed to the wall. There was something about the brutality of the act that told her that—no, she wouldn't be finding Presley alive.

"No," the word came out almost as a grunt. "I don't."

Roscoe bobbed his head. "Ya know, there are some cults who abduct kids to indoctrinate them and raise them as their own. Easiest way to get members if you ask me."

"But you don't think this is one of them." It wasn't a question.

Roscoe took some time to answer, but eventually shook his head.

"I may need to contact your armory guy," Felicity said. Roscoe apparently had some hookup that allowed him access to weapons most civilians didn't even know existed.

"What for this time? I think you got enough guns."

"It's not a gun I want. I'll get you the specs."

"Sound good." An awkward silence passed, then he said, "Ya know, a word keeps coming up in my searches. I've seen it in their browser history too. I even saw one of the crime scene photos from those guys you hit last week. One of the men had it tattooed on their arm."

"What is it?" Felicity asked. But she already knew. She had seen the same tattoo. What she didn't know was what it meant.

"*Drakfalett*. It's Trilodian, which is an obscure dead language."

"What does it mean?"

Roscoe shifted on his seat. "Child Eater."

• • •

THAT NIGHT, Felicity watched the video again, as she did every night. It had been taken by her brother's security system. The camera at the door began recording whenever someone approached and the camera in the living room began recording if the alarm went off.

She had come home one day to find the flash drive shoved through her mail slot. The device was small and only had two files on it: livingroom.mp4 and frontdoor.mp4. On each side of the drive was the picture of a cup. No, a chalice. The image was bizarre and caught her off guard. The idea that the cults might be branding electronics came off as borderline hilarious. Then she watched the videos.

The men were unremarkable. The leader was thick and gruff-looking, like a construction foreman. The other two, both flabby men with wide chests, looked somewhat less than sure of themselves. They followed the foreman's every word though, regardless of how heinous they were.

When the videos were done, Felicity leaned back and considered the implications.

First: the men wore no masks, which meant they either didn't care what happened to them or they had some pretty powerful friends on the police force that would see to it that they wouldn't be pursued.

Second: someone on the force had given her the drive in secret. It had come in a plain white envelope with her name written on it. Nothing else. If someone had leaked the information to her then that probably meant she had a friend on the force.

She'd have to think about that. No way of pursuing either of those leads at the moment. The most she could do was break down the lead investigator's door and squeeze him for answers. She didn't want to do that though. Not yet. 50/50 that would bring the heat down on her even more than it already was.

For now she'd sit on it.

FELICITY WAS in her brother's living room, crouched behind the entertainment center. The lights were out, her surroundings eerily grainy like in the security vid. She could hear voices. A light flashed across the ceiling as they searched for her.

They were getting closer.

At her side was Presley, her niece. Her face was scrunched up in fear, tears leaking from her eyes. Eyes that had seen her parents taken apart like animals. She whimpered into Felicity's sleeve.

"*Hide,*" Felicity whispered.

Presley looked up at her, her lips forming a word she could barely make out. *Where?*

And before Felicity knew what she was doing, she was opening her mouth wide. The joints clicked as they came out of place, her cheeks stretching apart. Carefully now, she lowered her mouth over Presley's head. The child began to struggle but there was nothing for it now.

Felicity reached down and grabbed Presley by her little ankles and slowly eased her inside. The shoulders made it past her lips, then barely down her throat. Then, just as the feet were about to follow the rest of the child down, Felicity quickly removed the purple light-up shoes she had bought her for Christmas.

SHE WOKE up choking and coughing. She flung the comforter off of herself and stumbled toward the bathroom, not bothering to turn on the lights. She gulped water down straight from the faucet. It was cold and refreshing and she couldn't get enough.

The sound of her throat gulping was loud in the still

apartment and eventually made her gag. Her stomach convulsed and she just barely made it to the toilet before a spew of vomit came up and out.

Felicity's body heaved a few more times and then went still. She curled her arms around the cold porcelain and cried.

COLE FOGEL CHUCKED his half-eaten turkey sub in the trash and lit another cigarette. He took a drag and exhaled slowly, the smoke leaking out of him as if his insides were a trash can that had been set on fire.

God, how he wished he could live off of nicotine. Food was becoming less and less appetizing, considering the things he had seen over the last year. Now he couldn't eat a chicken wing without thinking of a little hand or a burger without seeing raw human flesh.

He wasn't no lefty screwball, but Hell, maybe he'd become a vegetarian or something here soon. Better to eat rabbit food than no food at all. It's not that he didn't like meat. The idea was just too wrapped up with his work now.

And it *was* work. That's how he thought of it at least. It was hard, it was fulfilling, and it pushed his boundaries. In many ways, it was the perfect job. Unfortunately, there wasn't a single meaningful job out there that didn't require something of you. That didn't take some piece of you. This was no exception.

Cole had worked a lot of jobs in his 46 years. From retail to construction worker to warehouse manager. All of them were tough and rewarding but this was by far the most meaningful. This job actually gave him purpose. Unlike those other jobs, now he was actually tasked with caring for a living thing.

He thought about it as he smoked. Thought about how fast the thing had grown. Some people might look at it and just see a monster, but not him. He had looked the thing directly in the eye and seen the spark of intelligence. And that spark had done nothing but grow.

What would it look like in five years? Ten years? How big would it be then and what would it be capable of? Cole shuddered at the thought.

The warehouse was empty. All of his employees had been shuttled off on some other task tonight, leaving just a few guards outside and him up here in the main office to smoke and twiddle his thumbs.

There was a sharp tang in the air leftover from all the blood and Cole suspected it was there to stay. In his time in this position, he had seen hundreds of cows, sheep, chickens, and pigs brought through here to be processed. No amount of scrubbing or elbow grease could remove that level of death from a place.

When he had asked about the animals, the man in charge had told him that the thing they were feeding needed the animals to survive but it needed the *other* stuff to grow. It had seemed repulsive at first, even evil. But now he understood it as just another gruesome fact of a hungry world.

Things died so that other things could live. That was that.

And the thing they had on their hands was so rare and magnificent. It was one of a kind. An endangered species even.

Cole had read somewhere that most poaching in Africa was actually committed by people who couldn't feed their families any other way. The poor and destitute who were pushed to extreme acts to provide, because after all, what did the preservation of some lion or rhinoceros mean to the survival of your own family?

But still, the world saw poaching as wrong. And in a way, they were right. There were billions of human lives on this planet, so many as to be practically expendable. Who cared if a couple kids died to preserve a whole species? Hell, who cared if a thousand kids died?

Mankind would continue to exist, but those species were gone forever.

A heavy *boom* sounded from outside and Cole suddenly found himself covered in hundreds of pieces of broken glass. He shook the sharp little pebbles off of him and staggered to his feet, just as something flew through the large window that overlooked the warehouse and bounced off the wall behind him.

He turned around and looked at it, then the world went white.

As soon as the stun grenade detonated, Felicity used the heavy battering ram Roscoe had procured for her to knock down the flimsy office door. The man inside was on his feet but barely. His arm was flung over his face and wherever there was exposed skin there were tons of tiny red cuts where the broken glass had dug in.

When the man lowered his hand and revealed his face, Felicity felt something grow cold within her. It was him. The man from the video. The one who looked like the foreman.

She dropped the battering ram to the floor with a loud *clunk*, drew her pistol, and then smashed the butt of it into the man's face. There was a light rattling sound and when Felicity looked down, she realized it was his teeth bouncing off of the chair he had been sitting in.

She hit him again. He screamed, blood pouring out over his lips.

"*Stop,*" he raised his hands feebly.

"Where is she?" Felicity asked, her voice like the rasp of steel.

"Who?" The foreman wailed.

Felicity stepped in to hit him again. This time the heavy butt of the gun connected with his nose. She felt the satisfying crunch of cartilage as it folded.

But as she tried to draw back from him, he suddenly wrapped his hands around her arm. He grunted, pulling her in, trying to wrestle the gun from her hand.

Felicity tried to pull free again, but couldn't. She was surprised by the move but wasn't unprepared for it. The man was strong, adrenaline mixing with rage in a potent cocktail. There was no outmuscling him.

Moving quickly, Felicity reached behind her back and pulled out a folding knife. There was a light *snap* as she flicked it open with her thumb and the man had just enough time to stop and look at it before she rushed forward and plunged it into his stomach.

Now it was Felicity who was fueled by rage and adrenaline. The steel flashed in the harsh industrial light as she pumped the blade into his gut again and again. The man began screaming, which turned to grunting, and then died into whimpering.

She finally stopped and stepped back. The foreman looked up at her, pain and tears in his eyes. He slumped to the floor, holding his guts in. He sobbed and looked at the wound, then pulled a face and looked away.

"Where is she?" Felicity repeated.

But the man was just shaking his head.

Felicity reached down to her hip where the large leather sheath was. She unsnapped it and slowly drew out the heavy meat cleaver.

"They fucking did this to me," the man spat. "Those bastards."

"Who did?" Felicity asked. Her voice was all silk. She stepped in a little closer.

"I don't know their names. But they pulled my security. Why do you think it was so easy to get to me?"

"It wasn't easy. I killed five men to get your name and still had to scour every resource I had to find this place. There was nothing easy about it."

"But they knew you'd find me eventually," he said. "After you killed those men, they must have-" He suddenly winced and bent over, sucking air through his teeth. He took a few rasping breaths.

"The girl," Felicity said.

"Oh, lay the fuck off," he spat. "What do you think? I don't even know which one you're talking about at this point but they all go to the same place. The place you don't come back from."

"And where's that?"

The foreman pursed his lips and shook his head vigorously. "You loved your girl?"

"My niece."

"Right. You couldn't be a parent." He sniggered, his body beginning to sway. "The parents gotta go."

"Why is that?"

"We need the skins."

"For what?"

But he was shaking his head again. "You love your niece, then you understand. Understand why I can't tell you, even if they seem to be leading you there."

"I don't get it."

"I hope you never will." The man's eyelids began to flutter.

"Hey, hey," Felicity slapped him. "Look at me."

The foreman's eyes opened again and she looked deep into them. They were the color of dirty brown water. She exhaled and raised the cleaver, then began to slowly erase his face.

· · ·

"CHRIST." Bross felt something rise in the back of his throat as he looked down at Cole Fogel's corpse.

"Looks like tomato soup," Hawkins said casually.

It was late in the morning and the crime scene guys had moved on from this body to the two just outside. Bross and Hawkins were the only ones in the room.

"Ah, don't say that. Tomato soup is all I can afford with my pay."

Hawkins shrugged, looking down his thin nose at Bross. "We'll have to do something about that."

"Right," he muttered. He knew plenty of crooked cops and they were all pulling in massive amounts of dough. Buying expensive cars and hookers, the whole nine yards. Why did he have to fall into the gig that didn't pay shit?

No way the higher-ups would be able to help him out either, even if they were in-the-know. The organization he was in wasn't about money, it was about life. It was about beauty and transformation.

"You really want this sick broad to find the dam?"

"Ain't about what I want," Hawkins said. "The elders understand things about this world that we couldn't even begin to comprehend. We do what they say. No questions."

Despite how much he liked Hawkins and believed in what they were doing, Bross still felt that genuine American side of him twist at the thought of obeying without question. He wanted to say *fuck that* and have it explained to him. But what the Hell else was new? Two decades on the street had taught him that there's always someone above you pissing on your head, and sometimes you just gotta take it.

Hawkins tapped a cigarette into his hand, then flicked the lighter. Before he could light the end, Bross leaned over and blew it out.

"Not at the crime scene," he said, trying to say what he

couldn't say aloud. Trying to convey the fact that even though they were protected and the chain of evidence was worth less than the empty gum wrapper in his pocket, they shouldn't *flaunt* the fact.

Hawkins sighed and lowered the cigarette. "Where do you suppose his face is?"

"Look at this place. It's probably on the bottom of your fuckin' shoes."

"There should be more."

"More what? More face?"

"Nah," Hawkins said. "The bones. The pulp. The skin. A bunch of it is missing."

Bross let that sink in. "You still think she's taking trophies? Like the finger?"

"Could be. Not sure what you're going to do with a shattered face though."

"She may not have shattered it at first. Possible she peeled his face off while he was still alive, then bashed it in afterward."

"She's mad." Hawkins scratched his chin. "Real mad."

"And they want her…"

"They do."

FELICITY HAD GOTTEN home before the sun came up and proceeded to drink herself into unconsciousness. She didn't want to shower. Didn't want to eat. Didn't want to dream.

She just wanted to sleep.

And when she finally stumbled off the couch and into the bathroom 14 hours later, she had the vague notion of having dreamt but couldn't recall what about. Good. Her life was enough of a nightmare. She didn't need that following her into her place of rest.

Still though, she couldn't shake the feeling that she had

dreamt of something unpleasant. The back of her neck prickled and her head pounded, putting her in a generally sour mood.

And she stank. Like blood and puke and piss. She looked down and saw that she had indeed urinated on herself in the night. Great. She'd have to burn the couch now.

After guzzling down about a half-gallon of water, she padded into the bathroom and brushed her teeth. As she did, she tentatively opened the lid of the toilet and saw a horrible brown soup floating in it with a few suspect chunks bobbing around. The worst part was, she couldn't remember which end it had come out of.

She dropped the lid back down with a clack and flushed it. Then she stripped her clothes off, walked naked into the kitchen to chuck them in the garbage can, and then returned to take a twenty-minute shower in water so hot it nearly scalded her.

Once she was out, she dried her hair, popped a few Advil, watched the video of the three men killing her brother and his wife and abducting their daughter, then she climbed into bed knowing full well the nightmares were on their way.

"You look like shit," Roscoe said as he stood in the doorway to his garage.

"Shoulda seen me yesterday," Felicity said. "I was so gross you probably wouldn't have let me on your property."

"C'mon in," he waved her inside. "I'll let you on my property but I'm not quite sure I want you *seen* on my property right now. You're lucky that ATM vid they got was grainier than my butt crack after a day at the beach or you wouldn't even be able to go outside right now."

Felicity sat down and took off a backpack she had been carrying. She unzipped it, dug inside, and then produced about ten manilla envelopes stuffed thick with papers.

Roscoe made a sour face. "You know I don't do analog, right? Paper doesn't have a search function."

"It does today, because I've already gone through a bunch of it."

"And?"

"Most of these are shipping manifests. They seem to be buying livestock hand-over-fist."

"For what?"

Felicity shook her head. "Dunno. But it looks like they're all going to one place. Gotta map?"

"Of where?"

"Blackburg and the surrounding areas."

Roscoe walked over to the bank of monitors along the wall, sat down in the chair, and began typing. A few seconds later, he had a map up on the biggest monitor. Felicity walked over to join him.

"They tried to hide where everything is going but I think I figured it out." She pointed at an intersection on the southwestern outskirts of the city. "This is one of their frequent drop-off points."

Roscoe blinked. "There's nothing there."

"There is though. If you look closely, you can see a service road. The trucks also make drops here, here, here, and here." She pointed at a number of intersections, making a rough circle.

"So what's in the middle then?"

"Only thing I could find online is an old water treatment plant for the Wokanom River. It's shut down but here's the thing: I did some digging and it sounds like places downstream have been experiencing a drought."

"What are you thinking?"

"Let's review." Felicity cracked her knuckles. "The place I hit the other night had been turned into a meat processing plant, that much was clear. They ship animals in, butcher them, and then ship them out, apparently to this old treatment plant."

"Okay, I'm with you so far."

"Meanwhile, people downstream of the river say all the water's dried up."

"Okay."

"Plus, in my digging it sounded like they sent an EPA guy upstream to check it out. But get this: he's disappeared."

"So they're doing something at this old abandoned plant that involves a heaping shit-ton of meat and water. But what? Like, a ritual or something?"

"I don't think so." Felicity smiled. "I think they're keeping something there."

"Something like..."

"Like a creature of some sort. I think they dammed the river to fill this gorge here," Felicity pointed at a small dark spot on the map. "And I think they're holding something there in a manmade lake."

They had both heard the stories about incomprehensible creatures in the city. At first, they had thought they were just that: stories. But the more they watched the cultists, the more they believed. Whatever was happening in Blackburg was otherworldly. And once you had seen a man in a black robe use a ceremonial dagger to perform a ritual sacrifice online, a lot of things suddenly seemed a lot more possible.

Roscoe paled. "Felicity, that's a *lot* of meat they're shipping."

"Yup."

An uncomfortable look formed on Roscoe's face and he shifted in his seat.

"So," he began, choosing his words carefully. "What are they doing with the children?"

Felicity felt her own countenance diminish a bit.

"I'm not sure. But if they're feeding it livestock, I can't see why they would feed it children as well. Hell, maybe Presley's still alive."

"What's next then? We go knock on their door and ask for her back?"

"Yeah," she said. "And we're going to need your hardware hookup again."

"Why?"

"Because I'm gonna knock really fuckin' hard."

DETECTIVE BROSS WATCHED the sun come up over the water. He would have thought it beautiful if it weren't for what lay beneath that placid, glass-like surface. Hell, maybe that's what made it beautiful. The knowing.

He thought about what they had done. About the gift the forest animals had given them over a year ago. The gift they had brought into this world as a loose collective of cops, lawyers, construction workers, senators, and about every other profession. You name a job in Blackburg and they had someone working it.

In reality, this was what Blackburg had made. This was the sum of their combined effort. Something they could take pride in. Something that could give their lives meaning. They had given birth to something... magnificent.

A cloud of smoke drifted across his field of view and he turned. Hawkins was standing on the balcony of the old plant with him, a scoped rifle slung over his shoulder.

"You think she's gonna show?" Bross asked.

Hawkins didn't say anything. Instead, he squinted and took another drag on his cigarette.

Out of the corner of his eye, Bross saw a puff of white smoke along the South Ridge. Then, before he could say anything, something streaked across the ground, hit their car, and exploded.

"What the fuck?" Bross said, looking down at the smoldering wreckage that had been his Lincoln Town Car.

"She's here." Hawkins stubbed the cigarette out on the railing.

As the echoes of the explosion rolled over the manmade lake, the sound of men shouting became audible, along with a buzzing sound. Bross lifted the binoculars to where he had seen the puff of smoke, but there was nothing there.

Down below, a large metal door clanged open and men with rifles came pouring out. Within seconds, they were packed into trucks and ATVs and went speeding off.

"Wait," Bross said, turning to Hawkins. "Get them on the radio, tell them to come back."

"Why?" Hawkins asked.

"It's a diversion. She's gotta be working with someone. Ah shit, of course she is. She's making her play."

"I think she's already made it."

Just then, the door to the balcony cracked open and a black automatic pistol came jutting out inches from Hawkins' face. He didn't move. Didn't look at it.

Bross scrambled for his gun but as soon as he did, a voice said, "Stop."

"Not another move or I blow his face off."

Bross froze, his hand on his gun. The holster still snapped tight.

"Take it out slowly, then throw it over the edge. After that," she shoved the gun into Hawkins' ear, "You do the same."

The two men did as they were told, their pistols hitting the cement below and sounding like pieces of snapping plastic. The rifle followed. Bross tried to peer around the door, but it opened out in his direction, making it so all he could see was the woman's hand and forearm.

"Where are they?" the woman asked.

No one said anything. Bross considered slamming the heavy door shut on the woman's wrist but Hawkins shot him a look.

"The children!" she said more forcefully. "Where are they?"

"Where do you think they are?" Hawkins asked calmly.

"If I knew, you'd be dead."

"We can take you to them," Hawkins said after a moment. "If you promise to let Detective Bross here live."

"Detective Bross." A note of uncertainty crept into her voice. "But not you."

"You won't kill me."

"No? Why's that?"

Hawkins remained silent, fixing his eyes on Bross.

"Answer me!" she shouted.

Bross opened his mouth to say something, then there was a deafening bang and a tuft of hair on the side of Hawkins' head puffed out as a bullet passed through his brain. The man's body went limp and crumpled down to the metal grating that served as the balcony's floor.

Before Bross knew what he was doing, he rushed in to slam the door on the woman but she was already halfway through. The heavy door crashed into her chest and she grunted. Bross took the moment to duck down and go for his backup piece he had strapped to his ankle. Before he could, however, there was another bang and his right knee exploded.

The pain was like nothing he'd ever experienced. He had been shot once by a little .38 revolver two decades ago. The bullet had hit him just inside the shoulder and, at the time, he hadn't felt any pain. It was just like a heavy weight had been added to the left side of his chest. This was different.

This was like having pain itself dig its hands into the core of his bones and start fishing around. It felt like he had been shattered. Knew that if he tried to walk it would hurt so bad he'd want to die.

The woman tried to make him walk anyway.

"Get up." She swung the pistol across his face and he felt the metal sights dig into his cheek. A Smith and Wesson. 9mm, probably. Different from whatever automatic she had had the night the five men had died. But no less lethal.

Bross felt a hand grab him by the collar of his coat, then shots erupted from somewhere inside the plant. They were close, the sound of lead pinging off of metal rending the air apart. The woman ducked down and fired back a few times through the doorway. Three quick shots.

"Stop shooting or he dies," the woman yelled.

The firing from inside the plant stopped.

Bross looked up at her for the first time, trying to see her through teary eyes. She was thin and pale with red hair tied into a braid that fell across her shoulder. On her back was some large metal contraption he didn't recognize. She seemed unremarkable yet familiar. As if he had seen the face before.

Oh shit, he thought. *She's the sister.*

He had interviewed the friends and family of one of the murdered couples and she had been the man's sister. What was her name? He couldn't quite place it, but he definitely recognized her. She must have seen it because she glanced over at him then did another take. She recognized him too.

A moment passed and then she grabbed Bross by the shoulder and tugged him toward her. Pain shot through his leg like a bolt of electricity and he didn't bother trying to hold back the cry.

"Drop your weapons or he dies," she yelled, then continued to tug him along until they were both through the doorway and standing at the top of the stairwell inside the plant.

Down below were two men, each with automatic weapons pointing up at them.

"I said *drop 'em!* You're not getting backup anytime soon. Most of your friends are on a wild goose chase and the ones who aren't are already dead."

The two men hesitated and began to lower their weapons.

"Don't-" Bross began to shout but the sound was drowned out by the woman's pistol as she quickly extended her arm and shot the man on the right once in the neck, followed by the man on the left in his lower abdomen. He tried to bring his gun back up but she shot him two more times and he dropped.

Bross had recognized them. Benny and George. They had eaten and laughed together on a few cold and lonely nights out here after all the work was done. They were good men. And now they were dead.

"Why did you have-" but before he could go any further, the woman shoved him toward the stairs.

Bross stumbled and heard a crunch as his knee folded sideways. His scream was cut short as he tumbled down the steps, the world spinning around him as he fell. Every time he hit one of the metal stairs, it was like getting punched by the bumper of a car. His knee was fire. His entire body, pain.

He let out an *oof* as he hit the cement below. His head was swimming, his injured knee slowly pulling him into shock. All of a sudden, the woman was crouched next to him. She pressed the barrel of the gun against his cheek.

"Where?" she asked quietly.

FELICITY COULDN'T CARRY the injured man, so she dragged him by the feet. He moaned as his body thumped over every bump and step but she didn't care. He had pointed at the wall and she understood. She knew what lay beyond the wall. With a cold fist clenching her stomach, she had known where to go all along. She just hadn't had the courage until now.

"They're dead," the man said, his voice sounding like a whimper. "Just go. There's nothing for you here."

"All I have left is here," Felicity said flatly. She reached a large iron door and threw it open, the metal contraption that was slung over her shoulder bouncing on its strap.

Before her lay a rough dirt path leading down to the lake. At the edge of the water was a shed, dock, and some sort of large container. They all looked relatively new. The water appeared unnaturally calm, and as she approached, Felicity felt everything inside of her tighten harder and harder until it felt like she was going to fold in on herself.

Once she was at the water's edge, she dropped the detective's leg and walked over to the container. When she looked inside, something inside of her throat actually felt like it snapped. As if her body wanted to push tears out but it was wound so tight that it couldn't. Her chest heaved with a silent sob and she turned away, raising a hand to her mouth.

"Why?" She finally managed to squeeze out. She wanted to add more but she couldn't. And even if she could, what more was there?

She looked back at the container, a sudden fever washing over her. She hurled herself in and began pulling the items out.

Tiny shoes. Hundreds of them. All scuffed and dirty and soggy from rain. She hurled them aside, digging deeper and deeper until she was almost at the bottom. Then she found one. A faded purple shoe with a white flower on it. One from the pair she had gotten Presley for Christmas.

She turned it over in her hand like a delicate egg, then turned her gaze back upon the detective.

He was awake and watching her, sweat running down his face.

"It won't eat the rubber," he said hoarsely.

She narrowed her eyes. "What?"

"The rubber," he repeated. He swallowed hard. "It won't eat it."

Felicity felt white-hot anger ignite in her. She reached around and grabbed the contraption from her back.

It was a speargun with an explosive tip. It hadn't come like that so Roscoe had had to jerry-rig a device that attached to the end. The explosive part was much like a grenade, but more cylindrical. When the spear was fired, it ripped the priming pin out and detonated roughly five-seconds later.

She had brought it for whatever she suspected lay within the murky depths of the lake but at that moment she wanted nothing more than to see this man's body splatter apart into a rain of red mist.

She had two more spears strapped to her back. They should be enough.

Felicity raised the speargun. She pulled a lever on the side and three deadly-looking blades snapped out and locked into place at the end of the spear. Then, just as she lined the detective up in her sights, something shot out of the water behind her and latched onto her ankle.

Before she knew what was happening she was yanked down onto the ground, the speargun falling from her grasp. She spun quickly, drawing her Smith and Wesson and firing at the thing.

The tentacle was long and pale, looking less like something from a squid or octopus and more like some underground worm. A fetid stench washed over her and she saw the water roil as bullets hit the tentacle and the sand around it. One of the rounds hit its mark and the appendage went limp.

Without wasting a single moment, Felicity lurched to her feet and dove for the speargun. The beach was rough and gravelly and she felt the stones dig into her palms as she hit the ground and grasped the gun by the handle.

Multiple tentacles slithered down her arms and legs and ripped her off the ground and into the air. The speargun fell from her hands but she managed to catch the strap. The thing turned her around and began lowering her to the water. As it did, it slowly rose above the surface to meet her.

It was...her brother.

The sight sent a chill through her body as more and more faces came into view. It took a moment to realize that it wasn't her brother. It was his skin. That and the skins of other adult victims had been stitched together and stretched across the creature's bulbous form. An amalgam of dead parents, silently screaming for their lost children beneath the murky depths.

Then its true face was revealed.

Flesh at the center of its body parted into lips, revealing a mouth that looked like a giant nostril full of hair and icicle-sharp teeth. The flesh inside rippled and undulated and the disgusting reek Felicity had smelled when the creature had first arrived increased ten-fold.

The thing was massive, easily the size of three 18-wheelers parked alongside each other.

It didn't cry or howl. The sound it made was more of a deep and hollow clacking, like the sound of joints being pushed out of place. A fat, swollen purple tongue slithered up out of the dark hole.

Felicity had seen enough. She flipped the speargun up and gripped it with her right hand. It was heavy and wobbled as she tried to aim but it was so close it barely made a difference. She pulled the trigger and there was a metallic *clack*. The spear lodged itself in the upper part of the creature's mouth and it recoiled slightly.

Then the explosive detonated.

Something warm sprayed Felicity's face and she went tumbling through the air, splashing down into about two feet of water. She managed to hold onto the speargun but as she landed, she heard a dull snap and pain exploded in her right wrist and up her arm.

Waves rocked her as the creature thrashed, but she managed to pull another spear from where it was strapped to her back, lock it in place, and pull the lever to extend the blades before something wrapped around her ankle and yanked her down below the surface.

She couldn't tell which way was up as the brown water raced by her. It was all she could do not to let go of the speargun, but she knew that if she did then she was dead. If she didn't get air soon though, she'd die anyway.

Felicity felt herself suddenly slow down and then change direction. She was moving slower now and as she opened her eyes she saw a dark form slowly materialize in front of her.

It took less than a second for her to realize what was happening and it was barely enough. She hefted the speargun with both arms now, swallowed the pain in her wrist, and pulled the trigger.

It still took a moment for the explosive to detonate and by the time it did she was damn near on top of it. Best she could tell afterward, was the spear had hit the monster on the rounded edge of its body. When it finally detonated, she was half-inside of its mouth.

The experience was like nothing she had ever felt before. There was a loud *thump* and then it felt as if she was struck by a giant fist made of water. Felicity tumbled end-over-end through the murk, feeling the monster's teeth knick her shin and boot as she exited its mouth.

Once she was able to orient herself, she swam hard toward the surface and burst out into the cool morning air. The sky was grey above her and she looked around to find herself in the middle of the lake.

Cursing, she pulled the third and final spear from her harness and attempted loading it into the gun. The maneuver was much more difficult while treading water with an injured wrist. As she worked, she saw the wake of something huge begin circling her about forty feet out.

Dammit. The spear wouldn't lock in. She jammed it, twisted it, jammed it again, and finally drove it home. There was a click as it locked in and she took a crucial second to figure out what she was going to do next.

The two explosives hadn't done anything. For all she knew, the thing was impervious to damage. She needed to get out of the water and fast. But even on a good day it would take her no less than fifteen minutes to swim back to shore.

She looked around and saw a big pile of something near the southern end of the lake. It looked like sawn wood but not quite. It was too yellow and gave her a sickly feeling looking at it.

Oh shit, she thought to herself. *Are those bones?*

No time to think about that. Felicity raised the spear gun up out of the water, prayed that she judged the trajectory right, and pulled the trigger.

Wasting no time, she dropped the gun and reached around to grab the steel cleaver from where its sheath hung on her back. She unsnapped the strap, yanked it out, turned, and swung just as the mouth of the thing closed down on her waist.

The tiny sharp, sliver-like teeth skewered her legs in multiple places as the cleaver came down. She swung again and again as the creature ravaged her, then there was a loud boom.

At first, nothing happened. The monster continued to shake her in its mouth as she swung at it. A few tentacles lashed out and she chopped them away.

Then the water began to move. It was slow but noticeable.

Then it picked up. Before long, Felicity was able to cast a glance over her shoulder and see that her aim had been dead-on. The explosive had torn the dam apart and now the lake was emptying.

A tentacle suddenly wrapped around her neck and she swung the cleaver. She hacked at it once, twice, three times and if finally severed, blood spraying from the stump. Felicity took a quick breath and was then plunged underwater as the creature dove.

As she was tugged along, she felt her energy beginning to ebb away. She was bleeding from multiple places in her thighs and shins and had been fighting this thing for God-knew-how-long now. There was a bump as the creature settled to the bottom and just sat there, content to drown her.

When she looked up, however, she saw the surface of the water coming toward her fast. What was more was that they were close to the busted dam now. As the surface finally broke over her and the last of the water drained away, the creature's full form was revealed.

It looked like some sort of decomposing tadpole. Layers and layers of human skin were stretched over it in a macabre tableau of faces locked in silent howls. Its eyeless face contorted in the open air and spat her out into the mud. It began to thrash.

The tentacles seemed to be coming out of random points on its body, like stray bristles. It began using them to wriggle toward what was left of the lake as it flowed through the broken dam.

Felicity felt anger and rage flare up inside of her and without thinking, she got to her wobbly feet and took a few steps and hurled herself onto one of the trailing tentacles. She raised the cleaver, hacked at it, climbed a few feet, then hacked at it again.

It was at this point that she realized the dam was actually located at the edge of a pretty steep drop. The sound of water falling down below was loud, even over the noise of the struggle. She held on for a few more seconds, then let go as the creature tumbled over the ledge.

There was a loud crash down below, followed by the sounds of something whipping against the air.

Moving a little more carefully now, Felicity crept up to the ledge, grimacing at the human bones that had made up the dam, then she pushed them aside. Peering over, she saw that the giant tadpole creature had fallen over a hundred feet and skewered itself on one of the dead trees down below. It was convulsing, its tentacles flying out in every direction as it smacked the stone wall and tore down any other dead trees or bushes in its wake.

Felicity worked up a thick wad of blood and saliva from the inside of her mouth and spat it down at her defeated foe.

THE EXTENT of her injuries was more severe than she had thought, and she collapsed three-quarters of the way back to the treatment plant. The form of the detective lying on the ground was visible now and she made the rest of the journey on her hands and knees.

All of her weapons were gone now. The speargun had probably washed downriver, her gun was so soaked it probably wouldn't fire, and the cleaver had fallen from her hand at some unknown point after the creature had fallen.

It didn't matter. She would kill the man with her bare hands if she needed too. The others would be getting back soon, having likely figured out Roscoe's diversion. It didn't matter either. All that mattered was that that thing was dead. It wouldn't be eating any more children or collecting any more skins.

The detective seemed to wake up once Felicity was a few feet away from him. And when she looked into his eyes, a strange feeling washed over her. It was some mix of hunger and hatred. The feeling almost made her sick, like swallowing meat you knew was rotten. But she couldn't turn away. She continued to crawl.

"This is the final sacrifice," a voice said.

Felicity looked up to see a man standing there. A familiar man. A dead man.

"Detective Bross will give his life gladly, won't he?" the man asked, looking down at Bross.

"Hawkins?" the detective croaked out.

The man named Hawkins smiled and turned his head, revealing the exit wound from Felicity's bullet. Smoke drifted out of the wound and Felicity thought she caught something in the man's eye. A dull internal light that hadn't been there before.

"The ritual was long and arduous for you, I'm sure," Hawkins said to Felicity. "You have endured much heartache but it was necessary."

"What?" It was all Felicity could manage.

"Bringing a life into this world is painful. Always has been. But we delight in the pain. We recognize it for what it is: a gift."

Hawkins knelt down next to Detective Bross.

"You can think of this artificial lake here as an incubating pond. Like a nursery for the *Drakfalett's* first life stage."

"It's dead," Felicity said, making no effort to hide the satisfaction on her face. But the man only smiled.

"It cannot be killed by conventional means," he said, as if explaining something lovingly to a child. He tilted his head, a plume of smoke puffing out of his bullet wound. "And neither can you."

"I don't understand," Bross said, taking the words out of Felicity's mouth. "Hawkins, what the fuck is going on?"

"Exactly what you signed up for," Hawkins said. "We're bringing the Child Eater into the world. Children are characterized by feelings of wonder and nothing devours wonder like thoughts of revenge."

Hawkins stood up.

"Getting the hex into your hand was easy. We knew you'd never stop until you found your brother's killer, so a flash drive with a video of the act was the perfect Trojan horse. Every time you watched it, your body was being prepared for something. A transformation."

Felicity shook her head. "No. That's not...What?"

"It's already begun. The hunger. Tell me: when you look at Detective Bross here, the one who colluded to have your brother and his family killed, what do you feel?"

She couldn't help herself. She looked at the pathetic man on the ground whose knee she had shot out. And when she looked at him—*really* looked at him—she felt something deep down inside of her. She felt hunger.

Hawkins was nodding now. "It was the same with the others. The missing finger. The other man's face. You haven't been dealing justice out to these men, you've been *consuming* them. Because that's what you are, Felicity. You are what the ancient race of Trilodians called *Drak Trakem*. Do you know what that means?"

She didn't. Of course she didn't. How could she? Hawkins saw it on her face and answered his own question.

"Loosely translated, it means the same as *Drakfalett*. It means Child Eater. But the *Drak Trakem* is the other side of the coin. The *Drakfalett* eats the children of men. It eats other things too, of course. It eats cows and pigs and chickens like you wouldn't believe. But it eats livestock so that its flesh can grow. The children-" He reached up and tapped his forehead. "It eats those to nourish its mind."

"You, on the other hand," Hawkins continued. "You eat the Children of God. You feed off of a living soul that you have minimized down to an act or a series of acts. By making them killers rather than full-fledged human beings, you have turned men and women—these tiny image-bearers—into nothing more than meat. And the consumption of this meat is your entire purpose."

"I'm going to *destroy* you," Felicity snarled.

"I know," Hawkins said casually. "But first, you are going to eat him." He pointed down at Bross, who looked up at him in surprise and then over at Felicity.

"You are going to eat him. Then you are going to eat me. Then you are going to go find the *Drakfalett* and you are going to breed with it. Then, one month later, when the full moon is at its highest, you will give birth to a demon."

Felicity felt as if she had just been run over by a car. The man's words were ridiculous. Beyond believability. But when she looked down at Detective Bross, sitting there in the mud, holding his wrecked knee-cap, she felt something open up inside of her.

She felt suddenly weak. She felt defeated, like an old rope bridge finally snapping and sending its occupants plummeting down into the dark below. She felt angry. She felt despair.

Felicity continued to eye the man on the ground and as she did, she felt suddenly very, very hungry.

Without thinking, she reached up and grabbed Bross's shoes, then began to untie them.

"What are you doing?" He said, panic plain in his voice. "What the fuck are you doing?"

Felicity cast one shoe aside, untied the other one, then tossed that one aside as well.

"Hawkins," Bross pleaded. "You can't do this. I've been good. I've sacrificed everything for you. Please don't do this."

Felicity felt a click in her head as her cheeks began to stretch. Her lower jaw sank down with surprising ease and she began to push the man feet-first into her wide-open mouth.

Bross was screaming now. He sat up straight and began hitting her in the head but she didn't feel the blows. She didn't feel anything. She just consumed.

As her lips slid over his body, she felt the warm glow of oblivion begin to slide over hers. She felt all of her fears and sadness and desperation begin to melt away and slough off like something dead.

Bross's wrecked knee stabbed the inside of her mouth as she moved over it but the pain was muted and distant. Every inch of her body seemed to open up for the man. She stretched and gulped and before she knew it his muffled screams were echoing against the inside of her throat as she pushed the top of his head down and past her teeth.

Felicity gave one more hard swallow and Detective Bross slid into her stomach.

Roscoe cranked the engine of the ATV as he raced back toward the treatment plant. He had fired the RPG at a car in the parking lot and the reaction had been predictable. Men had come swarming out of the building to chase him down.

He hadn't waited for them to see where he was going, the tracks of the ATV would take care of that for him. He just hoped that enough of them would leave and let Felicity sneak in and take care of what she needed to do.

The trail he had been following ran parallel to a dirt road a few miles from the plant and once he reached it, he wrapped a piece of duct tape around the throttle and hopped off onto a patch of shaggy grass. The machine buzzed on down the road until it hit a curve and continued on over a cliff. By the time it hit the bottom of the ravine, Roscoe had already doubled back to where they had hidden another ATV on the side of the road.

With luck, the people chasing him would see the tracks and follow it to the cliff. They wouldn't see his body at the bottom so they'd have to split up, trying to figure out where he had gone and if he had somehow survived the crash. They'd figure it out eventually, but by then, he and Felicity would hopefully be long-gone.

Right before he fired up the engine though, he heard a loud *boom* off in the distance.

Good, he thought to himself. *She's fighting the creature.*

Now he was almost back, approaching from the South. He didn't know what the monster Felicity was fighting looked like but he sort of wanted to see it for himself.

The idea that they inhabited a world with monsters in it was terrifying. He had yet to see one with his own eyes, but the stories he had found on the dark web had been so numerous and consistent that he had begun to believe them whole-heartedly.

As he drove, he noticed the tiny trickle of a river become suddenly gushing with water. He had to swerve to the side so as not to get washed away by the river's rising edge.

Continuing to follow it, he came to the bottom of a cliff face that—if his sense of direction was correct—was right beneath the manmade lake.

Roscoe took a second to look at where the water was crashing down. Hundreds of bones seemed to be scattered by the cliff face and it looked as if something had swooped down and knocked a bunch of trees over. Whatever it was was gone now.

The ground running perpendicular to the cliff sloped steeply up at this point and Roscoe turned the ATV on and began the climb. The machine beneath him whined and groaned as he ascended, his tires spitting mud and gravel out behind him.

Once he had come level with the area where the lake had been he turned toward the treatment plant and floored it. All appeared quiet. No monsters. No gunshots. No explosions.

As he peered around, however, he noticed something moving slowly toward the river. He squinted.

What the fuck?

Whatever it was, it was big. Like some bloated tick dragging its massive belly through the mud. It was only a few feet from the water and as he drew closer, he felt his body tense.

Oh God. Felicity.

The thing that had been Felicity looked at him with a feverish glare burning in her eyes. Her jaw seemed to be tilted downward at an unnatural angle and her belly was the size of a giant beach ball. Her pale skin was stretched, and when he looked closer he saw red lines where it had torn.

She looked at him, something desperate in her eyes. Without words she seemed to be simultaneously asking for forgiveness and telling him to back off.

Roscoe skidded to a stop in the mud, the ATV's wheels sinking down. He stared in horror at his only friend as she dragged herself into the muddy water and disappeared.

THE SPACE BELOW

Selby greeted me when I walked in, his teeth clacking into a smile like an ivory firing line.

"Good to see you," he said, shaking my hand a little too hard. "How's the music industry?"

"Limping along," I said lightly, despite how heavy the statement actually was. I was making money but the big record companies as a whole still seemed to be desperately clawing away from the hungry lion of internet streaming and file-sharing. But I knew the question wasn't a real question. It was a dig.

How is wasting your life going, brother Vel? Think you'll ever make something of yourself someday?

As soon as my hand left my brother's, it began searching for the nearest drink. Thankfully, my mother always kept a full wet bar stocked in the hearth room. I wandered over and poured my third drink of the evening. One to think about coming. One to get in the car. One as soon as I got there.

Brandy on the rocks. I barely tasted it.

As I drank, my eyes wandered to the shotgun above the mantle. It used to belong to my grandfather, Theodore

Westchild and his father and grandfather before him. Dad said he always kept it loaded but I knew the truth. He had taken the lead out of the shells a long time ago. Now, if you pulled the trigger, it would just make a loud *bang* and nothing more. A perfect metaphor for the Westchild family.

"Vel, you can't enter the space below while intoxicated," my mother said, striding into the room. She was wearing a handsome black blouse with a pair of gold earrings that inexplicably matched her pants. "It's unclean."

"I'll be sure to throw up before I get down there," I said. "That should set me right."

"I'm serious," she said, her harsh glare backing her up.

"What is this even for?" I asked. "I thought we were too young to do the ceremony."

I was 24, which seemed plenty old. But according to my father we couldn't be initiated until we were 35. Then again, things might be different now that he was out of the picture.

My mother didn't respond. She just walked up and plucked the glass out of my hand.

"Dad would want it," Selby said. "It's important. For all of us."

Important for you, maybe. I didn't derive my power from some underground cosmic entity. I did it the good, old-fashioned way. With my dad's money.

I smirked to myself, feeling wretched.

"Go wash up," my mother said. "You can't enter dirty."

"I took a shower this morning," I lied. What I had actually done was wake up next to a stranger after a night of sweaty sex and sprayed myself down with a bottle of cologne.

There was a loud crack as my mother slapped me across the face. I barely felt it through the haze but the point came across well enough. Out of the corner of my eye, I saw Selby turn away with a grin on his face.

To be honest, I didn't fully understand why I was so resistant to the idea of engaging in the old family rituals. It was probably tied to the same rebellious impulse that drove me to music rather than politics. The impulse that kept me from speaking with my father for months at a time. The impulse that made me smile when I learned my father had disappeared a few months ago.

Without another word, I left the hearth room, ascended the stairs, stripped off my clothes, and took a shower.

When I was finished, I dried myself off and wandered into my old bedroom. Despite the pop sensibilities of my own music, I had grown up on punk and hardcore and the posters on my bedroom walls testified to that fact. I slipped on a white, silk shirt and a pair of designer jeans.

I thought about walking down barefoot, but to be honest, I had never actually been in our basement before. The entire time I had been alive, that area of the house had been off-limits. So I didn't know if the floor was warm, cool, carpeted, or dirt. I ended up opting for comfort and slipped into a pair of old sneakers I had bought from a prominent NBA star for $1,250.

If they weren't considered clean, then nothing was.

Once I was dressed, I stopped to take a look at myself in the mirror. Despite the strong sense of dissonance I felt buried deep inside, I liked what I saw. Still young. Still successful. And most importantly: no longer under my father's thumb.

I thought about the phone call I had received from my mother that morning. She had told—not *asked*, but *told*—me to be at the house by seven that night. She said my brother and I were finally going to go into the basement.

Where the secrets were. Where the power was.

· · ·

AFTER GETTING the call from my mother, I had spent the afternoon driving around town in a daze. Traffic was heavy, like usual, but once I got out on the freeway I was able to open up the throttle a bit. The air whipped by me through an open window as I wove in and out of the cars. A few times I even closed my eyes, feeling nothing but the road beneath me and the bite of the wind.

At one point, I opened them to see a billboard with my face on it. I was standing there shirtless, wearing a pouty look and a few layers of airbrushing. Next to my head in bold white letters were the words "*My art is my activism. I am my art.*"

The billboard was part of a larger anticapitalist campaign designed to sell Nova Louxx cologne to the new revolutionaries. The whole thing kind of made my head hurt but the paycheck was nice and at least it was for a worthy cause.

Some of the other billboards featured actors and celebrities. Some had guillotines in the background and one particularly striking one had a football player holding a torch.

"*Time to start a revolution.*" it said. The implication being that one had to buy the cologne first, of course. No proper revolution could begin without cologne.

If my dad had still been in office, my involvement in the campaign would have created a nice little stir among his voter base. Even with him missing and out of the mayor's seat, the story still got picked up by a number of podcasters, AM talk show hosts, and other content creators.

The light controversy drummed up more traffic and interest for the cologne than the ad itself.

A part of me felt as if I was violating something sacred by continuing down my career path with my father missing. But as soon as I started feeling that way, I thought about how he would have handled my disappearance if our positions had been reversed.

I could see it now. The tearful press releases. The interviews. All the media attention he could have ever wanted.

He would have loved it. It was simply who he was.

A few months ago, he had disappeared from the family home north of the city. The home I was procrastinating driving to. My mother had been away attending some fundraiser and when she had returned, he was simply gone, the only strange thing being a crudely drawn picture of an hourglass stapled to the back of his leather office chair.

I had neither heard nor seen sign of him since.

My brother, Selby, had taken it hard. Always the pleaser and the kiss-ass, he took my father's place in all of those press releases and interviews. Any day now, I expected him to announce his own run for mayor. Hell, he might even call for the current one to be impeached.

Crime rates were up along with joblessness. People were obviously struggling under the new mayor. All Selby needed now was to dig up some scandal. Real or not, he could always drum up some "facts" to lend credibility to the attack.

I felt my knuckles turn white and glanced down at the dash, only to see I had just ticked over 100 miles-per-hour. I eased off the gas and transitioned back into the right lane.

As if I'd get a ticket anyway. I was pretty sure I could talk my way out of any violation at this point but the Blackburg Police Department was in such disarray that I doubted they even had patrol cars out.

Even so, I eased off. To be honest, I just didn't like the effect my brother had on me. Him and my father both. Just the mere thought of them made me grind my teeth and I was trying to get better at that. For all I knew, I'd never see my father again. If that were the case, then what would I do with all my bitterness and resentment?

If I could never lay into him again for being a manipulative piece of trash, then those words would fester in my chest like a disease. I had to let them out, or rather, never give birth to them in the first place.

Selby would be there at the house tonight and while it was hard to look at him without thinking of my dad, my mom would also be present to absorb some of the tension. She had a way of doing that. Would have had to, really, considering who she had been married to for almost thirty years.

She was the glue that held our family together. She made the tough decisions when my dad tucked his tail and ran. For all intents and purposes, she acted the part of both my parents while my father simply used us as photo props for his campaigns.

My mother was the hero of our family and tonight she was going to prove that. Tonight, my brother and I would take our next steps on the long road toward ultimate power.

The thought made me simultaneously giddy and sick to my stomach.

FOR SUCH A LARGE and expensive house, the basement was awfully cold and leaky. Lit only by candles, the subterranean area of the property would have looked more at home in some ancient French catacombs than in an upper-class mansion on the East Coast. The floor was solid cement without any carpeting or tile laid over it. I got the sense that it would be impossible to tell where you were in reference to the rest of the house.

Rooms slanted and led off in strange directions. Hallways opened up and dead-ended without reason. It was almost as if the Westchild household had been built upon some sort of elaborate maze.

Despite this, my mother seemed to know where she was

going. She walked out ahead with an oil lamp dangling from her right hand and a cloth bag slung over her shoulder.

Selby walked beside me, wearing a suit that was way too nice for these conditions. I had barely said a word to him since arriving and he returned the favor. I noticed that his brown hair was neatly trimmed and swept back, enunciating his strong jawline and gentle lips.

My brother had always been classically good looking and I suspected that that was why he turned out the way he did. Take one look at him and assumptions are made. He got handed things. Not just girls and polite handshakes but opportunities. He slid right into my father's shoes as if he had already received his inheritance.

The thought had occurred to me that he was actually responsible for my father's disappearance but then I had to ask myself, "why?" What did he actually have to gain from my father being gone? He already used him as his virtual ATM in addition to the massive amount of money he made at his own job, so inheritance wasn't a factor. Any controversy my father managed to drum up always seemed to draw my brother into the spotlight as well.

Selby was the District Attorney for Blackburg. His position was largely political but required a lot less *gimmicks*, you might say, to keep it going. Even so, an occasional boost in attention caused by my father always managed to highlight Selby's squeaky-clean record. The media always looked at him but there wasn't much to see. He didn't break the unspoken rules. He was good at his job.

And I hated him.

It was hard to say why, really. Maybe I just saw too much of my dad in him. We were seven years apart and he had always treated me more like a subject than a brother. And just like my father, he didn't approve of my career as a musical artist.

The Westchilds were politicians to the bone. Born for the game. What they didn't understand though was that these days, power wasn't derived from voters, it was derived from a following. A fanbase. People may have voted for my dad but they *worshipped* me.

He had a voter base. I had a cult.

When my career really began to take off, I legally changed my name to my artistic persona, Veles Mir. This served to inextricably combine my artistic self with my everyday self. We were one. Are one. Until the end.

My fans worshipped me. The comment threads online were rabid. And despite the declining record industry, my numbers continued to climb. Tonight would bring me to the next level though.

I wasn't exactly sure what I would find among the dank stones and flickering candles beneath my house but I knew it would be something powerful. I remembered my father coming down here on occasion with groups of other prominent city leaders. I also remembered that not all of them would come back up.

My brother and I had never been allowed down here until now. This was actually due to my mother more than anything. Being someone who married into the Westchild family, she acted as the guide where the basement was concerned. She said the power was unpredictable and had been known to devour those who were unprepared for it. She said that sometimes it *wanted* us down there but she never acquiesced.

Until now.

In many ways, my mother was more powerful than all the men of the family. They made the final decisions but she was the one that guided the pen when something needed to be signed and spoke truth to my father when no one else could.

Her family was powerful. What her father did exactly wasn't

all that clear but as far as I could tell, he developed polymers that were used in weapons manufacturing. They made most of their money from government contracts and while his position was far less public than my own father's, it was arguably more powerful.

Together, my family was unstoppable. Or at least, it probably seemed that way from the outside. In reality, both my father and mother had had a number of affairs. I had been embroiled in several scandals over the years. And while my brother seemed perfect, there was something cold and untouchable about him. As if a part of him wasn't there.

"We're here," my mother said as she led us into one of the rooms.

At this point, we had been walking so long that I couldn't tell if we were still underneath the house or had traveled underground to someplace else entirely. The room itself looked similar to most of the others we had passed through but with one exception: in the center there stood something like a water basin. In fact, it almost looked like a birdbath.

It wasn't a birdbath though. That much was for certain. I couldn't explain why exactly, but I got the feeling that if a bird were to land in the center of this thing it might suddenly cease to exist.

The basin was four feet high and stretched to a diameter of about three feet at the top. It was made of some sort of carved stone and held intricate abstract designs. I stepped hesitantly up to the edge and peered in.

"Be careful," my mother warned. "It looks empty, but it is not."

Then, before I could respond, she reached up and unscrewed the bottom of the oil lamp she had been carrying. She held it over the basin, letting the clear liquid run out onto the stone surface. The flame inside the lamp slowly guttered and died, eventually plunging the room into darkness.

Suddenly, there was a loud *whoosh* as flames shot into the air, their yellow tips licking the ceiling before dying back down. The flames roiled and seemed to twist above the oil as they sank lower and lower. But instead of dying away completely, they sank all the way down until they looked as smooth as a liquid themselves. Indeed, they were no longer even identifiable as flames but resembled a glowing piece of orange glass.

Without wasting any time, my mother reached around to the cloth bag she had been carrying over her shoulder and produced some long semi-translucent piece of meat.

"Phallus of the squid," she said in monotone before dropping it in. The orange glass made the same *whooshing* sound it had before but the flames looked more like waves now, as if we were actually watching something get dropped into the ocean.

My mother then produced another chunk from her bag that somewhat resembled a shredded flank steak with a hole punched in the middle.

"Orifice of the stag." She dropped it in and the orange glass reacted the same way. A belch of fire. A wash of crimson sea foam.

We waited while the strange thing inside the basin calmed down and then my mother turned first to my brother and then to me.

"Your father is gone," she said. "I don't know where, but this might be able to tell us."

It suddenly dawned on me that she looked nervous. Uncertain. Desperate. I had always considered my parents' marriage to be somewhat loveless for most of my life but this new side of her seemed to cast doubt on that assessment. Maybe she *was* genuinely worried about my father. Or maybe she was in love with the public status he granted her. Either way, she seemed desperate to get him back.

"I thought we were here to be initiated," my brother said impatiently, irritation plain on his face.

"You must be 35 to undergo the initiation," my mother said. "The power here is—it must be submitted to. It inhabits your father right now. It says he's somewhere dark." Apprehension passed over her face. "It requires the minds of his sons to see."

"Then why are we here?" Selby asked. "Can't you do this on your own?"

"I have already tried. It needs more images to pull from. More minds. More memories." Her face twisted. "It needs the right blood."

"Get someone else to do it," my brother said, turning away. "I don't care where dad went."

It was difficult for me to understand that these words were actually coming out of my brother's mouth right now. He had always been closer to my father, if not in personal relationship then at least in admiration. His refusal was a shock.

What bothered me more though was that I actually wanted us to go through with it now. I had been somewhat indifferent before but now that we were down here there was something about the orange glassy substance that made me want to stay. That made me want to...*partake*.

"Selby," I said, giving him my best little brother look. "Stay."

"Why?" he said sourly.

I thought for a second. "Because I don't think this is the kind of thing you reject once and get to come back to. Once you walk away, I think you're out for good."

"It doesn't want to help us," he snapped. "It wants to *use* us, don't you see? Dad's gone and it's hungry. It wants to *feed* off of us."

"It can't hurt you," my mother said. "I have seen men die

down here but it was their own doing. It can only see into your mind and show you things. It can't possess you in any way."

"Then how did they die?" Selby asked. "These men you speak of that never made it out? How did they die if they weren't forced into anything?"

My mother blinked a few times and then straightened. "Sometimes the reflections of a person's heart are too much to bear, especially when others are in the room to witness it. Sometimes when someone peers into the Speculum, they don't like what they see."

"Are you saying they killed themselves?"

"Or each other," my mother explained. "But you must remember: when you gaze into the Speculum, you are only seeing yourself and no one else."

"Then why does it need us?" I asked. "If all it will show us is what we already know?"

"First of all, one does not know their own heart. Not fully. Second, *I* can see what you do not. The Mir resides in your father's blood. It must use someone from his bloodline to establish a connection to the other part of itself. Once it does, it will show me where to find him."

"And what if I don't want him found," Selby said coldly.

Now it was his turn to be slapped. I relished the look of shock that was plain on his face. My mother spat at his feet.

Something tightened in Selby's cheeks. He turned his head away for a moment and then looked back. I could see the wheels turning. He looked at me.

"You really don't think it will accept me again if I walk away?"

There it was. The possibility of power weighed against the risk of death or madness. In the end, it was no contest.

"I can't say for sure," I replied. "But from what we've heard, I don't think this thing takes rejection gracefully."

"Fine," he sniffed. "But whatever we see, don't trust it."

"Take my hand," my mother said, reaching out to Selby. She tilted her head and the orange glow of the basin reflected off of one of her earrings.

Something seemed to slide over her. A sort of self-assured calmness and gentleness. Gone was my mother, slapper of adult children. Now she appeared as something else. Now she was my mother, the guide.

Selby hesitated, then reached out and took her hand.

"Remember when the police investigated us after that snitch down at the docks disappeared?" my mother asked.

My brother nodded.

"We were fine. Remember when your brother hit that tramp a little too hard and her father came sniffing around a few weeks later?"

Selby nodded again, then reached up and wiped his forehead with the back of his hand.

"We were fine then too." She turned to me and held out her other hand. "We will always be fine. This family will always be fine. And even if your father is burning in the depths of Hell right now, then we will use the power to scoop him out and *we will be fine*. Got it?"

My brother and I both nodded. I took my mother's hand and then reached out for Selby's. He seemed hesitant but he eventually took it.

"Your father is the head of this household. The Mir resides in him and when people look at him they see the Mir. This is why some love him and others loathe him. Staring into the face of such concentrated power is enough to drive normal people mad." She gave each of us a reassuring smile. "But not us. We are different. We have the same power, in one way or another.

We are like the demigods of old. We traverse the plains of the underworld without flinching. And when we bring your father back we will be that much more powerful for it."

"Now, I'm going to ask you a few questions and you must answer them truthfully. I am not asking for me. I'm asking for the power, got it?"

My brother and I nodded. My mother closed her eyes and we all squeezed each other's hands tightly.

"Great Mir," she said. "We come before you, humble and unworthy."

Silence.

"Tonight we ask you to find Gregory Westchild. He is of your blood and you know him. We are of his blood and we know him. Bring us together."

The orange liquid swirled in the basin. Images began to swim up to the surface but I couldn't make anything out.

"Children, do you submit to the power?"

"Yes," my brother and I both answered, somewhat out of sync.

"Do you know where your father is?"

"No," I said. For a second, Selby didn't answer and I began to think he might actually know.

Then, a moment later, he said, "No."

"Do you accept the burden of yourselves?"

What? My mind began to race. I hadn't been prepared for this. I didn't even know what she meant. The burden of myself?

"Yes," Selby answered.

I thought back to myself earlier that evening, seeing my face on the billboard. Assessing my adult self in the mirror hanging in my childhood bedroom.

"Yes," I declared.

Then I was plunged face-first into Hell.

. . .

AN ANSWER to who was responsible for my father's disappearance presented itself immediately.

I saw an hourglass, my father in the bottom half and my brother in the top. My brother was clawing at the glass beneath him, trying to get down into the space below where my father was. The neck of the glass was too tight but my brother's body slowly dripped down into the bottom as if he was made of liquid.

Eventually, Selby's entire body passed through the middle. The liquid in the bottom sprang into the shape of my brother, wrapped a chain around my father's neck, kicked a hole in the glass, and then dragged him away kicking and screaming.

Next, my brother was speaking with someone in a grey cloak. The cloaked figure handed him a sack of gold coins in exchange for my father's leash. They shook hands and the world began to fall apart around them.

MY FATHER WAS GONE NOW. Lost in the dark. He was in a wire cage somewhere, hunched over like an ape. There were other cages around him with other men who were also turning into apes.

He defecated in his hand and threw it at someone cowering in the cage next to him. The rest of the apes howled with laughter.

THE HOURGLASS TURNS SIDEWAYS. Time stands still. The present is here. My father is gone. I am its prisoner now.

I WAKE up in my apartment. I rollover. No stranger sleeping next to me this time.

I walk into the bathroom and consider a shower. Instead, I pick up the cologne by the sink and stare at the bottle.

My art is my activism. I am my art.

I hurl it against the mirror. Shards of glass crack and fall apart, miscellaneous pill bottles spilling out.

I walk back into my bedroom to find Selby standing there. He turns around and sees me. He smiles, those big obnoxious teeth gleaming like LEDs.

"Why did you do it?" I ask.

"Get rid of father?"

"Yes."

Selby shrugs. "Because I hate him."

"Could have fooled me," I say. "I didn't think you could hate someone while voluntarily having your tongue up their ass."

"I guess you don't know much about hatred then."

"I'm young," I say, striding over to my bedside table. There's an alarm clock sitting there. It's stuck on 11:59. "I can learn."

Without thinking, I yank the clock from the wall and beat my brother to death with it.

The first blow hits him in the side of the head and he falls to his knees. The second hits him in the soft spot in the back of his head. He's on the ground now so I roll him over. The rest of the blows are aimed directly at his white and shining teeth.

When I'm done, I collect the teeth and put them into my pocket. I catch a cab to the family home. Once inside, I grab the shotgun from above the hearth. It's a twelve-gauge side-by-side with a selective trigger. I break open the barrels and pull the two shells out.

It's not easy prying the ends open. Packing my brother's bloody teeth in is even more difficult. I manage however, finally bending the tough plastic back down with a pair of pliers from the junk drawer in the kitchen.

I load the shells back into the gun and snap it closed. I have a monster to hunt.

Now I'm upstairs in my old bedroom. Black Flag and Minor Threat stare down at me from their posters. I assure them that I'm here to make things right.

I walk up to the mirror and look at myself. Older now. Aged by murder. I raise the shotgun and put the tiny bead that serves as a sight on my own head. I must look ridiculous now, pointing a shotgun at the mirror. But it will work. I know it will.

I have faith in the power. The power to set things right.

I pull the trigger and watch the top of my head sheer off in a spray of blood, brains, and bone. A chunk of gore drips down the front of a Bad Brains poster and I snort out a single laugh.

The hourglass turns. Time resumes.

I felt my mind wrench back to reality. The orange liquid was pure glass in the Speculum. There were no images. No fever dream visions of the world. Just me.

Me and the bodies.

My brother was lying crumpled on the floor with his entire face bashed into a pulp. Next to him was my mother, the top of her head missing. The light coming from the basin was just strong enough to let me discern a single tooth sticking out of her left cheek.

I spun and threw up, vomit coursing out of me and into the Speculum. The orange liquid didn't seem disturbed by it. In fact, it seemed to drink it.

Am I clean now, mother?

The question stayed with me as I walked back upstairs and sat down in one of the leather chairs in the hearth room. A fire crackled in the fireplace, reminding me of the strange orange liquid in the basement.

After a few minutes, I stood up and walked over to the fire.

I thought about seeing myself in the mirror. I thought about seeing myself in the billboard. I hated it. I hated myself and my family and the entire world.

The worst part was that I didn't know why. I didn't know what any of it meant. I had looked into the power. Into the Speculum. And all I saw were the things that I hated and nothing else. No point. No lesson. Just myself.

I steeled myself for a moment, staring at the fire. One of the logs was particularly hefty looking and completely engulfed in flames.

"My art is my activism," I said. "And I am my art."

I reached into the fire for the log. I absentmindedly watched my skin begin to bubble and crack against the red coals as I lifted it out. I let it burn me for one more full second and then threw it on the ground next to one of the heavy curtains. Flames began to climb.

It was time to start the revolution.

A HIGHER PLACE

They found him lying at the back of the apartment like a burst balloon. His body swollen and staining the floor beneath, legions of flies coating the walls and ceiling like a black fur. His skin was a pallid grey, eyes eaten by the building's vermin.

It was the smell that finally drove them up there. The landlord knocking six times before using his own key. The cops came soon afterward, holding cloths over their noses. Snapping pictures and unspooling police tape.

The room they found him in was empty, a stark contrast to the rest of the place. Stacks of magazines, boxes, and other assorted trash lay everywhere. Piles of refuse so old that their contents could not be discerned.

The professionals processing the crime scene thought they had died and gone to Hell.

The cataloging was intense, revealing nothing but the victim's own personality. A hoarder of the highest sort. They found boxes of restaurant napkins, hotel towels, and pens from banks. His credit cards were maxed. His computer showed multiple web pages open with full shopping carts, the orders denied for lack of a valid payment method.

The man, Hope Lundgen, was a man obsessed with *things*. Possibly even *possessed*, depending on one's definition of the word. So what to make of the empty room, thought detective Maynard. Did the killer do it somehow, or was this the work of the victim? The sign of a mind more complex than previously thought.

Maynard stood in the room, the stench an actual physical assault on his senses. He'd rather have been hit by a closed fist. But he stood there and endured it, letting it seep into him. Letting the *victim* seep into him.

This was the first body, but he already knew that there'd be more.

"WOULD YOU LIKE ANYTHING TO EAT?" Darlene asked, her face crinkling into a smile. She was about 53 and looked 70. Her body was flabby and unused, much like the rest. Bodies that had been molded for hundreds of thousands of years, all that sweet biological data packed into their genes, ready to launch them into a future of running and playing and fighting.

Not sitting and collecting. Not wasting away like bad fruit.

The man thought that he couldn't eat something if his stomach was opened and filled like a safe deposit box. The smell of cat piss was so strong it made his eyes water. They jumped up in his lap, walked in a careless circle and then jumped off again, leaving tiny red marks where their claws dug in.

"I'm okay for now," he croaked. "Do you have the room ready?"

"Of course, dear," she said, but she seemed uncertain.

"And it's clean?" He prodded. "Absolutely nothing inside?"

A moment of hesitation. He cursed inwardly. Of course it'd be her, the cat lady. The room was probably full of piss and shit. Undoubtedly. She couldn't control them. She couldn't even control herself. That was why she had come to him in the first place.

"Clean it," he said.

"Excuse me?"

"Clean it. Or you can't have it."

"I can't help what they do," her voice was suddenly shaky. "They're *free* here and they do what they want. It'll be easy to clean. You'll see."

"I don't need to see. I need it to be done."

"And if I do," she said. "You'll give it to me?"

He nodded.

She got up, grabbing a spray bottle and a sodden rag.

"You're going to need more than that."

She kept walking as if she hadn't heard him.

"Darlene."

She stopped and turned around. The flesh hung off her face like curtains, tears beginning to run down the folds.

"You'll need more than water," the man said. "The whole room has to be clean. Not just the floor and walls but the air. The atmosphere. If it's not clean then you won't get it."

Her shoulders quaked with barely contained sobs as she changed direction and made her way to the kitchen. She moved slowly, literally wading through the sea of cats.

Ten minutes later and he heard crying coming from the room. The apartment was too saturated with the cat smell. It couldn't be cleaned and she knew it.

He got up and left quietly, a small wooden box tucked under his arm. She'd never see the inside of it.

THE SECOND BODY turned up three weeks later. The fact that they found it at all was a miracle. This place was almost worse than the last. The man had taken to hoarding Business Reply inserts from magazines and his floors were literally covered in them down to the last inch.

Except for the one room, of course.

That's how they knew it was their killer. The one clean room. The body in the corner with his chest open.

A nosy neighbor had come poking around the back of the house, looking for him. He hadn't seen the body but he sure smelled it. The victim's house didn't smell all that nice to begin with but this was on a different level. And after having gone over a week without seeing him in the driveway or getting the mail or even through the living room window, he knew something was wrong.

"He's taking the ribs," Detective Maynard said.

"What?" One of the crime scene techs lowered his camera.

"The last one was missing their ribs. This one is too."

The man with the camera made a face. "Why?"

"I don't know." Maynard stepped back from the body and looked around. "But this is the pattern. Hoarders. A clean room. No forced entry. Victims missing their ribs."

"How'd he remove them?" the tech asked. He was a wiry man with a thin mustache. Half the techs would have just shrugged and moved on but Maynard appreciated the guy playing along, letting him work through it verbally.

"Autopsy on the previous guy showed they'd been taken off by a small handsaw. Lots of internal damage around the wounds. It's rough and messy. Guy would have been covered in blood by the time he left."

"Post-mortem or ante?"

"Post," Maynard said thoughtfully.

"Post? So what killed them?"

"Doc says cardiac arrest."

"Their hearts stopped?"

"Yeah."

"Why?"

"They're not sure."

The tech thought to himself for a moment. "So this guy walks in-"

"Is *let* in," Maynard corrected. "The preparation of the room suggests the victim knew the killer."

"Is *let* in. Then he brings them to this prepared empty room. And what, stops their heart?"

"Yup."

"And takes their ribs?"

"Mmmhmm."

The man shook his head. "I don't get it."

"Me neither. But I will."

DARLENE CALLED the man the next day but he didn't answer. He had his own business to attend to.

Unlike the others, he only had the one room and it was small. He had to keep his collectibles in the corner. The flies did a good job of cleaning them but if the rats got to them it would be a problem. He hadn't seen any but that didn't mean he'd stop checking. They were too precious to him. Too pristine.

He hadn't really paid for them in any meaningful way, other than his time. The thing in the box was eternal. He knew that and the others knew that. But it was rare nonetheless and as far as they knew, he was the only one who had it.

But the thing in the box could not give him what he wanted. What he wanted was beyond such things. What he wanted wasn't a single thing; it was many things.

What he wanted was to stroll in the After Wood as his ancestors had before him. He wanted to escape this horrendous world and return to the trees everlasting where the fog was as empty as it was promising. Where the streams ran clear and cool and the stag strode with both majesty and assured masculinity.

The stag. Oh, the stag. He wanted to walk with it and run with it through the endless fields. To live by sense alone, his movements graceful and without a single modicum of waste. He wanted it so bad it hurt.

The phone began ringing again. He thought about picking it up and asking her if she had cleaned the room yet, but then the screaming started from down below and he rejected the idea. He didn't need this. The phone calls *or* the noises that seeped up through the floorboards. Some day he would deal with it, but not now.

Right now, he would dream of escape.

MAYNARD MET the tech in a small diner near the precinct a few days later. Staffing in the precinct was short and he was currently between partners. The tech's name was Francis Delgota and he was both dedicated and sharp. He may not have been a detective, but he was good to bounce ideas off of.

"We got anything yet?" Maynard asked after ordering a cup of coffee.

Francis shook his head. "Not yet, as far as I know. Lots to process there. Most of it meaningless."

The crime scenes had been so dirty and cluttered that it served as a sort of white noise for forensics. They were able to figure out when and where the victims had died but that was about it. Canvassing turned up next to nothing and there didn't seem to be much in terms of hair or fibers.

"I got something on my end," Maynard said. "But so far it hasn't led anywhere."

The waitress came over and dropped two mugs of coffee on the table.

"Y'all looking to order?" she asked.

Maynard turned and looked at Francis. "Get whatever you want. I'm buying." He turned back to the waitress and ordered a plate of biscuits and gravy.

When she left, Francis leaned in. "Whatja got?"

"Both victims made numerous phone calls to burners in the week leading up to their deaths. We've been able to trace the burner phones back to little mom-and-pop shops on the Southside of town but they were bought over a year ago and most of those places don't have security footage from last week."

"Over a year, huh? That must mean this guy's been thinking about this for a while now."

"Right," Maynard said. "So why did he start now?"

"Maybe he finally got the confidence up," Francis said. "Or he's recently experienced some stressor. Lost his job. Lost his girlfriend. Lost his dog. You know, all the normal country song culprits."

"Maybe so. Then the next question is *why* is he doing it? What does he get out of it?"

"Ribs," Francis said. "Seems to like ribs."

"You can get those here for $11.99. And we don't think he's eating these people. The muscular tissue around the ribs is pretty torn up but it doesn't look like anything's missing. So what would he need ribs for?"

"Maybe he wants to build a girlfriend," Francis ventured.

"Why you say that?"

"You know: Book of Genesis. God took one of Adam's ribs to make Eve."

"Huh." Maynard leaned back. "Could be."

"So we looking for a religious nut?"

"There is something religious about the crime scenes," Maynard said. "They're so clean. The lack of struggle and emergency calls kind of make me think these people knew what was coming. Maybe not *exactly* but you'd expect something of a last-minute fight if they realized what was about to happen. There's none of that here."

"It's like he's offering them something holy," Francis added. "Like last rites or something."

"Okay. So how does that tie into the hoarding angle then?"

"Maybe they know they're sick and he's offering to put them out of their misery."

"So these people are looking to die?" asked Maynard. "That's hard to believe. What's the suicide rate among hoarders?"

"Something wild like 25 percent," Francis said. "I heard it a few years ago on that show Clutter Crisis."

"Clutter Crisis?" Maynard asked. "What's that?"

"Pretty much what you'd expect. They go around and talk to people with Hoarding Disorder. Interview their friends and families and whatnot."

"Interesting." Maynard reached up and scratched his chin. "You think he might be choosing his victims that way? Off this show?"

"Possibly. I haven't seen every episode but they could have been on. Might be worth checking into."

"I think I will," Maynard said. He was going to say more but just then the food arrived.

The biscuits and gravy were good if not a little salty. But with every bite, he had to make a concerted effort not to think about barbecue ribs.

Maynard spent the next morning making his way through a maze of phone trees until he finally got ahold of the right admin at the network in charge of Clutter Crisis.

"Everyone on the show has to go through an application process," she explained. "I can send over copies if you'd like."

"Yeah, that'd be great," Maynard replied. "How many are there, would you say?"

"Applications? Oh, I don't know. The show has been on for about eleven years and we must get something like two to three thousand a year."

"A *year*?" Maynard was flabbergasted. "I didn't realize that many hoarders existed."

"Yeah, there's something like ten million right here in the U.S. Plus, there's a ton of apps that get disqualified, either because it's obvious it's just someone trying to get on television or it's a frustrated family member who exacerbates the extent of the person's problem."

"What do you mean?"

"Oh, you know. A wife is mad because her husband owns too many fishing poles or maybe someone's mom has a large collection of ceramic chickens or something. Weird stuff like that."

"And they don't qualify?"

"No, Hoarders Disorder is an actual clinical condition. Lots of people just collect strange things."

"I guess so." Maynard sighed. "Gotta say, I'm not looking forward to going through something like 30,000 applications."

"Not sure what to tell you there."

Maynard decided to take a shot. "Hey, I don't suppose you have any strange folks that work with you that might have access to these?"

"It's TV," she said. "Half the people I work with are strange."

"Damn. Thought I'd ask."

"This is about the two killings, right? The ones in the newspapers?"

"Yes, but please don't spread that around to your colleagues. I'd like to control the flow of information as much as possible, you get me?"

"Sure thing. Say, why don't you check with some of the local support groups? He might be choosing them that way."

"Support groups for hoarders? They have those?"

"Of course," she replied. "Kind of surprised you haven't checked there already."

What could he say to that? Could he tell her that the precincts were as understaffed as they'd ever been? That the city had been rocked by crime wave after crime wave over the last few years? That there were literally bodies piling up in the streets and their budgets were cut and it was everything he could do not to drink himself to death every night when he stepped back into his little apartment?

"We probably got somebody already working that angle," he reassured her. "Just a matter of comparing notes now. Thanks. You've been a big help."

He rang off and tilted his head back.

Over the last year or so, he had been putting murderers away as fast as he could fill out the paperwork. Domestic disputes gone sideways. Gang wars. Spree shooters. And recently, a huge spate of what looked to be cult-related crimes.

At times, his desk looked like the homes of these hoarders. Reports piled past his head. Empty coffee cups and half-eaten sandwiches. It was a mess but instead of cleaning it he had just moved the mess to his apartment where he could let it continue to grow.

He wondered what it would take to stop it. If maybe there was some killer to end all killers out there. A proverbial head of the snake to cut off. The individual acts of violence seemed random but the general trend didn't.

At first, he had blamed poor economic conditions and crime policies but now he wasn't so sure. Something about the most recent crime wave seemed to have an *intention* behind it. And if so much of it was truly cult-related as people had been speculating, then that would imply some sort of cult leader, right?

And cult leaders could be stopped.

He was still thinking it over when his email beeped and showed a new message. Then another and another. Soon his inbox was drowning in new messages, all from the same address.

He opened one and saw a few zip files attached to it.

"That'd be the applications," he sighed to himself. He thought about digging into them but decided to procrastinate just a little longer.

He pulled out his phone and punched in Francis's number.

"Delgota."

"Hey Francis, it's Maynard. Got a second?"

"Sure thing."

"You got those crime scene pics saved somewhere?"

"Yeah, why?"

"We haven't released any of those to the public, right?"

"Nope."

"Well, I got an idea that might help to stir some things up. But it might be a little..."

"A little what?" Francis asked hesitantly.

"Against the rules."

Maynard explained what he was thinking and Francis agreed to it. Then he hung up the phone, looked at the emails for another few minutes, then finally opened another tab on his web browser. He punched a few words into the search engine, clicked on a link, and then took his phone back out.

"It's not clean enough," the man said. "Nowhere near."

"Bullshit." Darlene was angry now. "I scrubbed this floor on my hands and *knees.*"

"I told you. It's not just the surfaces. It's the atmosphere. The smells. It still reeks of cat piss."

"Oh, and I'm sure the others' places smelled like roses," she snarled. "Why are you doing this to me?"

"Others?" The man said innocently.

"Don't think I haven't caught on to what you're doing. I watch the news. I get the paper."

"I know you get the paper. It's what you use to mop up all the piss."

"You're killing them, aren't you?" She said, ignoring the comment.

"No," he said. "But you already know that. You know the deal. You know the consequences. I haven't killed anyone."

"But you're desecrating the corpses. I've seen it. The photos leaked online."

This was news to him. Most departments didn't just *leak* photos unless someone was paying a high price for them. And while his crimes had made the morning paper both times, it wasn't exactly high profile. Nothing worth risking a job over.

Which meant they had been leaked intentionally. Why would they do that?

To cause problems like they were at this very moment. The cops knew people were letting him into their homes but they didn't know why. Not exactly.

If they did, then they would have understood that nothing would keep him out. The draw was too great. The promise too much.

He had time. He knew he'd be caught eventually but for now he could go about his business. He could collect. He could dream.

"You know I can take it, right?" Darlene said.

The man turned and looked at her. "No, you can't."

She fixed her beady little eyes on the box he had sticking out of his coat pocket. "And why the Hell not?"

"Because I'll cut your head off," he said simply.

She recoiled and he took no small amount of pleasure in that.

"And because that's not how it works," he said. "I am the keeper of the box. I've been tasked with it and no one else. And for my work I am allowed a glimpse at the world to come."

"The world to come?" She was genuinely confused now.

"Yes," he said. "And the world that was and the world that is. I am allowed to dream there and no one else. And when my time finally comes, you'll just be a smear of blood on this abandoned rock. Just a bug on a windshield."

"You can't talk to me like that. I-"

"You what?" he asked, his voice threaded with steel. "You'll throw me out of here? You'll call the neighbors? Call the cops? Do it. But then you'll live the rest of your life like this." He knelt down and swiped a finger over the rough floorboards. "Empty. Unfulfilled."

She had tears in her eyes again and he relished in it. The power. The way he could make her twist. He practically came to tears himself.

"Get out," she said.

He stood back up and nodded.

"You know how to get ahold of me."

MOST OF THE support groups for hoarders were either hotlines or groups that people ran out of their homes. The places that met in person didn't have phone numbers but they had email addresses, so Maynard spent a solid two hours reaching out to them that way. He explained the situation briefly and asked if they could please call him at their soonest convenience.

Then, just as he was finishing the last one, his phone rang.

It was a bust, ultimately. The person who had called him couldn't seem to think of anyone who might be perpetrating the murders. She knew all of the members personally by now and though they were troubled, they were all very sweet people. A few had even gotten rid of the things they had been collecting. It had been hard, she said, and would continue to be hard, but community support was the key.

He thanked her and hung up the phone. As he did, however, he noticed two missed calls on his screen from two separate numbers. One of them had left a message. He listened to it, then hit redial.

"Hello?" Answered the voice of a woman on the other end. It was the same voice that had just left the message.

"Hello, this is Detective Maynard. I just missed your call."

"Yes. This is Cindy Paulson. Thanks for calling me back, Detective. I got your email and wanted to talk?"

"Go for it."

"Well, I saw some of the photos that leaked online. Of the murders?"

"Right, yeah. Officially speaking, you should know that we don't condone seeking out leaked department information."

"Of course," Cindy said. "But I saw them and they really disturbed me. Then I got your email and—well, this is going to sound crazy but I think I know who one of the next victims might be."

THE SOUND of wailing drifted up through the floor and the man ground his fists into his eyes. The noise was endless, like falling off the edge of the world. It was so loud he couldn't hear himself think. Couldn't escape. He couldn't escape.

"*Fuck*," he yelled to himself. He punched the wall, sucked on a bloody knuckle, then punched it two more times. He had to get out of here. Had to make the wailing stop. Choke the urge. Eat the need. Slip into the After Wood.

But he needed silence to do that. He needed peace and the gruesome noises coming from down below wouldn't allow it. He looked over at a small wooden shelf on the wall and considered the small bottle of tablets.

When the Children of the After Wood had set him on his task, they had given him the pills. *They* got 'em from the squids, apparently. They weren't *actually* squids. Or at least, the ones who dealt the junk weren't. The ones he had met were practically kids, maybe not even out of high school yet. Some of the elders insisted on working with the Cult of the Black Tide but the idea made his skin crawl.

More than that, he didn't like having to take drugs to walk in the wood. He felt that it somehow tainted the experience. Soiled the gift.

But he had to step into the glade. Had to escape to a higher place. And if the drugs let him do that, then so be it. He shook out one of the tiny blue gel tabs into his hand, turning it over in the light. The purple image of the lizard stared dumbly back at him.

He popped it into his mouth and swallowed.

Maynard drove fast but not too fast. It was the middle of the afternoon and the streets were busy. Eight hours from now and that would be a different story—most people had begun deserting the streets at night. But now, he had obstacles to weave through if he was going to make it to the destination in any reasonable amount of time.

The chance that the potential victim was in danger wasn't all that likely but he still had to act as if she was. The last thing he wanted was to show up ten seconds too late because he took his time on the freeway.

Flashers on, he sped around someone not paying attention in the fast lane and then found himself behind two semi-trucks driving side-by-side. They seemed to waver a little bit but didn't quite commit to moving aside. Maynard eased onto the shoulder and sped past, spraying dirt and gravel at everyone behind him.

Five minutes later, he turned off his flashers and slowed down. Three more blocks and he was there.

THE HOUSE WAS small and in need of desperate repair. The trim around the windows was rotted and hanging off. The yard was dirt and weeds. The front door appeared to lead into a screened-in porch that, even from here, Maynard could tell was heaped with garbage.

The woman's name was Darlene Travis. She had a form of Hoarding Disorder that involved the collection of cats. Maynard had known a few "cat ladies" in his life, his mother being one of them, but from what Cindy had told him, this was on a different level. There was a line between wanting companionship and feeling an uncontrollable impulse to have as many cats as possible.

According to Cindy, Darlene had stopped showing up after two-and-a-half years of pretty regular attendance. She had called her a few times but been sent to voicemail. She had even dropped by and knocked on her door but no one answered.

It made her worried, of course, but not nearly as much as seeing the pictures of the crime scene. Then when Maynard had called her, the dam had probably broken, flooding her mind with every horrible possibility imaginable.

Maynard could smell it before he even got to the door. The sharp, ammonia smell of cat piss. This had to be the place. He hurried up the rotted steps to the screen door, opened it, wove his way between piles of old broken children's toys, and knocked on the door.

While he waited, he looked down at the toys. A wooden rocking horse whose black eyes had been worn down to the wood underneath. A plastic lever-action popgun with an orange cap on the end of the barrel.

What would it have been like to grow up here with a mother who hoarded cats? Had she become ill after he had left home? Shit, had he left home at all?

Maynard had done some hasty research on Darlene before heading over. 53 years old. Divorced. Mother of Anthony Travis. He hadn't done much digging into Anthony, and if Darlene was dead or missing, he figured that he would have to be the first person he notified after calling it in.

Unless, of course, he still lived with her. It was possible, though if Maynard had been in that position, he would have left as soon as possible.

To his right, Maynard caught the quick flash of a curtain being pulled aside for a second. Without having to think about it, he swiveled his head and smiled. In his experience, people instantly believe they've been seen if they see you smile at them. Maynard hadn't actually seen who the person behind the curtain was, but now the secret observer would feel more obligated to answer than if he had just kept staring straight ahead.

The door opened to reveal a short, sunken-in woman with a rounded face. The smell of urine wafted out into the open air and Maynard caught himself taking an involuntary step back.

"Darlene Travis?" Maynard flipped his identification open for Darlene to see and watched her immediately recoil.

"What?" she said, and Maynard couldn't tell if the darkness

in her voice was born of irritation or the desire to hide something.

"Would that be you then?" Maynard said, seeking clarification. "Are you Darlene Travis?"

She evaded again by saying, "I'm busy." She began to shut the door.

"The way you're answering might lead one to believe that you're *not* Ms. Travis," Maynard said hastily. "I'm here investigating some concerns of Darlene's disappearance, so if you're not her but you're occupying her house without explanation, then one might say that gives me probable cause to enter."

Maynard had tiptoed around the implication very carefully without actually saying what he thought or what he was going to do, because in reality, his basis for a forcible entry was pretty shaky. He wanted to see how she would react though, so he held his breath.

"Come in," she said after a moment's hesitation. "But don't touch anything."

If the woman was trying to establish some line that Maynard would invariably cross just so she could throw him out, she was succeeding. Because as soon as he entered the house he found that he couldn't move an inch without touching anything. The place was just like the other victims' houses. Stuff was piled everywhere and it was nearly impossible for him to follow the woman inside without actually touching something.

She didn't seem to be actually concerned about him touching stuff, however. She simply led him inside without even turning around to follow his progress.

If the smell had been bad outside then the smell inside was almost unbearable. His eyes were watering so bad he could barely see. Through the blur, he saw feline shapes slinking around the mountains of trash.

"Is there somewhere we can go to talk?" Maynard asked, reaching up to wipe the tears from his face.

"Living room's fine," the woman said curtly, which Maynard seriously doubted.

He gritted through it though and eventually they were both seated in a cramped little space with two worn-out recliners directed towards an ancient tube television. The screen was blank but Maynard would have guessed she had been watching it before he arrived.

"So first off, for the record: you are Darlene Travis, correct?"

"Is this an official interrogation?" the woman asked, still suspicious.

"No," Maynard said. "I would just like it for the record in case anyone asks why I didn't probe further on someone who, up until this point, has refused to give me her name."

"Am I being recorded?"

"No, you're not being recorded."

"You have to tell me if I'm being recorded," she said. "It's the law."

"I am aware of the law."

A beat of silence, then. "Yes, I'm Darlene Travis."

And Maynard believed her. The look in her face spoke of some sort of insecurity or self-betrayal, as if giving anything to the police, even a name, was tantamount to giving away some valuable piece of property.

Maynard nodded. "So the reason I'm here is because your support group leader was concerned about you. She said that it wasn't like you to stop showing up to group."

"I don't have to show up to group," Darlene all-but spat. "It's not the law."

Maynard's impulse was to remind her that he was aware of the law, but he swallowed it.

"So, you're okay then? No one is threatening you?"

"No."

"Has anyone reached out to you?"

"No."

Maynard waited a beat. He had left the question purposefully vague. The most reasonable response would have been something along the lines of "What do you mean *reached out*?" But she had simply said, "no." Now the question was *why*? Was she caught in a pattern where she was determined to answer "no" to everything or was she concerned because she actually had been contacted and she was trying to keep it secret?

"Have you been in contact with your son recently?"

Darlene's eyebrow twitched. *Trying to decide if she's going to lie.*

"Yes," she said, suddenly calm.

Maynard switched tacts. "How old is he?"

"Huh?"

"Your son's age," Maynard said casually. "How old is he?"

She thought for a second. "32. But he hasn't been by."

Then something in her face changed. She became panicked as if she had just thought of something or made a mistake.

"That's okay. I was just-"

"I think you should leave now." Darlene stood up.

"I still have a-"

"Now," she said, her voice forceful but restrained.

It occurred to Maynard that if she really wanted to intimidate him she would have raised her voice, but she hadn't. It seemed an inconsistency and it bothered him.

Then the floor above them creaked.

ANTHONY WAS CLIMBING THE MOUNTAIN, the warmth radiating from within.

It was fall now, the leaves just beginning to turn. He felt the crisp air blow through his antlers, the velvet hanging off of them like bloody rags. He smelled the grass. The trees. The frigid streams and animal musk. He was full. He was at home.

Now there was just one thing left to do. He had to reach the High Place. The top of the mountain. He didn't know why but he felt it in his gut the same way he felt he had to scrape his antlers on the trees in autumn and chase the does during spring. It was an integral part of him.

The problem was that the forest had changed as of late. He had seen less and less of the herd. Had smelled something strange on the wind. It wasn't the faint scent of ash that signaled a fire or the fresh signs of some new animal. No, it was something else.

The scent he occasionally caught on the air was almost mineral. Sometimes it smelled like the fetid stench that occasionally wafted out of a dark cave and other times it gave the impression of water like a big lake. It made the hairs on the back of his neck stand up.

He snorted and pawed the ground with his hoofs. The peak of the mountain was close. The climbing was tough but doable.

The sun was beginning to set.

"Ms. Travis, are you alone in this house?" Maynard asked urgently.

"Of course, I-" she began to say but was interrupted by another sound, this one being more like someone scuffing their feet against the floor on the upper level.

Whoever was in the house with them, they were in the attic.

Maynard reached down and drew his sidearm. "Stay back, ma'am."

Ignoring Ms. Travis's protests, Maynard made his way through the cluttered house until he found a hallway. He looked up, saw the drawstring for a pulldown staircase, and gave it a yank.

The entire contraption squealed as the wooden steps folded out and descended to the ground. If whoever was up there hadn't known Maynard was coming, they knew now.

BUT ANTHONY DIDN'T KNOW. Anthony was climbing the mountain. The High Place was right in front of him but no matter how hard he strove, he couldn't quite reach it. His chest heaved with the chilled air. His legs strained as they powered him up the stony ridge.

But it was useless. The High Place was unattainable. His feet slipped, his energy waned, his mind faltered. And with every step, the goal seemed that much further away.

Something pricked Anthony's senses and he spun around.

There, on the stone ledge with him, was a hunter. The man was crouched, his piercing eyes boring into him. It raised something above its head. What was it?

A flaming spear. A weapon touched with divinity. That first technological step toward ultimate doom. Anthony knew this in his core. Saw the danger for what it was.

He lowered his head and charged.

MAYNARD STARED at the man before him.

He was gaunt and malnourished, pale skin heaving as he breathed the hot attic air. His pupils were frantic and dilated. The worst thing though were the antlers.

The man he presumed to be Anthony Travis was completely naked, but on his head he wore a ghastly crown of bloody antlers.

Made from ribs, Maynard realized. *Human ribs.*

There was a small foggy window at the end of the room and the soiled daylight filtered through, turning the man's silhouette into something Maynard could only describe as a demon from Hell.

The demon lowered its head and charged.

Maynard cried out for him to stop, almost in unison with Darlene who had just stumbled up into the attic with them. The man didn't listen.

Up until this point in his career, Maynard had shot three people and none of them had died. He had been surprised by this, actually. All three had been hit center-mass in accordance with his training. All of them were potentially fatal wounds. But they all somehow managed to pull through.

The man who was eventually identified as Anthony Travis, did not. Due to the angle at which he had been charging, Anthony was hit in the top of his right shoulder. The bullet entered and exited cleanly, knocking him down to the ground.

Maynard quickly radioed in the shooting and rushed to his side, surprised that he hadn't kept coming. After all, he had heard story-after-story from his colleagues about people high on meth taking multiple bullets without even slowing down.

This was different. As soon as Anthony was hit, he crumpled and lay twitching on the floor. Maynard grabbed his hand tight and held it, trying to catch the man's focus. Seconds later and the twitching stopped. His body slackened and his bowels released.

A silent moment passed as the reality of the situation sank in, then Maynard turned around in search of Darlene. Panic momentarily swept over him as he observed she too had fallen to the floor.

Just as he had done with the woman's son, Maynard rushed to her side. And just like her son, she was dead.

Maynard stared down in mute confusion. He considered the possibility that the bullet that had hit Anthony had ricocheted only to hit his mother as well. As he searched her body, however, he didn't find a mark on her.

He checked and rechecked her pulse. Nothing.

A cat popped up from the steps below. It meowed and sniffed her, then disappeared again.

"So this is the guy," Francis said. He had found Maynard sitting outside on the curb while the techs did their thing.

"Yup," Maynard replied. He had a hard time lifting his gaze up off the ground.

"I was talking with some of the other crime scene guys. They're not sure who leaked the photos."

"It didn't work. Not really. It didn't quite tear them apart like we were hoping. Did you see the room? That woman was going to die no matter what she saw. She wanted it."

"She may not have even seen the photos," Francis tried.

"She saw them."

"How do you know?"

Maynard hesitated. He reached into his pocket and fumbled with his new possession. The thing he had found in the attic. The thing he never knew he needed. He felt a drop of sweat roll down the back of his neck.

"She saw them," he repeated.

"The photos probably motivated the support group leader, so it wasn't for nothing."

"Yeah, I guess."

"What's up? You got the guy."

"Suppose so." Maynard looked up above the tree line across

the road. The sun was beginning to set. That lonely golden star. Solitary. Life-giving. Unattainable.

He stood up and looked down the road. The shadows were beginning to lengthen and grow deeper.

"There'll be another, though. There's always another."

CASE OF THE UNDERGROUND HEART

This is how it ends.

In the dark sewers beneath the city of Blackburg, Richard strained against his bonds as he was dragged into the heart of darkness. The air was dank and full of fumes, what little he could get through his broken nose.

They had beaten him badly when he was abducted and he had not resisted. His wife was dead. His daughter was a cultist. And now she was going to kill her own father or at least be responsible for his death. He had failed his family in the most spectacular way.

As far as he saw it, everything that he got now was nothing more than what he deserved.

The two men carrying him weren't teenagers. To be honest, he couldn't even tell if they were men. They wore dark robes and black masks on their faces. They gave off the smell of something dead and rotten, like old seaweed.

Richard shuddered at the smell. The smell that had washed over him from that thing when it tore Samantha limb-from-limb. Whatever *it* was, it wasn't human. It had had tentacles like some sort of octopus or squid but stood like a person, silent in its long grey cloak.

He hadn't seen it since being taken from his house. He hadn't seen his daughter either for that matter. They had beaten him so badly he had slipped into unconsciousness.

And now he was here.

His feet made a scuffing sound as they dragged across the wet stone floor. The walls around him were sporadically lit by sconces, their orange fires flickering low like the glancing light of a setting sun.

He looked up. The narrow passageway they were in opened into a large stone atrium. Lord, he had no idea anything like this existed beneath the city. Small clusters of candles and torches fought the surrounding darkness to a stalemate, casting everything in a blood-red hue as impenetrable as a moonless night.

Off to the left were massive ornate pillars stretching up to the ceiling. They had figures carved into them that Richard couldn't quite make out at this distance but they gave the impression of ancient Greek sculptures.

To the right were rows of wire kennels full of people. They were ragged-looking with brown bloodstains on their soiled clothing. Some sat huddled on the hard ground while others threw themselves against the cages and screamed obscenities. It was like every prison movie Richard had ever seen, except the harsh lighting of a penitentiary was replaced by the ominous glow of candles, making the people inside seem more like primitive animals at the dawn of mankind.

That was where they were dragging him.

Once they were amongst the cages, some of the men cursed and spat at Richard's captors, managing to hit him in the process. The figures dragging him couldn't have been any less concerned.

As they walked, Richard noticed that the caged men gradually became more civilized. In fact, the ones at the beginning had been the ones spitting and screaming while the further he went, the tamer they became. This puzzled him for a second until he finally put it together.

The men in the first few cages had been down here the longest and the further he was dragged, the more recent the captives were. This was confirmed when they reached the last of the occupied cages and Richard was hurled inside.

Still weak from the beating, he collapsed to the hard earth and groaned, pain slicing up his side. He managed to open his eyes in time to see one of the masked figures lock a padlock on the door and then turn around and leave with the other.

"Don't curse them like the others," a voice said behind him.

This seemed like a strange thing to say, and Richard tried to turn but couldn't quite manage without feeling like his lungs were collapsing.

"Hadn't planned on it," he croaked.

"Good," the man said behind him. "It helps if you can keep from cursing."

"Helps what?"

"Helps you stay alive."

Richard laughed in the form of a wet cough.

"Who says I want that?" He wheezed.

"You cannot say that," the man said urgently, stepping around in front of him.

In stark contrast to some of the more willowy men Richard had seen in the other cages, this man was thick with broad shoulders and a bit of a belly. He had a bushy beard, thinning hair, and gentle brown eyes. He was sporting a black eye and wore faded jeans with a dark dress shirt Richard couldn't quite make out the color of in the low light.

"My name is Brunson," said the man, extending his hand.

Richard assessed it for a few seconds and then reached out and took it, shaking it weakly.

"Names help," Brunson said. "So does talking. Some of these men have stopped talking altogether. Hard to blame them but that's when you know the enemy's won."

"The enemy?"

"The Devil," Brunson said, as if mentioning a casual acquaintance.

"You think the Devil did this?"

"I don't think God did."

Richard fought down the impulse to get into a religious conversation with the guy and steered the talk elsewhere.

"What is this place?" he asked. "Why are we here?"

Brunson sighed. "I don't know where we are but it's gotta be somewhere under the city. This place looks older than anything I've seen. Possibly older than the country itself. But the tunnel that leads into this place looked a lot like a sewer. Old brickwork to be sure, but I recognize Blackburg masonry when I see it."

"Now, as for *why* we're here?" Brunson looked up to the stone ceiling for a moment, then back down at Richard. "I'm not going to sugarcoat things for you. We're here to die."

The answer hit Richard a little harder than he would have expected. Of course, he didn't think his captors had brought him down here to hang out and watch the playoffs, but hearing the words out loud had an edge of reality to them he could damn near cut himself on.

"Why?" Richard shook his head slowly. "Why are they doing this? Why do they want to kill us?"

"Well, as far as I can tell," Brunson pursed his lips and raised his eyebrows. "We're here to die for our failures."

———

FOUR MONTHS after her partner had disappeared, Nora found herself sitting inside a hotel lobby looking for a stranger.

After all the people involved in the case had disappeared into thin air and every lead had dried up. After the BPD had failed to find a partner to replace Richard. After she had taken up a drinking habit and started watching movies and broken about every other rule she had made for herself. After she had sunk into a depression she couldn't seem to pull herself out of, something grasped her by the hand and yanked her out.

That something was a simple note she found beneath her windshield wiper one winter night after stumbling out of a bar at 1:35 in the morning. It simply said:

Meet me in the lobby of the Danica Hotel tomorrow night after the sun sets.

That was it. No explanation. No hint about what it could be about.

But there was only one thing it could be about as far as Nora was concerned. It was the thing that torpedoed her life four months ago. The thing that broke the small semblance of normalcy she had been able to build after emerging from the clutches of a cult nearly a decade ago.

The meeting had to be about Richard's disappearance. It had to be about the murder of his wife, Samantha. The vanishing of his daughter. It had to be about that because as far as Nora could tell, that's what everything was about these days.

It was as if the city had fallen under some sort of dark spell. Average citizens were fleeing at record rates. Abandoned houses and storefronts could be seen on every block. The constant high-profile disappearances and brutal murders were creating an insurmountable backlog. And the police department had become so corrupt and ineffectual that Nora was basically going through the motions at this point.

Something was happening to Blackburg and the moment

Nora read the note, she decided that she was going to figure out what. The problem had seemed too large and amorphous before. Lawyers and politicians had made almost anyone involved untouchable and even on the occasion that a seemingly good police officer broke and showed up at a suspect's door with a metal baseball bat determined to get some answers, no answers ever came to light.

The crimes of whoever these people were were so ubiquitous and out in the open at this point that it felt as if nothing could be done. But now she had a thread to pull.

Nora didn't know where it would lead or what would unravel but she was willing to give her life for it. As far as she was concerned, she had died at the age of eighteen when she had awakened one morning to find the cult she had lived with for fifteen years lying in pieces all over a field in southern Iowa.

She still didn't know what had happened or why she was the only one left alive but the people she had lived with for so long had been into some dark shit. Her aunt and uncle had abducted her at the age of three from her parents, effectively becoming her new unofficial guardians. Nora remembered picking up her aunt's severed head and turning it over in her hands, the face frozen in silent agony.

That had fucked her up. Her whole *childhood* had fucked her up. Even after the cult deprogrammer, the legions of psychologists, and the awkward reunion with parents she didn't even recognize, she was still learning just how much her upbringing had warped her.

The fact that she was able to become a police officer was a complete fluke. She began consulting on a few cult-related murder cases in her mid-twenties and eventually found herself becoming more and more involved with law enforcement as she went on.

She had been working with a detective named Palowski at

the time, who was now retired somewhere in Nevada. He had taken her under his wing, showing her everything she needed to know. Two years later, she went through the police academy and ended up as a beat cop on the same streets she had worked with her mentor.

Palowski worked his connections and Nora excelled in her position until she was made detective. At that point, it was apparent that something was wrong with Blackburg. They couldn't keep police on the force to save their lives and relatively green detectives were shooting up through the ranks faster than they could celebrate their promotions.

The work was grueling. Crime rates were up and solve rates had bottomed out. Nora was thankful to be promoted to detective so soon but a part of her doubted whether or not she had earned it. In fact, her experience was so different from everyone else's that she couldn't tell exactly what she did or didn't deserve to have.

So she took what she got and did what she could with it.

Richard's disappearance, however, had been the first major hurdle in both her career and her faith in the system. She knew that people in her precinct were involved in these cults and she didn't doubt that they were hampering her investigation after she had shown up at Richard's house to find him gone and Samantha's body dismembered and stacked up in the living room, that strange hourglass symbol written in blood on the wall.

The kicker though, was that she felt as if she should be able to do more. Nora was almost certain now that those kids they had talked to were involved. Hell, Richard's daughter had probably been involved. The pattern was there. Abducted dad, torn apart mom. And since they hadn't found Hannah butchered in the streets, then she was probably a part of it. Nora should have seen it. Should have recognized the signs.

But she hadn't. And now they were gone.

The night Nora found the note pinned to her car, she felt a fire light inside of her. To Hell with the department. To Hell with feeling sorry for herself. To Hell with the whole lot.

She folded up the paper, considered driving back to her apartment, then finally called a cab.

AND NOW SHE was here at a table near the back of the lobby nursing a bourbon poured neat. The hotel was upscale without a pair of jeans in sight. She was wearing a slim black dress with a compact CZ 9mm in her handbag and a small folding knife strapped to the inside of her left thigh.

She had practiced removing the knife and flipping it open with one hand the night before. Had repeated the action again and again until she could do it in less than a second without thinking.

Then she had done her eyelashes and put on a very light application of blush and mascara. The touches were minimal. Makeup often irritated her face and she wasn't particularly good at applying it.

When she assessed herself in the mirror, it seemed okay. Not too little and definitely not too much. She had seen better but it would have to pass tonight.

And so far it was. The bartender had treated her just like any other customer and she had even been hit on a few times, which had been a strange feeling. Granted, she had come across her fair share of men in bars over the years, some of them creeps and some of them genuinely kind, but the rate of occurrence here was more than she'd ever experienced in a single night.

Nora wasn't sure if she liked it or not. On one hand, it was flattering. The men were gentle at least and she had even caught a glance from a woman in a red dress a few minutes ago. But it was also a little unsettling.

This wasn't her crowd. She didn't know who these people were and if they were in positions of power—and it looked like they were—then they were probably at least peripherally involved in the steady decline of the city.

Hell, maybe she was just being paranoid.

As if on cue, a handsome man wearing a black tux broke off from his group of friends to come over to Nora's table. He had a square jaw and had his dark hair slicked back. Late twenties, maybe early thirties.

"Is anyone sitting here?" he asked politely, a warm grin cracking his face. He sat down before she could answer.

"Just waiting for my husband," Nora replied casually.

"Husband?" The man laughed. "You've been sitting here for over an hour now."

"He comes from a country where their view of time isn't quite as strict as ours," Nora lied. "I got him a watch last Christmas. He even wears it. Hasn't made a difference from what I can tell."

The man narrowed his eyes and held out a hand. "Marcus."

"I don't shake hands with people I'm going to forget," Nora said.

Marcus laughed. "That another one of your rules, Nora? I hear you haven't been keeping them as well lately."

Nora felt whatever semblance of a smile she had on her face slide away. She looked over at the party of men, who were all gathered around the bar, preparing to do shots together. Nora could have sworn Marcus had been a part of their group.

"I *am* actually with those guys over there," he said, answering her unspoken question. "Bachelor party. I knew I'd be here tonight."

"So what? You just stood there and watched me?"

"I have people who keep pretty close tabs on me, which makes it hard to slip away. So I had to manufacture a 'chance encounter.' As far as they know, I'm just hitting on a girl at a bar. That, and I wanted to see how committed you were."

"And?"

"You lasted a while," Marcus said. "Enough for me. I just had to make sure you had the patience and demeanor to care. People who spiral like you tend to give up on things easily."

Nora felt a twinge of annoyance. "Have you been watching me?"

"Watching? No." Marcus looked at Nora's bourbon, then motioned for a bartender to bring two more. "More like keeping tabs."

Nora thought about that for a moment, then said, "So. Why am I here, Marcus?"

"Because I know where your partner is. Or at least, I know how to find him."

Nora felt her whole body clench involuntarily. This is why she was here. She knew this was tied into Richard's disappearance in some way but she had no idea it would be so direct.

"Before we go any further," she said slowly. "I need to know why you're helping me."

"The people you are chasing belong to the Cult of the Black Tide. They want to tear this city down. *Literally*, tear it down. This entire city is built upon a sacred site of the ancient Trilodian people."

"Trilodian?" The word felt uncomfortable in her mouth.

"An extinct civilization. They sailed here from ancient Antarctica. They worship the Void and an entity called *Rakathreev*."

Nora blinked a few times. "You say they're extinct but it sounded like you just referred to them in the present tense."

A man set two drinks down on the table. Nora and Marcus both flashed a smile at him and nodded, then returned to their conversation.

"There are certain artifacts and books that have made their way onto the black markets. Artifacts and books unearthed in Antarctica."

"So you're saying there has been a resurgence in interest in these...*whatever*."

"Trilodians."

"Right. Trilobites. Is that why there are so many cults right now?"

"Yes and no. We've always been here. It's just that most of us are having light shed on us for the first time in almost a century. Some of us don't like what the Cult of the Black Tide is doing and some of us do. We're coming into conflict."

"We?"

Marcus took a sip of his drink and sank into his chair a bit.

"I belong to the Children of the After Wood. I'm helping you because I don't want to see the Cult of the Black Tide succeed. Unfortunately, not all of us feel that way."

"Children of the After Wood," Nora tried, rolling the words over her tongue. "And what would *you* like to happen?"

Marcus exhaled slowly and looked up at the ceiling.

"We recognize that our place is in the trees and on the plains. We don't belong here in these concrete prisons. It's not our genetic environment."

"Genetic environment? I think you'll have to explain that one to me."

"The environment that we spent our crucial evolutionary years in. In other words, the place we have evolved to inhabit as a species."

"And you don't think we'll evolve to inhabit our cities?"

"Maybe." Marcus shrugged. "I doubt it though. We'll probably be dead long before then."

"So, what are you planning on doing about it?"

"That's not what we're here to talk about," Marcus said curtly.

"I'm a cop, remember? If something illegal is happening then I need to know about it."

Marcus pursed his lips. "And I'm an *informant*, remember? That means we need to come to an agreement."

"What do you propose?"

Marcus relaxed a bit. "In nine months, they will be sacrificing the entire city of Blackburg to *Rakathreev*. This is when they will be most vulnerable."

"How do they intend on sacrificing an entire city?" Nora asked.

"Remember how I said Blackburg is built on an ancient site? I wasn't being metaphorical. Blackburg itself is built over an ancient lake. It's held up by sacred pillars that, once broken, would allow the city to sink down into the black waters of the lake."

"The lake can't be that deep," Nora said. "I don't know what they're hoping to accomplish."

But Marcus was shaking his head. "The lake has no bottom. Think of it like a hole in time and space. If Blackburg falls in, it will be like falling into an abyss from which there is no escape. You might even be falling into the jaws of *Rakathreev* herself."

"I hear you saying 'you' a lot. Does that mean you won't be sticking around for the festivities?"

Marcus took a large sip of bourbon and swallowed.

"No," he said. "None of us are. Regardless of how we feel about it. Ultimately, the affairs of modern people are not ours. What happens, happens."

"You seem to be sticking your neck out to make sure that it *doesn't* happen."

"The Cult of the Black Tide doesn't just want to wipe Blackburg off of the map, they want to plunge the entire world into chaos. We just want to return to the After Wood." Marcus leaned back and spread his hands. "But not all of us believe the Cult of the Black Tide are dangerous to the Children's plans. More importantly, the ones in charge don't. Centuries of laying low have made them cautious and docile."

"Docile?" Nora snorted. "I've seen crime scene photos of some shit that I'm pretty sure you folks had a hand in."

"The Cult of the Black Tide either converts your children or butchers them in the street like the Shepherd girl whose death you were investigating. They disarticulate your mothers and wives. They sacrifice your fathers and husbands. We are *not* the same."

"Are you saying you're any less brutal?" Nora asked.

"Maybe not," Marcus admitted. "What you've seen is a fraction of what we were once capable of. And what we will be capable of again. But our goal is a human goal. Theirs is not."

Nora felt a chill run down her back. She looked Marcus in the eye.

"So what do you want me to do?"

"The ritual is on the first full moon of September. They'll be careless, certain that they're unstoppable at that point. Mark your calendar because that night you'll have to flip through your radio and listen for reports of numerous minors succumbing to a hallucinogenic drug. Those in-the-know have tried to keep it quiet but I'm sure you've caught wind of it by now."

"Blue Chameleon," Nora said.

Marcus nodded.

"We found a guy wanted for questioning in an open murder investigation a few months back. Dude was on a real bad trip.

Still is, from what I hear. Doctors say he might be like that forever. Nasty stuff."

"For some people, yes. It seems to depend on if you have a guilty conscience or not."

"From what I've seen, teenagers deal with it significantly better. Why do you suppose that is?"

"*Zealots* deal with it significantly better. And most of the teens you've come across who've done Blue Chameleon are exactly that."

"Why's that?" Nora asked.

"The Cult of the Black Tide is primarily made up of minors right now. 'Kill or convert' is their motto. They're easy to influence and they've been looking for some sort of solid identity for the last few decades. Your youth are in search of meaning and some have found it in anti-meaning."

"I wish I could say I didn't believe you," Nora said. "But I know the statistics. Not just in Blackburg but in developed countries around the world. Suicide. Mass shootings. Just watching the news these days sorta makes *me* want to trip balls and sink into an abyss."

"It would seem you're halfway there," Marcus said seriously.

Nora flashed a smile and took another sip of her drink.

"Seriously," Marcus said. "When this is over, you should leave. We weren't meant to live like this."

"What would you suggest? Going and living with the monkeys in the jungle?"

"Tribal living is what we are built for. You have to find your tribe, wherever that is."

"I had a tribe once. They abducted me when I was a toddler and then one day fifteen years later I was holding the head of the closest thing I had to a mother in my bare hands."

Marcus flinched.

"That detail probably wasn't in the reports," Nora explained, then tapped her head with an index finger. "It's up here though. And it's there forever." She sighed and smiled. "I don't think I have a tribe."

"Do you know what it means then? To be truly alone? Without a people?"

"I do," Nora replied. "It means I'm like everyone else in this country. I'm stuck in a maze, trying to find my way out before the clock runs down. Trying to figure out why everyone around me is dying. But there is no reason they're dying. There is no way out. It simply is."

"Don't say things like that, Nora. I'm putting-" Marcus looked around. "We're putting our faith in you. There is no one else. Everyone else is bought. Either by money or threats. We don't need you spouting the rhetoric of the enemy."

"Maybe that's the reason I'm your only hope," she said grinning. "In a city full of self-interested assholes, I'm the only one who doesn't want anything." She slammed the rest of her drink and hailed the bartender for another. "I'm the one who doesn't hope for anything."

"Do you hope to save Richard?"

Nora thought about that for a moment, then nodded reluctantly.

"Then listen to your police radio on the first full moon of September. Find where the kids came from. If it's a nightclub, then it probably has a back room. In the back room, if this is one of the places you're looking for, you'll find a golden pool. If you look at the edge of the pool, you should see a narrow channel carved into the concrete. Follow that channel with your eyes and you'll see that it leads beneath a doorway. Follow it. Follow it and you will find Richard."

"What makes you think they'll let me in?"

"Isn't it obvious?"

Nora shook her head.

"Because they want you," Marcus explained. "Because when you speak, you sound like one of them."

———

RICHARD HAD no idea how long he had been down here in the dark being treated like an animal. At first, he tried keeping track of the days by making scratches in the hard ground they had to sleep on. But every morning—or night, it was hard to tell—the guards would come and scratch them out.

One of the times the guards came in, he tried to overpower them. But the figure was strong. Unnaturally strong. It turned and looked at him with its impenetrable mask, grabbed him by the hand, and then sawed it off.

Two others came in to cauterize the wound. Richard tried to keep his eyes squeezed shut for the duration of the procedure, but on the occasion that he opened them and looked feverishly around the cell, he saw Brunson watching from where he was leaning against the back of the cage.

Richard's cellmate had made no move to rescue him. In their time together, he offered no plan of escape and gave no heed to the idea that they would find their way out of this somehow. He seemed to have accepted their situation. And while Richard was having his hand removed with a rough metal saw, Brunson just kept his gaze steady on him, maintaining eye contact.

And somehow, that made things better.

Richard couldn't explain it exactly. The experience was like holding your father's gaze in the midst of a punishment. It neither condemned nor absolved. The time for such things had passed. Now was the time for comfort, strength, and responsibility.

Halfway through the cauterizing of his wrist, Richard passed out.

· · ·

WHEN HE AWOKE SOMETIME LATER, the stump of his forearm throbbing worse than anything he'd ever felt, he found Brunson carefully cleaning his wound with some of the precious water they had been given that morning. He was appreciative of the act, but he still couldn't keep himself from asking Brunson directly why he hadn't helped.

"Because these guards are not men. They were never men. Some of the people who wear their robes and walk the streets on the surface are, but these are not. These are beasts and they cannot be overcome. As I'm sure you're well aware now."

"But we should still try," Richard pleaded. "We have to at least try."

Brunson reached up and rubbed the top of his head.

"Do you believe in hope, Richard?"

"Yes," Richard said, feeling as if he was walking into some sort of trap.

"Hope in what?"

"What do you mean?"

"What I'm asking is, what do you hope for?"

"I want to *leave*," Richard shook his head. "That's what I'm trying to say."

"And before that—before you were captured and held here —what did you hope for?"

Richard thought about it for a second and shrugged. "My family. This country."

"But what specifically? What did you hope your family would experience or accomplish? What did you hope your country would look like further on down the road?"

"I guess I hadn't really thought about it."

"Think about it now," Brunson said.

Richard took a second to gather his thoughts. He had hopes

for his family, of course. He wanted them to be safe, healthy, and prosperous. He told Brunson as much.

"And what happens when they die?" Brunson asked. "Because they *will* die."

"They *have* died," Richard sneered. "I..." He took a moment to compose himself. "Samantha. I...I shot her. In the end. When the thing was..."

Brunson held up his hand. "I know what they do. No need for you to relive it."

"Then why the fuck are you asking me these questions?" Richard found that he had tears in his eyes. They stung his face as they rolled down.

"I'm sorry," Brunson said softly. "But what we are talking about is of the utmost importance. It's why we're down here."

"What the Hell are you talking about?"

Brunson lifted his hand and pointed to the cell adjacent to them. Richard had seen the man a number of times. Had recognized him instantly. Had watched him slowly degrade.

"Who is that man?" Brunson asked.

"That's Stephen Shepherd. His daughter was murdered and I was tasked with finding her killer."

"Yes, but who *was* he?"

"I don't know," Richard admitted. "My partner, Nora, told me that he was some hotshot CEO."

"And?"

Richard thought back. "She said he played a little fast and loose with the women. Ran his mouth. That sort of thing."

"Good. Now, did you recognize the man in the first cage to the left when you were brought in?"

"No," Richard said, trying to remember the faces. In all honesty, the men he had seen in those first cages were more animal than man. Long hair, wary eyes, hunched over. He felt as if he could have seen a nature documentary on them at some point.

"Mayor Westchild."

Richard felt his jaw drop slightly open. "That was Westchild? I knew he had sort of disappeared from the public eye after he had been voted out but so do most politicians. I had no idea he was kidnapped. Shit, I voted for him."

Brunson nodded. "Me too. I had my reasons but what were yours?"

"Well, he was an asshole of the highest caliber but his policies were good. Blackburg really thrived for a bit there."

"And of course, there was the other guy he was running against."

"Right, well," Richard waved his good arm and cracked a smile. "Look around. This is where we are now under the other guy."

"I thought the same thing. That is, until I started watching these people down here."

Richard gave him a questioning look.

"Let me ask you a question: what do you think upholds the world we live in?"

"What do you mean?"

"I mean, we live in an age of technological wonder. Where a massive percentage of the world has been lifted out of poverty. Where we can travel to the other side of the world in a day. Where common people live better than any king did six centuries ago. How did we get here?"

"Progress." Richard shrugged. "Human ingenuity."

"Parts of the equation, for sure. But what binds us together? What allows us to *make* progress and demonstrate ingenuity?"

Richard stared blankly. His arm was throbbing. His family was dead. His life was essentially over. Whatever Brunson was talking about was so far removed from his situation that it might as well have been in a different language.

Yet, Brunson was in a similar situation. And he was saying these things, nonetheless.

"I don't know," Richard admitted.

"There is one thing in our society that lets us be a society at all." He held up a single finger. "Trust."

"Trust."

"Yes, trust."

"I suppose," Richard said, chewing that over. "I don't find myself trusting anyone these days. And some that I did—even some of those closest to me—have turned that trust against me."

"Would you say you don't trust anyone anymore?"

Richard looked up at the man sharply. "I don't suppose I do," he finally said.

Brunson only nodded.

"Is this the part where you tell me that I'm right. That trust in others will only get me killed?"

Brunson smiled. "You're half-correct. Trust in others will get you killed, but you should do it anyway."

"Are you saying I should trust *you*?"

"I'm saying you should trust *someone*. It doesn't have to be me. But you should do it knowing that trust entails risk. That is the human problem and the divine solution."

"Solution to what?"

"To everything." Brunson folded his hands together. "Do you mind if I slip into preacher mode for a second?"

"I feel like you're always in preacher mode," Richard said flatly.

Brunson laughed. "I guess you got me there. But I feel as if I should ask nonetheless. Once again: trust. I don't want you to feel like you're my project. One last soul for Heaven and all that."

"Hey, I go to church just like a third of this city."

"We all go to church, in our own ways," Brunson said. "But that's not the point. The point is: I believe that the God of all creation died for us. I believe he sacrificed himself for a vision of a better world. That is what trust is. That is what love is."

"Love is sacrifice," Richard said.

"Yes, and so is trust. They both accept risk in exchange for vision. They are the scaffolding upon which creation stands. Not peace. Not policy. Not power. All of those things are necessary to the equation of a successful civilization but they are not the foundation."

"Let me see if I'm hearing you correctly: you believe trust is what allows us to become better than what we might be without it. And if a society doesn't trust each other, then they will all be worse off because of it."

"Correct," Brunson said. "At least, that's how I see things. As I said, trust is always a risk. You put your whole heart, body, and mind on the line when you trust someone. Or—if you will—you hang it on a cross."

"A sacrifice," Richard said bleakly. He smiled. "Your religion is another blood cult."

"It is," Brunson replied. "I believe every man and woman is made in the image of God and to sacrifice yourself is to model the very idea of a God become man, willing to die. Sacrifices are what push the world forward. Life itself is sustained by the sacrifices of plants and animals. So with that in mind, there are only two true religions in the world. The one where you sacrifice another person for your own livelihood or the one where you sacrifice yourself for theirs."

"Take up your cross," Richard said. "Is that what you're saying?"

"I am."

Richard thought about that for a long time. The hoots and hollers of the men around him rising and falling like waves.

Finally, he asked the question that had been on his mind since the beginning of the conversation.

"Mayor Westchild. How does this apply to him?"

"Right," Brunson laughed a deep belly laugh. "The question that brought us here. I'm glad you were able to keep hold of the thread in the maze, as it were."

"My dad always said there were two kinds of preachers: those who bring a candle into a dark room and those who fumble for the light switch until they find it."

"Ha!" Brunson laughed again, this time much louder. The noise felt unnatural down there in the cage.

"I'd have liked to have met your father," the preacher said. "But to answer your question, men like Mayor Westchild are willing to make good decisions until it demands they sacrifice themselves."

"I don't know," Richard said. "Even if you don't like the man, you can't deny that he sacrificed everything to the job. He had his entire past dredged up. His private life upended. His youngest son practically disowned him. He was dragged through the mud by the media and slandered by anyone with a platform."

"Yes, but he never sacrificed the thing that actually mattered to him: his ego."

Richard wasn't quite sure what to say to that. He tried to think of a retort but came up empty.

"I get it," Brunson said. "I voted for the man too. Him and a hundred others like him. Whether it was with my actual vote or my money or simply my attention. The truth is, there are countless men and women like him out in the world and we love them. We idolize them. We literally base superheroes on them."

"So, what's your point?"

"My point is this: we want peace, freedom, and security. Right?"

"More or less, yeah?"

"These men offer it. And not only do they talk about it, they actually do it."

"Okay, still not seeing a problem."

"The problem is, they pursue these things while undermining the very ideals that make it possible."

"You mean like trust?"

"Trust, integrity, loyalty, charity, grace, kindness, and respect. These are not products of a society, they are the foundation. And when they are damaged or attacked outright, they undermine the bedrock of what allows us to be reasonably safe, happy, and free."

"I always thought the foundation of civilization was bloodshed, enslavement, and exploitation."

"Those things are nothing but holes in the foundations. Cracks. Flaws. Or in the case of Blackburg: chasms."

A thought suddenly staggered Richard. He looked at the people around him, then considered himself. He gave voice to the thought.

"We're not in here because of who we voted for, are we?"

"I do not believe we are," Brunson said solemnly.

"My partner, Nora. She said I was a fundamentalist."

"You are. Except your fundamentals aren't what you think they are."

"Tell me then," Richard said. "What are my fundamentals?"

"You want to control things. You want to dominate your neighbors and either make them live as you do or become so small you can ignore them entirely. You don't want to persuade them because that would require you to be vulnerable with them. It would require trust and patience. So instead, you force them. Either into submission or into exile. You justify your actions by saying you are building a better world for your family, a family that disintegrates beneath you.

Your fundamentals, Richard, they are not family or God or country. Those are but masks. Your god is much simpler and far more common. Just like those you despise and lock up, your god is a god of domination. Your god is power."

Richard closed his eyes. His arm throbbed and now, worse than ever, nausea overtook him. He wretched, his throat spasming. He wanted to ask how the preacher had failed, if for no other reason than to take that gaze of judgment off of himself.

But before he could, exhaustion overtook him once again and he drifted off into darkness.

———

THE NIGHT WAS cloudy but Nora had verified the stage of the moon's cycle with multiple sources. Tonight was the night.

The first report of minors strung out on hallucinogens came in just after 11. She didn't know exactly what was going to happen or how long she had but by that time she had been patrolling the streets for five hours and was properly nervous. When the dispatcher's voice called it in, she felt relief and adrenaline begin pumping through her simultaneously.

Seven minutes later and she was parked in front of a nightclub called The Vortex. Two squad cars were already pulled up with their flashers on. A group of too-young-looking teenagers were sitting on the sidewalk as an officer spoke with them.

Nora would have immediately tried to figure out her way in if she hadn't recognized one of the youthful faces.

"*Hannah*," she breathed. And before she could second guess herself, she got up out of the car and began walking towards the group of kids. As she approached, she also recognized the dark-haired kid she had lightly interrogated with Richard the day he disappeared. And next to him were the two girls.

Coming up alongside the officer who had just been speaking to them, she flashed her badge and watched the man's forehead crinkle into a question mark.

"Detective Nora Kane," she said, then jerked her head towards Hannah. "This young woman is a person of interest in a murder investigation. Along with those three."

She wondered what exactly the kids were doing. Marcus had said they'd be careless. Were they simply cutting loose and throwing caution to the wind? If Hannah was willing to show her face in public all of a sudden, then that meant she probably didn't think there'd *be* a public for that much longer. Nora didn't have much time.

Hannah smiled. "You're too late. You'll never find them in time."

Nora turned to the officer. "Get three more squad cars down here right now. Watch these kids and call the city. We may need to enter the sewers."

"The...what?" The officer was clearly confused. The man was cut and sturdy without an ounce of fat on him, but he looked barely older than the kids he was standing in front of. His nameplate read "Gunderson."

"Just do it." Nora pulled out a pair of walkie-talkies. "And take this. I'll keep you updated."

Gunderson took it reluctantly. Nora gave one last look at Hannah and her friends, resisted the urge to spit on them, and then walked inside.

THE MUSIC WAS LOUD, pulsing along with an expensive light display that cut through the heavy shadows. Bodies seemed to melt into each other as they danced.

Nora found she was having a hard time discerning where the actual walls were. To her it just seemed like undulating darkness, punctured by an occasional laser or dazzle of flashing lights.

As she made her way in, she could eventually discern a catwalk that led to some closed-off VIP area. She traced the rail down and to the right where it met with some thin metal stairs and began making her way towards it.

Before she reached the base of the steps, however, she glanced up to see someone watching her. A woman, as far as she could tell. She was wearing a slim dress and had her head tilted at an odd angle. Her silhouette against the lights had a familiarity to it. One that she couldn't quite place.

Nora moved on.

Once she had huffed it up the stairs and across the walk to the VIP area, she found the woman standing just on the other side of a thick golden rope.

"What's the password?" the woman asked.

Nora assessed her for a moment. It may have been the lights but it almost seemed as if one of her eyes was green and the other nearly black. The woman smiled.

"*Rakathreev*," Nora said, putting as much confidence behind the uncomfortable word as she could.

"Close enough," the woman said, unhooking the rope to let her through. "Follow me."

The VIP lounge was lit with a soft amber light and the sound of the club seemed to immediately retreat as Nora stepped inside. There was no door or soundproofing that she could tell, but the room seemed to envelop her all the same once she had stepped through.

The lounge was comfy and surprisingly spacious. There were a few expensive-looking leather couches along the wall with an unattended bar on the opposite side. In the middle of the room was a tall table and sitting on the table was a large party bowl filled with blue tablets.

Blue Chameleon.

"I've been waiting for you," the woman said, turning around. Nora could now see that she was wearing a red dress and had long dark hair. Something niggled in the back of her mind but she couldn't quite catch it. She had seen this woman somewhere before.

"Waiting for me to come bust you for possession?" Nora asked.

"My name is Marion." The woman said, ignoring Nora's jab. She turned around and walked toward a door at the end of the room.

Nora hesitated, felt the reassuring grip of her sidearm and checked the knife strapped to the outside of her leg, then followed.

The door led to a winding red staircase. They descended the metal steps for what seemed like a very long time and Nora couldn't help but admire Marion for her ability to navigate the metal grating in her high heels.

Once they reached the bottom, Marion opened another door and led her into another room. This space was wide but the ceiling was low. Flames flickered along the walls, lighting the interior. And at the center was a large golden pool.

Nora felt her pulse begin to quicken. This was it. The room with the golden pool. The one Marcus had talked about.

The pool wasn't square like others she had seen but had a circular bottom. It looked to be about four feet deep at its deepest point and due to the curvature of the bottom, one would have to either stand directly in the middle or risk sliding down beneath the surface. The gold seemed to glow in the firelight and as she looked closer, she saw that there were images carved all along the inside. Simple but elegant pictures of severed arms and legs and hourglasses. They appeared to run together into a counter-clockwise spiral that wound its way down to the center, where there was a drain.

If you look at the edge of the pool, you should see a narrow channel carved into the floor.

Nora had repeated the words in her head so many times that they were virtually etched into her at this point. Her gaze wandered up to the edge where there were indeed several channels leading away from the pool to meet at a single point. That channel then led across the floor and beneath a doorway on the other side of the room.

"What would you like, Nora?"

"Excuse me?" Nora blinked. The question had sounded almost as if she was asking what kind of cocktail she preferred but she knew better.

"You're here for a reason. Searching for your partner, I presume. But is that what you really want?"

"Of course it is." Nora yanked her gaze away from the mesmerizing pool at the center of the room and fixed it on Marion. Reflections of the water danced on her skin and over her dress. "Where is he?"

"Answer my question first and I'll answer yours."

"I don't have time for games." Nora drew her sidearm and pointed it at Marion.

"It is not the place of one of the city's guardians to point a loaded weapon at an unarmed woman. You should know better."

"I do but I don't care. Tell me where he is."

Marion clicked her tongue and slowly shook her head. "Nora, Nora, Nora. That's the kind of thinking that got you here. That blatant disregard for the supposed values of your profession are the reason the whole structure is crumbling."

"What are you talking about?"

"Trust is a wall, Nora." Marion smiled. "And when you tear it down, monsters come through."

"Tell me where Richard is," Nora demanded.

"You haven't heard what I have to offer yet."

Nora remained silent.

"Tell me dear, who has come alongside you in your spiral downward after losing Richard? Who has been there for you?"

"No one. But that doesn't matter. That's just the way it is right now."

"Just the way it is?"

Nora adjusted her grip on the pistol, trying to decide how much of her personal life to divulge. She had entered a game now. One she didn't think she could shoot her way out of. She'd have to speak carefully.

"You don't make a lot of friends growing up in a cult," Nora said

"In my experience, that's where you make the *most* friends. That's what a cult *is*, after all. It's community. It's *cult*ure."

"Well, even if I did. They're gone now."

"Oh?"

"Stop playing games. I know you've been watching me. You probably know about my past. You know about the cult I was rescued from and how they all died."

"*Rescued* is an interesting way of putting it. Are you implying that whoever or whatever killed all of your friends and family were doing it for you?"

"I was the only one left."

"So you think it was acting benevolently then."

"If you know something about what happened to them, tell me now."

"Slow down there, dear." Marion turned to the side and began walking along the edge of the pool. "Do you want to know what happened to your friends and family or do you want to know where Richard is?"

Nora hesitated. "Richard. I want to know where Richard is."

"Are you sure?"

Nora didn't answer.

"Remove your clothes."

"What?"

"Your clothes. Take them off, lay them in a pile, then step into the pool."

"Why?"

"Because the death of your previous family and Richard's disappearance are both part of a larger tapestry. A conflict as old as the world itself. Enter the pool and sink beneath its surface. Do this and you will cross the divide and discern the pattern. You will know all."

Nora watched as Marion reached up and slid the straps of her dress off her shoulders. First the left, then the right. The thin red fabric fell to the ground. Marion was naked beneath. She lifted her arms in the air, as if giving praise.

"Follow me, dear. And you will know everything. You will know the secrets of your family. You will see the tapestry of time. Follow me, and you will be as a god."

Then in one fluid motion, Marion knelt and slipped down into the pool. Her body slid along the curved golden bottom, black hair flowing out behind her. The darkness of her hair began to grow. It grew and spread throughout the entire pool until the whole thing was as black as a tar pit.

Nora stood there watching. She thought about the fifteen years she had spent with the cult. About the bonds she had formed. She thought about walking out of a tent one morning to find her friends and family lying in pieces on the ground.

She closed her eyes and made her decision. She turned to

follow the channel that led away from the pool and beneath the door. She would find Richard herself.

As soon as she moved, the darkness in the pool sprang up into the air. Nora swung and fired a single shot but it went wide and the dark shape crashed into her, sending her gun skidding across the tile.

The world tumbled end over end as she rolled. Her body came to a stop and she tried to get up but found herself pinned to the ground. She looked down at what was holding her and gagged.

Wrapped around her waist were thick grey tentacles. She tried to push against them but it felt as if the tentacles were made of steel. They tightened and squeezed, and as they did, a form rose in front of her.

The creature was massive. It had mottled grey skin and a large spear-shaped head like that of a squid. Eight spindly legs sprouted in multiple directions and more tentacles than she could count whipped and snapped in the air. The creature had short digits that looked like fingers dangling over its mouth and had one black eye and one glowing green eye.

Nora stared into the green one, mesmerized. It was like looking into the sun. She felt her own eyes burn and stars began bursting in her vision. Her mind began clouding over.

Her hands remembered their training and snatched the folding knife from where it was strapped to her leg, snapped it open, and then proceeded to plunge the steel blade into the green eye.

Black blood sprayed across Nora's face as the monster howled and fell backward. She felt the grip slacken on her arm and took the opportunity to twist free of the creature's grip and snatch up her weapon.

The squid monster was just beginning to turn back toward her as she leveled the pistol and pulled the trigger three times.

The sound of the gun was deafening in the tiled room and she watched the bullets tear three neat holes in the squid-like face.

Stumbling, the creature seemed to whip a long grey cloak out of the air, wrap it around itself, and then spin away in a cloud of black smoke.

Nora coughed and waved her hand in front of herself. Once the smoke was clear she looked around. The room was empty. She was alone.

———

"They're coming," Brunson said.

Richard looked up from where he was sitting on the floor. The men in the other cages had begun screaming unintelligibly but he knew what their cries meant. Brunson was right. They were coming.

Over the course of the next hour, Richard watched men get dragged out of their cages by the guards. Aside from Brunson and Richard, most of the other men were closer to animals by now. They hissed and spat at their captors, trying to claw their masks off and bite them whenever possible. It did no good.

Brunson had been correct. The guards weren't men. They were something else entirely.

When it came time to go, the two men didn't fight but they didn't make it easy either. Richard was limp as they dragged him, his feet scuffing the floor just as they had when he was brought in.

They strapped him to one of the pillars and then secured Brunson to the pillar across from him. They hadn't been the last ones to be imprisoned but there weren't as many afterward. The guards would be done soon, then the ceremony would begin.

———

THE DOOR in the pool room had led into some underground tunnel. She had no idea how far below Blackburg she was but she couldn't get a signal on her walkie-talkie. For all her efforts, backup wasn't coming.

She raced down the narrow stone passageway. A multitude of other tunnels branched off from the path she was on but she kept following the trench. There were no lights so she held her mini flashlight out ahead of her, using the back of her flashlight hand to keep her gun hand steady.

She moved quickly but carefully. The last thing she wanted was to run headlong into another one of whatever that thing was in the pool room. She hadn't killed it and she wasn't sure she could.

Nora noticed that the ground sloped gradually upward and the thought slowly began to form a pit in the bottom of her stomach. She glanced down at the trench.

Then the ground began to shake.

———

"LOOK AT ME," Brunson said. His gaze was hard and intense, like a medic about to perform an amputation in the field without anesthesia. "Do you trust me?"

"I do."

"Focus on the sound of my voice," the preacher said. "Remember: while you are living, they can take everything from you but your suffering. That suffering is yours and no matter what they force you to do, you decide what that suffering is going to mean. Now, what is that suffering going to mean, Richard?"

They had practiced this for when the time came and now that it was here, Richard found the words flowing freely from his mouth and from his heart.

"My suffering is for all the world. My suffering is a sacrifice for the God that suffers. It will not be used by lesser gods."

"Again."

"My suffering is for *all* the world. My suffering is my sacrifice for the God that suffers. It will *not* be used by lesser gods."

"Again."

Richard shouted the words this time.

"My suffering is for all the world. My suffering is my sacrifice for the God that suffers. It will not be used by lesser gods."

They repeated the phrases over and over again, drawing some looks from the other captive men. Some of them began moving their lips while others continued to thrash.

One of the guards walked up to Brunson, drawing some sort of ceremonial blade. Richard continued his own chanting as he watched Brunson get his tongue cut out. Then the guard moved onto him.

The pain was excruciating but he embraced it. This was his suffering. His sacrifice. They could not take it from him and make it theirs. He would not let them. He kept mouthing the words as blood gurgled out and down his neck.

Out of the corner of his eye, Richard saw something moving among the pillars. Eight legs protruded from its cloak along with numerous tentacles. Tentacles that had torn his wife apart. Tentacles that were coming for him.

The monster held its own ceremonial blade and it slithered from man-to-man, cutting each of their throats. After a few seconds, it would wrap all of its tentacles around the pillars and squeeze until the whole structure came apart with an earth-shattering groan.

The concussions of the breaking pillars acquired a rhythm as the monster worked, sounding almost like the beating of a heart.

NORA BEGAN TO RUN, the circle of light bobbing out in front of her. The ground shuttered again and again, threatening to bring the whole place down around her. As she ran, she began to hear the sound of rushing water.

No, not water. She glanced down at the trench in the floor and saw a river of blood flowing past. It rolled down the slight incline of the corridor, winding away behind her, creeping ever closer to one of the golden pools.

She began to sprint.

IN HIS LAST MOMENTS, Richard thought of his life. He thought of his mistakes. Of his crimes against the very structure of being.

As a child, he had dreamt of being a guardian of the city. A pillar of the community. A hero. A protector. And in some ways he had accomplished this.

But it hadn't been enough. He had failed his family. Failed his city. In his time on the police force he had sought power without virtue. Power had been the only thing he believed in and in doing so he had corroded the foundation he was trying to build his life upon. He had acted vengefully on occasion and cut corners when it came to certain legal procedures. Small sins, all things considered, but this country had been accumulating small sins the way one accrues spiraling debt and now the collector had come.

It was the way of all civilizations, he supposed. A society is built on imperfections and those imperfections grow, like spreading cracks in the city streets. You can patch the cracks but eventually there comes a point where the whole street just falls apart.

Richard found his mind transported to his father's study. He had been in there many times as a child, watching his father work to build a life for him and his mother. He saw a poem hanging in a frame on the wall. A poem he had probably looked at a hundred times but hadn't understood until recently.

"*Things fall apart,*" Yeats had said. "*The centre cannot hold.*"

So now, in the 11th hour when there was no hope of rescue, he sought to change the only thing he could: his heart. And he did it through his suffering. An act of holy purification.

In his suffering, he took responsibility rather than curse. In his suffering, he yearned for the preservation of all that was good in these doomed men around him rather than the destruction of what was detestable. He wished the same for the city.

Without words he prayed for the safety and preservation of what good was left in Blackburg rather than its complete annihilation. Lord knew he had wanted the whole thing to burn to the ground on more than one occasion. Scrap the plan and start over. He didn't know a single soul who hadn't thought that at least once in their lives.

The monster slithered to the pillar in front of him, blocking his view of Brunson. A final mercy that he didn't have to watch him die.

There came a sound like the sawing of meat and then a wet gurgle. A few seconds later and Richard watched as the creature tried to rend the pillar apart. And to his amazement the creature failed. It tried again and again but the pillar held firm.

The monster in the grey cloak eventually gave up and moved on. Now it was his turn.

He closed his eyes and focused his heart on the good he had seen in the world. On the precious moments he had spent with his wife and daughter before the end. He thought of Hannah and her part in all this. And even now he chose to believe that the good in her would endure. Beyond death. Beyond failure. For if all is plunged into darkness and nothingness, then what good is virtue and morality to begin with? If all things fall apart without renewal or preservation, then why build anything in the first place?

The steel was surprisingly warm against Richard's neck, heated by the blood of all the previous men, he figured. He hoped that some of the other men had found some sort of salvation in their final moments. Some awakening in their hearts just before they stopped beating.

The pain of the blade cutting through his neck was nothing compared to the removal of his hand or tongue. It was light. Easy.

Richard was filled with a warm euphoria, the kind one gets from choosing life, even as they feel it pumping out of them.

———

Nora halted as the corridor collapsed in front of her. She spun to go back the other way just in time to see her retreat crumble apart as well. Her chest began to heave as panic took hold. She looked up and saw massive cracks in the ceiling. They spread apart wider and wider, the sound of the stones grating together was so loud she couldn't hear herself think.

Then the ground gave out beneath her and she was plunged into icy cold darkness.

Light streamed in and Nora coughed black water from her lungs. She blinked and tried to sit up but immediately sank back down as red-hot pain sliced its way up her side.

She didn't know where she was or how she had gotten there. The last thing she remembered was blood flowing in the trench, a massive shaking as the earth came apart around her, then darkness.

I should be dead, she thought to herself. The walls had come apart around her. She should be crushed. Drowned. Destroyed. But she wasn't. It was as if the black water beneath the city had spit her out. As if something had snatched her away at the last second.

After a few deep breaths, she tried sitting up again, slower this time. She found herself leaning against some sort of broken stone wall. Water was trickling from the cracks and running past her to flow down a muddy bank.

Beyond the bank was a small creek and beyond that, a copse of ragged trees swaying in the evening wind. Nora turned around and looked up the stone ridge she was leaning against. It was tall, maybe fifty feet, and looked as if some part of it had recently collapsed.

She gritted her teeth and forced herself to her feet.

IT TOOK PROBABLY an hour to find a road. Nora's body was screaming and begging for rest but the sun was going down and the nights had been getting colder. If she didn't find shelter somewhere, she could just as well die of hypothermia.

She stood there for a moment at the edge of the highway, her chest heaving. She was covered in scrapes and bruises and was pretty sure she had a torn tendon in her leg and a few cracked ribs. What a sight she must have been standing there.

She turned left to look up the road and what she saw almost stopped her heart.

Off in the distance was Blackburg. Smoke seemed to be rising from multiple places, making black smudges against the orange evening sky. Then when she looked closer, she saw that some buildings were leaning sideways or had even fallen over.

"*In nine months they will be sacrificing the entire city of Blackburg to* Rakathreev," Marcus had told her.

And it seemed as if they had succeeded.

Or had they?

Marcus had said that there was a bottomless lake below the city and that the entire thing would disappear into it. He had made it sound as if there would be nothing left. So if that had been their plan, then they had failed, hadn't they? Blackburg had been ravaged, certainly, but it was still standing. People had likely died but some had probably lived, right?

Nora thought about Richard. She thought about the blood she had seen running in the trench, flowing down toward the golden pool. She had failed. Richard was dead.

The thought wrenched her heart and she slowly sank to the ground. Something tugged at the muscles in her face. She fought it for a second and then relented. There on the side of the road, with Blackburg burning in the distance, she began to cry.

Light bathed the area around her and Nora's head snapped up. A car had come around the corner, headed away from the city. She sat there motionless for a second and then raised her hand.

The car slowed and pulled to the side of the road. The passenger door swung open and a woman ran out to meet her.

"Oh sweetie, what happened?" The woman said. She was wearing a purple blouse with big white flowers on it.

Nora looked past her and through the open door to the driver. A skinny man with thick glasses peered out at her, concern etched plainly on his face.

"I think-," Nora said, her voice quaking. "I don't know. But I'm hurt."

The woman slowly helped Nora to her feet. Then they began moving slowly to the car. The woman opened the rear passenger side door and Nora slid into the back.

"I don't think the hospital in Blackburg is operational right now," the man said to the woman. Judging by their body language they were husband and wife. "The National Guard is setting up emergency medical stations but I don't think anyone's allowed into the city right now."

"That's okay," Nora said. "You can take me to the next closest hospital. I think I'm done with Blackburg."

The car pulled back onto the highway. Nora felt her eyes flutter closed. Blissful sleep washed over her and the next thing she knew was nothing at all.

THE END

ALSO BY FREDRICK NILES

The Omen Tree

ALSO BY FREDRICK NILES

Cold Water Forest

ABOUT THE AUTHOR

Fredrick Niles is the author of *Ash Above, Snow Below* and *The Omen Tree*. He lives in St. Paul, Minnesota where he writes fiction and plays music. In his free time he rants about movies, lurks in bookstores, and practices introversion with his wife.

facebook.com/fredricknilesauthor

instagram.com/fredrickniles_author

www.ingramcontent.com/pod-product-compliance
Lightning Source LLC
Chambersburg PA
CBHW050838190726
48286CB00007B/2131